An Unknown Woman

JANE DAVIS

ISBN-10: 1508578826
ISBN-13: 978-1508578826

Cover design by Andrew Candy using original artwork by
Vladimir Volodin (mature lady), Jason Salmon (young lady) and
Jeff Wasserman (detail from mirror), all at Shutterstock.

for THOMAS M. DAVIS

on the occasion of his eightieth birthday.

Happy birthday, Dad.

Identity (noun) pl. **identities**: 'An ever-evolving core within which our genetics, culture, loved ones, those we cared for, people who have harmed us and people we have harmed, the deeds done (good and ill) to self and others, experiences lived, and choices made come together to form who we are at this moment.' Parker J. Palmer

PRAISE FOR THE AUTHOR

'Davis is a phenomenal writer, whose ability to create well rounded characters that are easy to relate to feels effortless.'

Compulsion Reads

'Jane Davis is an extraordinary writer, whose deft blend of polished prose and imaginative intelligence makes you feel in the safest of hands.'

J. J. Marsh, author and founder of Triskele Books

CHAPTER ONE

"What's that noise?" Anita sat upright in bed, blinking blindly in the dark.

Ed rolled onto his side, dragging the duvet with him and groaning, "What noise?"

"That banging." She reached for the light switch.

"I can't hear anything," Ed insisted. "Go back to sleep."

But Anita knew she hadn't imagined it. She willed it to come again.

"There!" She grabbed at it, her lungs so tight with fear that she could barely breathe. "Someone's trying to break in!"

"No." All attention now, Ed was up on his elbows, staring at the ceiling. "It's coming from the loft."

Then a shrieking sound pierced the silence, relentless, heart-stopping, almost paralysing. The sideways leap from burglar to what else this might mean was almost too much to take on board. In disbelief, Anita asked, "Is that -?"

"It's the smoke alarm." Already on his feet, Ed commanded, "Get up!" His hands were fists. Perhaps he imagined an intruder might have set the alarm off, intending to draw them downstairs.

She saw a drift of air, cloudy and powder-grey, nothing so substantial that it fitted the description of smoke. Anita followed Ed out onto the landing. The door to the spare room was edged with a reddish glow. Before she could yell "Stop!" Ed had reached for the doorknob. He yanked his hand away - "Fuck!" - shaking it violently. Just as he hid it in the opposite armpit, the door swung inwards on its hinges. Slapped in the face by a fierce concentration of heat, they stepped back. The sight of flames devouring the wall was mesmerising, the sounds of snapping and popping surreal. A lungful of toxic black smoke escaped, then the door sucked closed. There was a moment when all she could do was blink, then Anita found herself being pushed in front of Ed, ordered downstairs.

"Passports and birth certificates," Ed shouted above the din.

"I'll get those."

It seemed so urgent, the need to make the right decisions about what to save. At the foot of the staircase Anita grabbed her handbag from the banister, shrugged on her coat. Venturing into the dining room, she checked that her route to the French windows was clear. Her laptop lay on the table. She had worked late into the evening, until her eyes protested. Anita ripped out the lead, ready to pick up on her way out. About to pull out the plug, she stopped short. An inch more and she would have been touching live electrics. The alarm was meant to induce panic. It was doing its job.

Calm down.

Think.

How long did she have? A minute, perhaps. She checked over her shoulder: Ed was going between the front room and the hall, throwing things out of the front door.

"Shut the door!" she yelled at him.

"What?"

"Oxygen feeds fire." Didn't everybody know that? "Go out the front and shut the door behind you."

On hearing a slam, she bent over the oriental chest. In it, household documents were stored in manila folders, their edges torn from regular use. Ed thought her filing system obsessive, but they never had to search for passports. She found them quickly.

"*Anita! Anita! You need to get out!*"

Christ, Ed was still inside! Where, a minute ago, there'd been a doorway, she saw a wall of thick black smoke. "So do you. I'll go out the back!"

"*I can't hear you! Where are you?*"

Important documents stowed in her handbag, she clutched her laptop under one arm. "*I said, I'll go out the back!*" She instinctively covered her nostrils and mouth and skirted the table. Black smoke rolled the length of the ceiling, determined to ambush her. Memory urged: crouch low.

Moments later she was standing on the patio, relieved to find herself breathing untainted air, marvelling at the miracle that was the night sky. It would have been a good night for star-gazing. Ed pointing and spouting facts about distant constellations whose names Anita would forget; trying to explain that they were seeing light from stars that no longer existed. "How can we see something that doesn't exist?" Anita protested against a concept so mind-bending, though she enjoyed Ed's enthusiasm, seeing his eyes light up. But tonight there was no time. "You need to keep moving," she scolded herself.

Anita's shoulders jerked violently at the sound of a heavy thud against the French windows. Ed must still be inside! "Christ!" Thank God the stars had held her attention for a moment. There was an orange glow in the dining room now. She pulled a coat sleeve down over one hand and tugged at the handle. Another thud and the door flew open. Ed staggered out, one hand reaching, the other clutched to his chest. His face was smudged black. "Why didn't you go out the front?" Anita demanded, angry that he'd been so stupid.

"I thought you were trapped..." He doubled over, hands

on his knees, winded. "Give me a minute to catch my breath."

"We don't have a minute." She made him straighten up, trying to offer support. He snatched his burnt hand away and returned it to the safety of his armpit.

"Anyway," he rasped, his head angled towards her, "what were you doing, standing there?"

"Looking at the light from all the dead stars."

"You *were* listening!"

"Just because I can't get my head around what you're telling me, doesn't mean I'm not listening. Come on!" she insisted.

They stood in the road watching as flames billowed from an upstairs window. Even in the darkness, the air shimmered. Lit from below, a swell of dense black smoke obscured the crescent moon. The night was alive with ungodly sounds: sharp shouts, the rise and fall of screaming sirens, a sickening crackling. To Anita's right, there was a violent explosion of glass. Theirs had been an incredibly narrow escape.

Thick, acrid-tasting air turned her throat to charcoal. Her lungs protested. The fire harnessed hypnotic power. With her gaze welded to the spectacle, Anita was only vaguely aware of the neighbours who had drifted out of silent homes. They were knotting belts of dressing gowns, hoisting up waistbands of tracksuit bottoms, looking for the cause of this unwelcome disturbance. Entranced, they grabbed the arms of partners, joined the vigil. Seeing the fire's merciless progress, some went in search of assurance that their loved ones, houses and possessions - "Christ, has anyone seen the cat?" - were safe. As liquid flames licked the eaves, lips silently thanked lucky stars - or whatever god they believed dwelled in the heavens. This was someone else's misfortune.

Ed pulled Anita closer as another volley of coughs wracked through her chest. Flames shot out of the letterbox, dulling the sheen of recently polished brass. She made no complaint.

Pain felt like an appropriate response. Watching the paintwork blister, it was easy to think of the house as having a skin.

"Is there anyone inside the building?" a fireman demanded.

As Ed appointed himself spokesperson - "No, just the two of us live there" - Anita pressed the laptop she had been clutching to his chest like a shield, moved forwards onto the path and began to pick up stray cushions that were strewn around the garden. They were damp and muddied, and she doubted they could be salvaged, but she stowed them in the boot of their Mini - the only place that seemed safe from the hosepipes.

The discussion continued behind her. "No pets?"

"None."

More firemen pounded up the path - kept on running, it seemed - armed with axes and sledgehammers. She returned to Ed's side. In Anita's initial flush of relief, it had felt comforting to hand responsibility to someone else. But now, though logic told her that the firemen were risking their lives, Anita tensed at the sight of them breaking down her front door, hacking it into splinters. She had painted the door twice, first British Racing Green and then, after fitting new brass locks, a glossy black. What had seemed substantial proved flimsy. Shifting her feet, Anita felt cold wet grit press into her soles. There'd been no time for shoes. She was dressed in what she had been wearing in bed - pyjamas would be a generous description for her tired yoga pants and camisole - topped with her winter coat. Her mother insisted on calling it her 'good winter coat', but it was Anita's only coat and she was glad of it. Despite the waves of intense dry heat that stretched the skin taut over her cheekbones, cold rose up through Anita's bare feet, into her marrow.

The smoke was blacker than she had thought possible; the flames redder, wrapping themselves around the guttering, licking the darkness, crawling on the concrete roof tiles Ed had always wanted to replace with terracotta, but Anita hadn't minded terribly much. Her mind conjured shapes within the writhing flames. Hellish beings with forked tongues. Demonic shadows. She saw a silhouette that looked remarkably like hers standing at an upstairs window.

Another sudden explosion of glass. Anita's breath caught. She tore her focus away from her ghost. Debris was falling now. Flaming things hit the ground and burnt themselves out. She watched the leaves of a rosebush turn from glossy green to black and then disintegrate, dropping away to nothing.

In spite of its ferocious heat, the fire was magnetic.

"We need to get back," Ed encouraged in an altered voice.

Anita pulled away from his embrace. "Shouldn't we move the car?" Her feet shifted of their own accord. The drive was awash with a soup of water and soot.

"For Christ's sake, Anita! It's too late!"

"But we haven't finished paying for it..."

"It's just a bloody car." Fingers handcuffed her wrist. Hauled backwards, she was encircled and rocked. Ed's frantic tone took her aback. "None of this stuff matters. Not compared with having you safe."

Anita knew he was trying to say the right things. He unbuttoned her coat, lending her his body heat. She settled against his chest, numbed by impotence, but knowing how wrong he was. Contained within those four walls was their fifteen-year history. Every Sunday morning lie-in they'd shared. Cosy evenings. Conversations shaped. Baths run. Culinary triumphs - and disasters. Every history book she'd ever read. Every Christmas, every birthday. That terrible party they'd held in celebration of their tenth anniversary, when friends and family had clearly expected an engagement announcement. The results of every hour of every trip to every flea market or antiques fair.

Ed was asking, "Aren't you going to put them on?" Paired

next to her feet were some wellington boots, cheerful things with a floral design.

This small kindness made Anita tearful. "Where did they come from?"

"Someone from up the far end, I think. I didn't recognise her."

Anita swiped grit from her feet, grabbing Ed's arm for support before stepping unsteadily into the boots. They were a poor fit, no good for walking in, but at least her feet were no longer bare. "How will I get them back to her?" Anita scanned the cul-de-sac for a sign of recognition, but the scattering of neighbours seemed determined to look anywhere other than at her.

"She didn't seem terribly worried."

Anita returned her attention to the house. Fingers of orange, liquid like lava. Prometheus was said to have stolen fire from the gods. They appeared to have been angered again. Anita couldn't decide which was more persistent: the flames or the jets of water firemen aimed at their home. It was a battle from which no victor would emerge. Everything they possessed would be destroyed by one element or the other. A fireman was standing in her flowerbeds, crushing the plants that she had watered and pruned under the soles of his rubber boots. It was impossible to voice an objection while flames lit the night sky like an erupting volcano, but Anita's splayed fingers objected; her fingertips objected.

"I've always hated those roof tiles." Ed returned to a favourite theme, but Anita didn't want pretence that there was a silver lining. From the cathedral of flames and the great chutes of water, the skeleton of their home emerged. It had always worn its timber beams - its bones - on the outside. Anita watched one of the timbers in the porch as it was overcome by flames, and thought of Joan of Arc. The firemen would sacrifice their home in an attempt to save the houses on either side. Ed had always complained that the house to the immediate left had been built too close, its tall chimney perching territorially at the very edge of the roof.

A man with a microphone. She clutched Ed's arm asking silent questions: Who was he? And when had he arrived?

"It looks as if he's from the local radio station," Ed said, following her gaze, almost as if they should expect someone to show up and record the destruction of their home.

She could hear the manager of the fire station saying, "Upon arrival, my crew was faced with a severe fire in the back bedroom of the detached property. It had already spread to the roof space. Firefighters wearing breathing apparatus are tackling the blaze with three hose reels and one main jet. The room that the fire started in has been completely gutted, together with much of the rest of the property."

"And the cause?"

"Impossible to tell at this stage."

"But if you had to hazard a guess?" The microphone thrust forwards once again.

"That's our house they're talking about!" Anita said.

Ed cradled her head to his shoulder. "They're just doing their jobs."

She delved into her handbag for her phone - an automatic reaction.

"What are you doing?" Ed asked, incredulous.

"I should give Roz a ring. Let her know I won't be in first thing." Her throat burned with the effort of speaking.

"Work is the *last* thing you should be worrying about!"

"I have to be there. It's the opening of the new exhibition. I'm introducing the speaker."

"Not dressed like that!"

Looking down at herself, Anita confronted an indisputable fact. She would walk away with only the clothes she was dressed in and what she carried, nothing more.

Underneath the fire's perpetual roar was a second layer of sound, a steady clap, like applause at a cricket match. The firemen were struggling to make their shouts heard, but somewhere beneath the chaos, a third layer emerged - a place of stillness - and it was there Anita sought refuge. The calm of knowing that nothing would be salvaged, nothing would remain. But even braving this inevitability, Anita wasn't aware of the full extent of what she was losing. News reports and insurance settlements wouldn't reveal the whole picture. It would be some months before the true tally of what she had lost in the fire finally emerged.

CHAPTER TWO

Patti's hands were occupied with a basket of laundered clothes, topped off with odds and ends that needed to be returned to their homes. Though she'd resisted Ron's suggestion of a retirement bungalow - one of those dreadful soulless places - no journey upstairs was wasted these days. With the basket balanced high on her stomach, her view was blocked. She sought out each step with a careful foot. Already a little out of puff, she had made it just shy of the small landing when a ringing sent her heart into palpitations. "Jesus!"

The telephone was only two weeks old. Ron had programmed it with a tinny version of *Swan Lake* - the least offensive option on the menu. Although her husband insisted he'd followed the instructions to the letter, an urgent tone joined with Tchaikovsky's masterpiece, jarring, like Patti's oven timer. Once the shock subsided, bristling with annoyance, she paused to shout over the banister, "Would you mind getting that, Ron?"

The lack of reply suggested he was in the back garden - dispatching any snails that had ignored his request to keep their distance from the potted herbs, no doubt.

"I suppose *I'll* have to answer it!" she said, setting the laundry basket down on the small square of landing, wincing as she straightened up. Keen to get back to her office (formerly known as 'the ironing room'), she went a little faster than was good for her. "Hang on a mo', will you?" she told the darned thing. At this time of the morning it was probably only some scally trying to sell her something she didn't want. Funeral plans were the latest insult. Registering with the Telephone Preference Service (or the 'Call Prevention Service', as Ron insisted on calling it) hadn't made the blindest difference. Three steps from the bottom, the answerphone kicked in. A robotic voice announced that they were not available to take the call right now, but if the caller would care to leave a message...

A voice wavered, "Mum, it's me."

Patti grabbed the receiver: "Anita, love? Just let me catch my breath. I was on my way upstairs." Fighting light-headedness, Patti perched on the chair by the telephone table.

"OK."

She willed herself, *breathe,* imagining this was how it would feel to be drowning in the Mersey. "You're normally at work at this time of day. Aren't you feeling well?"

"I'm fine. We're *both* fine, but we've had an awful shock."

Thoughts flicked on like light switches. *You've been made redundant. Or Ed has. Poor Ed. He works so hard. You've split up with Ed. No, no, it couldn't be that. Ed's a keeper.* Tamping them down one by one, Patti managed to repeat, "A shock?"

"It's the house. Last night. There was a fire."

She knew how a mother was supposed to set her own reactions to one side. "But you're both alright?"

"We've just come from the hospital. They had us both on oxygen, and they want us to see our doctor tomorrow. But, Mum..." She broke off.

"What, love, what?"

"We've lost everything."

"Everything?" Patti echoed stupidly.

"Apart from the clothes we're wearing. It's all gone."

"All of your beautiful things. Oh, love. I can't begin to..."

Anita sniffed. "And I can't afford to think about that now. Today's priority is finding somewhere to live."

One thing at a time. So sensible. Patti searched for the right sentence. "Do you want to come home? I can easily make up the bed in the spare room. Let me take care of you."

"Maybe, once we've got a clearer idea what we're doing. We both need to be in London for work. And then there's the insurance to sort out."

"Of course. I wasn't thinking." With nowhere to picture her daughter, and London's suburbs a mystery, Anita had never seemed so far away. "Where will you stay tonight?"

"A friend's offered us a room until we find something to rent. Natalie. I think you've met her. She's my godson's mother."

Patti couldn't recall individuals, just a sea of similarly smiling faces. A smart set. She found something fake in all the pleasantries. Could never get used to being kissed by people she hadn't met before. Feeling out of place in London, Patti was continually on her best behaviour. Conscious of her accent; of the need not to embarrass her grown-up daughter with a quaint turn of phrase (did these people say toilet or loo?); of the missing button on her cardigan (how had that escaped her attention); of her size. "Tell me what I can do. Are you alright for money?"

"I think so. We'll have to see how quickly the insurance company can pay us something."

Here was how they could be of use to a grown-up daughter who had never needed much in the way of help, being so capable and so very far away. "I'm sure we can give you a loan to be getting along with."

"I hate asking, but we might need to take you up on that."

"Don't be daft. Besides, you didn't ask. I offered. But you're alright, are you? Both of you, I mean?"

"To be honest, we're in shock."

A volley of coughing filled Patti's head. She jerked the receiver away from her ear and held it aside until the noise receded. "Of course you are. There'd be something wrong with you if you weren't."

"People at the hospital kept telling us how lucky we've been. One of the paramedics said there must have been someone watching out for us." What sounded like a bitter laugh might well have been the onset of tears. Patti knew only too well how thin the line between the two was.

She tried to personify calm. "Well, the main thing is that you're alright. You have each other. You hang onto that -"

"Mum, I'm sorry." Her daughter's voice was efficient again, her vowels elongated. "Ed's telling me I need to get off the phone. We're waiting for a couple of urgent calls."

Panic flared in the pit of Patti's stomach. There were other things that Ron would want to know. "You'll text me to let us know where you're staying? The address -"

"I'm really sorry, Mum. I've got to go."

"Of course you do." Patti found herself talking to a dead line. "Of course you do," she said again as she put the receiver back in its cradle. Cheap plastic. No attempt to make it easy on the eye. Even the font on the digital display was ugly. Look how they've squashed the 'g' in 'charging' so that it's the same height as the 'r' and the 'i'!

Patti opened the appointments diary she and Ron kept, so that one would know what the other was up to, and when the car might be available. Taking a biro from the pen tidy, she wrote the word FIRE in today's otherwise empty space. She stared for some time at the scrawl of capital letters. Having intended to cement the event as fact, instead Patti sat wondering, the weight of her failings pressing down on her temples. FIRE had already taken on the look of something she might have dreamt up. Her mother, Clemmie, had always accused Patti of having a morbid imagination: *'As if we don't have enough to worry about, Patricia!'* And, though she'd rubbished the suggestion, perhaps she'd had been right. Only recently, Patti had asked Ron if he'd heard the news about Stevie Gerrard, captain of Liverpool.

"I'm sorry love, but he's dead."

"Dead? He can't be."

"That's what they said." She dismissed an inner voice which demanded, *Who told you that?*

Ron had sat hunched and grim-faced, re-tuning the radio, working his way methodically, station by station. With his distress visibly increasing, Patti decided that she would just Google it, to be absolutely sure, astonished to discover she must have dreamt it after all.

There were other words she should have offered Anita, words of comfort and advice. Patti understood full well that now wasn't the time to indulge selfish thoughts, but she couldn't help thinking about the christening robe. Its silk and embroidery, its antique lace edging. She'd been baptised in it, and her mother before her. Neither Patti nor her mother had made much use of the robe. One child apiece. Quite normal these days, of course. The press called it the China Syndrome, referring to the child as a 'singleton' - a term previously reserved for Bridget Jones.

She'd presented the robe to Anita shortly after her daughter announced that she and Ed were moving in together, a conversation Patti couldn't imagine having had with her own mother, never mind that Anita had turned thirty. It had been bad enough telling her parents that she and Ron were getting married. Only the thought of what the neighbours would have said about the alternatives had brought her mother round. Respectability - that was the thing. As if the Roscoes were so much better than the Halls!

"I really want you to like Ed," Anita had said, her voice laced with urgency.

"Of course I like him. What a daft thing to say." Patti wondered if her modern young daughter hadn't been after her blessing and, never one to gush, she couldn't think of another way to give it. The truth was that she'd liked Ed from the moment she'd set eyes on him. There was no reason not to. She'd never been absolutely sure what it was he did for a living, except that it was something in a private bank. Possibly on the I.T. side of things (he was always good for sorting out electrical equipment when it played up). He was one of those capable sorts, practical and kind. The type who would have had her mother-in-law declaring, *'If he stuck his hand down the toilet, he'd find a gold watch'*, but then Mrs Hall always believed that everything came down to luck. *'You can't alter what's headed your way'*. Ed had grafted to get where he was and hard work was something both she and Ron respected. What's more, he and Anita looked good together, so Patti had decided not to fret about the absence of an engagement ring.

She'd waited until the men were installed in front of the rugby, Ron adding his tuppence-worth to the official commentary. Opportunity for a genuine mother and daughter moment.

"Here. You should have this now." Patti had placed the oblong-lidded box on the dinner table after Anita had helped clear the debris of Sunday lunch (although Patti noticed they'd missed a stray coffee cup and several abandoned After Eight wrappers). She positioned the box in such a way that Anita would realise this was something of considerable significance.

"What is it?" Anita had asked, tucking hair behind her ears.

"Why don't you take a look?"

She removed the lid - as if the cardboard itself were valuable - and peeled back the delicate layers of tissue with her long-fingered hands.

There was a word for the thing Patti wanted to capture. Not just significance, but - oh, what was it? That thing possessed by newsreaders and politicians. Even priests, if they were worth their salt. "It's the robe you were christened in." Gravitas, that was it!

"The embroidery!" Anita's gaze had darted towards Patti's face, her eyes widening. "It's exquisite." Her daughter's expression was the same one she'd worn the first time Patti had taken her to London for the weekend. The rain showed no mercy and, caught without a brolly, she'd suggested they took refuge in the V&A. *'You might like the costumes.'* There'd been no going back from that moment. Patti had barely taken in the contents of the glass cabinets. Instead, she had watched Anita's rapt face reflected in the glass. *Mantu gown by unknown maker 1760 – 70.* Jealous was how Patti had felt. She hadn't discovered the thing that could make her feel that way: enchanted, curious, hungry to gobble up every fact. But, of course, she'd never had Anita's confidence; never thought the world might be hers to conquer. Though everyone had drummed it into Patti that she was a clever child, the peak of her aspirations had been that, like her Aunty Nellie, she might one day live on the Wirral - 'over the water' as it was called. New Brighton, where the dance halls were the height of sophistication, but during Patti's childhood, as far as she was concerned, the beach had been the main draw. Days spent playing with Norris, Nellie's Labrador. *'All woof and no bite'* as her aunt put it, he tolerated having his tail grabbed when she lost her balance in the shallows.

It must have been Ron's influence, Patti supposed. Ron who had patiently sat Anita on his knee and read her the names and dates he'd written for the Family Notices in the *Liverpool Echo*. Ron who took her hand and twirled her around the front room as he played his 45s; Ron who, discovering she couldn't be encouraged to take an interest in his beloved football team - the Red Men - had taken her to the Walker Art Gallery.

Patti had thought Anita's fascination was with the clothes themselves, the outrageous six-foot-wide skirts, the rich silks, the intricate beading. On their return home from London, her daughter had sat sketching for hours on end, adding flourishes of her own to what she recreated from memory. Over the next few years, Anita would often be found with an open sketchbook. *'Doodling'*, Ron called it. It was easy to imagine walking into the kitchen and finding her there now. Patti had suggested they tried dress-making, something a mother and daughter could do together. But Anita wasn't interested. What had stirred her imagination was the mystery of the *unknown dress-maker*.

Now Anita pronounced the christening robe Victorian.

"So I was told by your Nan," Patti confirmed.

"Has it been in the family long?" This was the girl who'd taken herself off on the bus to Liverpool's Central Library and discovered how undervalued women's traditional skills and crafts were. She reported back. When the Royal Academy of Art allowed the first women to join, the committee barred them from life-drawing classes and lectures about male anatomy, and was quick to minute that needlework, artificial flowers, shell-work 'and the like' were strictly forbidden.

"This unknown dress-maker was a woman," Anita had pronounced, her confidence shocking Patti.

"One afternoon's research and you're the expert, are you? How can you be so sure?"

"Because if it had been a man, we'd know his name."

Something about her daughter's reasoning rang true, but what did you do with certainty like that? And what good would it do Anita in Liverpool where there might be a job for her behind the beauty counter at George Henry Lee's - *if* she was lucky? There'd been no job for Patti. Once Anita was in school, she'd hoped to help out with the family income. Something part-time, something to build on. But whereas before it was thought that what jobs there were should go to the men, now it was suggested that the 'young ones' be allowed a crack of the whip.

"Such a shame." Though she hadn't shared Patti's surprise, her mother, Clemmie, had shaken her head. "And you, with so much promise." Twenty-five years old, and even her mother had written her off.

Of course, though Patti hadn't known it at the time, Anita had never pictured staying in Liverpool. Careers' advice in the eighties had been blunt: leave - and, while you're about it, lose the accent. Another generation of the city's finest, siphoned off. Others found work in Chester or Conwy, but Anita chose London, and all Ron said was, "Good luck to her." She'd been a long time in planning her great escape, digging a network of tunnels. And then, after a couple of false starts, waitressing and bar work, Anita had netted her dream job - a curator at Hampton Court Palace.

Now Patti stared hard at the antique robe and said, "I was christened in it. And so was your Nan. Before that, I don't really know."

"So it might have been in the family for generations?"

Patti's shrug was non-committal. "Perhaps." Her own mother hadn't dispensed facts willingly. Sensing that questions would have been as welcome as a dose of the mumps, Patti had never given her curiosity a voice. "But there wasn't a lot of money going spare. My grandparents might have bought it second-hand." Cut and stitched with another child in mind.

"I should wash my hands before touching it," Anita enthused, removing her assortment of silver rings, stowing them in a cut-glass bowl on the sideboard. Patti's impatience relocated to her chest as her daughter paid what she considered to be unnecessary attention when drying her hands. Anita wasn't about to perform open heart surgery, for goodness' sake.

"Right. Let's take a look." Her touch was light as she smoothed the fabric out. "Of course, it shouldn't really be kept in tissue paper. Not unless it's acid-free. Was the silk originally this dark?"

No criticism was intended, and yet Patti felt its pointed end. She imagined her mother-in-law quipping, '*Who knitted your face and dropped a stitch?*' These sayings hadn't been part of her upbringing. She'd adopted them to spite her own mother, who thought Ron's family common. "It was always ivory, from what I remember," she offered.

And Anita had lifted the robe, holding it against her jersey dress. She looked down at it, eyes glistening with delight. "I had no idea. Aside from the slight discolouration, it's in beautiful condition. I wonder..."

This was more like it. Things were getting back on track. "What?"

"It wasn't uncommon for a single wedding dress to be cut up to make several christening robes."

"So the material could be older."

The corners of Patti's mouth twitched. It was impossible to see the christening robe unboxed without thinking of Anita wearing it. She hoped that her daughter would never know the heartbreak she had suffered. A child she'd been unable to bond with. But it would have been wonderful to see her in a wedding gown.

Patti's friends, Geraldine and Frances, had assured her over coffee that the lack of an engagement ring didn't mean anything. Young people did things differently these days, just as they'd all done things differently from their parents (and most were willing to admit they'd do differently now if they had their time again).

"Although we weren't so open about our love lives in the sixties - at least not with our folks."

"Time she got a move on," Geraldine had said. "The clock's ticking."

"I'd like to see her married, but I won't be too upset if there are no grandchildren," Patti said, enjoying their open-mouthed expressions - though, as always, the truth was more complicated. She seethed as, having refused a plate (*'I'll save you the washing up'*), Geraldine blatantly swept her lap free of biscuit crumbs. She could have murdered her, sitting there, flaunting her *World's Best Nan* t-shirt. The police wouldn't have needed to chalk her outline. It would have been there for all to see, marked out in crumbs. The pair had been close ever since their daughters were in primary school together, but there was no getting away from the fact that Geraldine had a gob like the Mersey tunnel. You might as well place an advert in the *Echo* as tell her a secret.

"Well?" her friends probed over the years. "Do we need to buy a hat yet?

"I expect it will be very discreet. Once you start paying a London mortgage, there's no money for diamond rings, let alone the fortunes people fork out for big ceremonies these days."

But Patti had taken note when Anita and Ed had found money for foreign holidays and a gleaming new kitchen. She and Ron never went to stay in London without a bottle of bubbly being cracked open in welcome (even though what Patti wanted after being stuck on the M25 for two hours was a nice pot of tea). There was nothing toffee-nosed about Anita and Ed, but you could enjoy a slap-up meal at the Adelphi for the price of the hand wash in their bathroom.

It was hard, what with Geraldine trumpeting about her daughter. "Our Lizzie's up to number four." Patti tried to keep her conflicted emotions in check, but when Jason took it on himself to have the snip, even Ron - who would have loved more children - had remarked, "About bloody time."

Though Patti sometimes felt as if her nose was being rubbed in it, Geraldine had more than earned her *World's Best Nan* t-shirt. She'd more or less brought the first one up as her own. At that point, Lizzie had still been living at home. Then she'd given up her own job so that Lizzie could go back to work, spending more time with the grandkids than her daughter or son-in-law did. But now that they were off doing their own thing, they rarely made time for her. It would have been unthinkable for a week to go by without Patti dropping in to see her grandad, even if it was only a quick visit to make sure he wasn't short of ciggies. Geraldine made excuses for her grandchildren, but Patti wasn't convinced. The t-shirt had acquired a washed-out look.

If only she didn't have to suffer Geraldine's pitying looks - the ones that suggested there was something missing - as she probed, "And how's your Anita?"

"Ah, she's doing great," Patti would reply, offering some snippet that Anita had fed her. A holiday. A theatre trip. Another exhibition at Hampton Court Palace. Something invented - because what were the chances of Geraldine checking up? No, all things considered, Patti thought it best that there was no grandchild. But it seemed sad and strange that the Halls and the Roscoes would end with Anita, their family tree an inverted triangle. Still, she wasn't a bad finale by anyone's calculations.

It could have been far worse, Patti reminded herself. *Imagine the smoke alarm had run out of batteries. Imagine Anita and Ed hadn't woken up in time.* Her heartbeat accelerated. Those things didn't bear thinking about. *She's fine.* Patti gave herself a ticking off. *They're both fine. Be grateful for what you have.*

But it didn't stop Patti's breath from juddering. The chris-tening robe had gone up in flames. There was a finality about it. Her family tree would peter out. No more branches. Patti tucked the pen inside the diary's plastic-coated ring-binder. Bin day tomorrow. She must get round to sorting out the recycling. Perhaps in a moment or two.

Ron kicked off his muddied shoes, paired them outside the back door, and entered the kitchen in sock feet. He could see his wife's outline in the hall. She was sitting at the telephone table, her back to him. There was a time when, at the sight of her swan neck, he would have crept up and kissed the cool skin below the line of her bobbed hair, and she wouldn't have told him not to be daft. "That's me done," he said, so as not to startle her. "The beer traps are out, the salt's down, and I've topped up the pots on the patio with grit. And, no, I didn't use slug pellets - though why you should give a damn about the neighbours' cats, I don't know."

Expecting a retort, he paused, but Patti didn't take the bait. In fact, she was so still that Ron felt the creep of inexplicable dread, something he found happening more frequently with age. He approached, feigning cheerfulness. "They'll be safe until the next time one of them uses the flower beds as a litter tray."

Still nothing. He reached for his wife's shoulder, relieved to find it warm, and gave a squeeze. "A penny for them?"

"Christ!" Her hand leapt to her chest. "You made me jump." There was a look of panic about Patti's face. Her skin was bleached.

"It's only your loving husband. I live here, remember? You've probably seen me wandering about the place occasionally."

"I was miles away." Patti's hand moved from her chest to her mouth and her forehead creased along the length of her worry lines. Her new haircut provided a slightly different frame for her face. It was shorter than usual and, knowing she wasn't terribly pleased with the hairdresser, Ron had declared that he liked it.

"Is anything wrong, love? You don't seem your normal chipper self."

She nodded at him, a look of forgetfulness - or of someone wanting to forget. "It's our Anita."

A seed of panic rooted itself in his stomach. "Our kid?" he prompted, feeling for the fourth step and easing himself into an uncomfortable sitting position. One that enabled eye contact. Provided he could see his wife's eyes, Ron could read her like a book.

A dark shadow shot across Patti's irises. "She says we're not to panic."

Don't let your imagination run riot, he cautioned himself. "*What* aren't we to panic about?"

"There's been a fire -"

Blood drained from Ron's face. "A fire?"

"But they're alright, both of them. They've been checked out at the hospital and they're not hurt."

His chest was tight, gripping and twisting. "When did it happen?"

"Last night."

"Do they know how it started?"

"I doubt they'll ever know." Her voice was gentle. "Anita says they've lost everything apart from the clothes on their backs. And, if that really *is* the case, I expect the evidence will have been destroyed."

"Good God," he heard himself whisper, a dusty voice coming from some forgotten airless place inside him. Something stirred, a vague memory awakening. Then, all at once, images crowded Ron's mind, images that didn't belong together - but he couldn't stop them from coming. His daughter's beautiful face, contorted. The night sky lit up like the Blackpool Illuminations. Bomb craters. A terrible tangle of metal and electrical cables. Wrought iron girders felled. A section of overhead track that looked like a ramp. Of being asked to identify Anita's body. His knees buckling in protest. Every fear he'd ever had for his daughter combined with guilty secrets. There was no logic. Patti had spoken to Anita. She was safe. And yet...

Then, from this frightful collage, a sound came. One Ron had hoped to never hear again: the wail of the banshee - the air raid siren. His father ushering him down to the cellar, the temperature dropping, the light dimming with every narrow concrete step. He remembered kneeling in the damp, scrunching his eyes shut until he felt dizzy and pleading, *Dear God, please make it stop. Make them go away.* Rocking back and forth, the touch of cold fingertips against his forehead, his nose between his index fingers, breath warming his palms.

His mother's voice: "Be still, Ronnie. Calm yourself."

It wasn't that he particularly wanted to live, in fact he was very, very tired. But Ron was terrified of being buried alive. The noise of the bombs, the shudders they sent rippling through buildings, the taste of plaster in his mouth. Calming down was impossible. Besides, he needed to keep praying. *Let them drop their bombs on someone else tonight.* If it was to be a case of us or them, he wanted it to be them: *Take Mr and Mrs Frenchman. Take Bart Nisbet.* But these were people he didn't like. A prayer needed a sacrifice: *Take our Aunty Magda.*

He remembered his mother standing by the front door, doubled over, biting down on her knuckles. No sound came from her. But when she allowed him to take her hand in his, he saw the individual tooth-marks cut into her skin.

Our Magda.

How could he have admitted that the bomb that killed her sister as she rode the overhead railway had been meant for them? That wasn't how it was supposed to work. You offered God the person you loved above all others and, at the very last moment, he was supposed to let you off the hook with that deep booming voice: *Now I know that you fear God.* They had lied to him at Sunday school and he could never forgive them.

He'd passed the supporting railway girders every day on the walk to his office at the *Echo*. It was unavoidable. They were there, buried in the road, by the high brick wall. The dockers' umbrella, that's what they used to call it. *Dear God, Please let them drop their bombs on someone else tonight.* Every day, a fresh reminder.

Ron looked up. There was Patti, hovering over him, asking, "Are you alright, love?"

Glad he was sitting down, Ron felt himself rocking slightly. "Thank God they're safe." His fingertips met his forehead. "But their house... and all of their things...?" he said, altogether overwhelmed.

The words - at least those he wanted to say - refused to come. He managed to blurt, "How was she?" but it sounded trite, so he added, "How did she sound?"

"She was in a good deal of shock. Of course."

He made a murmuring sound.

"I said we'd see how much we can lend them until the insurance comes through."

In many ways, his wife's ability to remain detached in times of crises was a good thing. Someone had to be capable of thinking of practicalities. "Of - of course." It was obvious to Ron that he should be taking charge, picking up the phone and trying to keep his patience while he battled with the telephone banking menu, struggling to remember his passcode and the answers to his security questions. But it was impossible to focus. "Do you think you -?" He stalled, realising that he had no idea what he'd intended to say.

"You sit there for a minute or two." Patti cupped his knee, then pressed down on it as she stood. "Get your breath back."

"Right." Ron took the hand of the woman he had loved

for most of his adult life and pressed it to his lips. Patti wore her pained expression, and he was grateful that she made it possible for him to push aside his own tortuous thoughts. But adult logic and the cold light of day couldn't lighten the ten-tonne weight he dragged around with him.

"I'll put the kettle on. Make us some tea."

His understanding of loyalty, and of marriage in particular, included a host of unspoken and unspeakable things.

"I'll make us that cuppa," Patti repeated.

It was as much as Ron could do to nod his head in agreement. Patti's secret was safe with him. So safe that he would never let on that he knew. At times, he blamed Mrs Roscoe. The *formidable* Mrs Roscoe, as he thought of his mother-in-law. There you were. The fact of it was that his wife could not feel as he felt about their daughter - but no one was harder on themselves than Patti.

CHAPTER THREE

"Anita! I've been trying to reach you! Are you on your way in?"

Anita had been crossing the hospital car park when her mobile phone began to vibrate. As she paused to fumble with the straps of her bag, seeing that she was struggling, Ed had taken her laptop in his good hand. It was Roz.

"I need to take this." Her eyes particularly sensitive to daylight, Anita squinted up at Ed's drawn face, grey with exhaustion. She motioned that he should go on ahead and put the money in the parking meter.

The voice on the other end of the line was breathy. Anita imagined her manager walking briskly along narrow cobbled passageways, over the stone slabs of the Tudor kitchen or across the broad sweep of the Great Hall, casting scalding glances at anything that was out of place. The warders abandoning their gossip and standing straighter as Roz charged by, announced by the clip of her heels. "Didn't you get my text?" Anita said. "I'm sorry but we've been stuck at the hospital all night." Reminded how physically and mentally exhausted she was, as if on cue, her eyes began to stream. She hardly had the will to keep them open.

"I didn't, no. Is everything alright?"

"We've got to come back for more X-rays next week but

they say it's just smoke inhalation." Speaking irritated her throat. Knowing she would be unable to stop coughing once she started, Anita swallowed.

"Smoke?"

"We had a fire at the house last night."

"Damn this reception! Did you say a *fire?*"

Anita ducked behind a red-brick pillar which supported an overhanging corner of the building, out of the range of a motorbike's roar. "I think the problem might be the noise at this end."

"Not your dishwasher, was it? I heard a terrible story about one bursting into flames. Smoked out the whole kitchen. I won't be using mine again at night in a hurry."

Anita could still taste charcoal. Even the hairs in her nostrils were coated in soot. What she really needed was a long, hot soak. "We honestly don't know what started it."

"Well, you can give me all the details once you get here. I've got Helena filling in for you, but I don't think we can trust her to do the introductions tonight. You know Helena..."

Anita bristled. "That's the thing, Roz. I'm not going to be able to make -"

"Can you still hear me?"

"I -"

"Listen, if you need to catch up on a couple of hours' sleep, do. It doesn't matter when you get here, as long as you're in time for the drinks reception."

Her body felt like a dead weight. Swaying slightly, Anita could have gladly fallen asleep on her feet. "Roz, I can hear you just fine, but I'm not sure you understand." She tried to circumnavigate the lump that had lodged in her throat. "Our house has burnt down! All we have left are the clothes we're standing up in." The magnitude of what had happened was still sinking in. It was unreal to think that she was homeless, that everything they owned was gone.

The phone seemed to have been stunned into silence. It was a moment before Roz repeated, "Burnt down?" Her incredulity still suggested that Anita's timing was inconsiderate.

"To the ground." The effort of saying those few words left Anita shaking from her core. *Everything they owned was gone.* Feeling as if her legs were about to give way, she threw out one hand in search of support. It grazed the red-brick pillar and, with this incidental action, she was transported to Hampton Court Palace.

Whenever Anita needed to escape from the library or the office, she walked the length of the Processional Gallery. Pausing by a deep windowsill, she placed her left hand within the etched outline of another hand. Others had engraved initials and dates, but this person chose to leave something infinitely more personal, something a child might have done. The cool stone had acquired a sheen, suggesting that ladies in waiting, grace and favour tenants and paying visitors had been similarly moved, and she felt connected to them all.

"Shit! I mean... Anita! Good God, that's *awful.*"

"Yes," Anita said, relieved that this much was appreciated. She rotated until the flat of her back was propped against the pillar, then she sank to a crouching position.

"I don't know what to say. I mean, here's me, going on... Tell me what I can do."

Anita massaged her forehead. "I'm going to need a few days to sort myself out. We need to find somewhere to stay. Buy a few basics."

"Right. Of course you will. Of course you will." Roz sounded distracted, her subtext almost as loud as her words. "Take all the time you need. You're not to worry about us." She would be pacing the floor.

Anita felt as if she was letting the side down, but not only that. This evening's event had been her baby. Now, she wasn't going to see it through. "It can't be helped," Ed had said, and it couldn't. Only Roz would understand how much it pained her to hand over the reins. "My notes for tonight are in a file on my computer called 'The Queen in the Tower' and there's a short biography for Alison Weir." Anita had learned the introduction off by heart. *Alison Weir has perfected the art of bringing history to life.* She had borrowed the sentence from a review by the *Chicago Herald*, but it was a good starting point. "And if you wouldn't mind apologising from me..."

"OK, I'm on my way over to the office now. Is there anything else you were down to do?"

"Probably." Items had been queuing inside Anita's head for the past few weeks, emerging when she was sitting on the sofa watching a film or when she woke in the early hours. Now it was as if her thoughts, too, were clogged by smoke. "I can't think straight."

"I'm not surprised." And then. "Christ! What am I going to do?"

"Go to the *Recently changed* files on my computer. That should give you an idea of everything I've been working on."

"OK, OK."

"And if I think of anything else, I'll call."

"I can say a few words. Anyway, Alison's been here so many times, she knows the score."

"As long as the projector's set up for her. Oh, and if someone could make sure she has a bottle of mineral water."

"Holy crap, you know how hopeless I am with the projector. I don't even know where to find it."

"Dan's good with things like that. Put him in charge. And try the Clore Learning Centre." She found herself staring at the borrowed boots. The bloody *Cath Kidston* wellingtons. Perhaps she could borrow some clothes... Anita felt the tarmac tilt. The horizon was a diagonal. No, it was impossible. "You'll be fine."

"Concentrate on yourself. Call if you need anything. In

fact call anyway, just to let me know how you're getting on."

"OK." As she thumbed the button to end the call, Anita experienced a cocktail of emotions she'd never entertained before. Disorientated, she stood and scanned the car park for the white roof of the Mini. Wearing his dressing gown and grey tracksuit bottoms, her laptop tucked under one arm, Ed was leaning against a pay machine.

And it struck her.

She strode over to meet him, shaking her head. "I'd completely forgotten. We don't own a car anymore."

"Just as well. These parking charges are outrageous. Come on. We'd better get a move on. I'm not walking to Natalie's dressed like this."

Up until that moment, Ed had resisted the idea of taking Anita's friend up on her offer of putting them up for a few nights, protesting, "Staying with friends always ends in disaster. Maybe Natalie felt she had to offer. She can hardly hide the fact that she's got a spare room."

Anita had baulked at the idea that Natalie had expected them to refuse. "She's trying to do something nice for us. It would be awkward to say no."

Perhaps Ed had remembered how caged they always felt in hotel rooms once the novelty of matching bathrobes wore off. Or perhaps, like her, he was too drained to argue.

Ed tightened the belt of his dressing gown. "We'll get the bus. But first I need to nip into Sutton."

Anita felt her jaw drop. Running on empty, she had nothing left to give. "What for?" The prospect of going anywhere was ridiculous, let alone walking around a shopping centre.

Ed was insisting, "There's not much point in having a shower if I haven't got any clean clothes to change into." He seemed to have located an emergency store of energy. "We won't be the first people seen in town wearing pyjamas."

"But they won't let us try on clothes smelling like this!"

"I don't need to try anything on. I'll just grab some jeans and a couple of t-shirts. It'll take five minutes."

"Oh, I see!"

"What now?"

"No, you're right." She relented, the realisation that she was beyond caring what anyone thought of her struck Anita as a comfort. "You can hardly borrow Natalie's clothes."

"What are you doing?"

Extraordinarily tired, she had reached for her mobile phone again. "I draw the line at going by bus. I'm calling a cab!"

He pointed with his bandaged hand. "Over by the entrance. There's a queue of them."

CHAPTER FOUR

Anita and Ed had only ever arrived at the house in separate cars once before - when they went for the first viewing (back in the days when a car had come with Ed's job). It had been an impractical choice, something they both recognised, but each trusted their guts and each other. Their thirty-three previous appointments with estate agents had proved fruitless. Sometimes they hadn't got as far as the front door before one of them looked knowingly at the other with a slow head shake. Everything else on the market felt like family homes, which wasn't what Anita and Ed were about. One of the first things they had agreed during the moving-in-together discussion was that they didn't want children and, but for a slight waver around the time of her thirty-seventh birthday, Anita was convinced it had been the right decision.

"Last chance to change your mind," Ed had joked, after catching her pulling faces at a baby dressed in blue who was being wheeled around their local park (a quiet baby, mind).

But for every well-behaved child, a riot of others ran amuck, cutting across their path on scooters and trikes, shrieking at the tops of their voices. And Anita could hardly complain that this wasn't the place to let off steam. Beddington Park had been teeming. Families were equipped with tents and folding chairs, swing ball sets and cricket stumps. Smoke from barbeques had turned the air opaque. Children were climbing onto and hurling themselves off tree stumps (*I'm the king of the castle, you're the dirty rascal*). "It's difficult to imagine where you might fit another eighty million people a year."

"They probably won't *all* come to our park."

Ed's ability to be flippant offset Anita's seriousness and she could laugh once more. "Not at once, anyhow." But navigating the crowds, the thought that crunch-time would arrive within fifty years *was* sobering. It was these children - this waist-height child, haring in their direction - who would have to find the solution. Anita found herself staring at a pregnant woman, focusing, not on her oblivious expression, but on the swell of her hard round belly. Sometimes Anita sensed that she was sealed behind a Perspex wall, outlawed from the life her ten-year-old self had assumed she would lead. And so she squeezed Ed's hand, assuring herself that he was real.

A child's demands for ice cream spiralled into wails of, "It's not fair. I hate you!"

"Fancy finding a beer garden and sitting outside with a pint?"

"Yes!" She jumped at the chance. This was the life she had chosen. Anita liked the fact that they were a couple, but weren't joined at the hip. They went out into the world separately but came back home together. Ed, crossing over London Bridge into the City, keeping one eye on the future. Her, at Hampton Court Palace, with one foot in the past.

What Anita saw as she stepped out of her car had curved her mouth into a smile. The small property was the house a child would draw: a square, topped by a triangular roof with a central chimney; windows either side of the door. Timber beams extended from the eaves, creating a large porch, the original black and white floor tiles still intact. Window boxes filled with wallflowers had been placed on the broad window-sills. It was a gingerbread house.

By the time Ed had parked his car behind Anita's and joined her, she was grinning excitedly.

"Try not to look too keen."

She hugged herself. "I might not be able to help myself!"

"Well, here goes," he said, leading the way up the path and using the brass door knocker.

The décor was hideous - Anaglypta walls competing with Artex ceilings. All but the front room, whose walls were covered almost entirely with small framed sepia photographs. Ed whispered, "What are they hiding?" and flared his nostrils several times. Though Anita widened her eyes in warning, he embarrassed her by asking the vendor - a woman of tiny proportions - "Has there been a damp problem?"

"The house will sell itself," she replied with a curt smile, confidence that proved impossible to dislodge. When Anita, armed with a measuring tape, raised a space-related objection about the sloped bedroom ceilings - "Where would be the best place to put a wardrobe?" - the woman's gaze suggested that she was looking backwards through the years: "I raised three boys here."

"Very small ones," Ed whispered, his breath warm in Anita's ear. She elbowed him in the ribs.

"The house talks to me," the woman said as they traipsed downstairs in an awkward procession. Ed, with one hand on the low angled ceiling, ducked his head. It was something they would learn was true, woken every morning as each beam and pipe, floorboard and roof tile yawned and stretched.

"So, what was this place?" Anita asked about the unusual property.

"The gatehouse to an estate, or so I was told. Didn't you see the photograph?"

Anita and Ed looked at the woman blankly.

"You must have walked straight past it!" She unhooked an Edwardian photograph that hung in the hall - just a few square feet (no room to hang their coats, Anita noted). "Here."

With Ed craning over her shoulder, Anita studied what she held in her hands. She *knew* instinctively that the story about the gatehouse wasn't true. Only half of the house was in the shot, but there was its chimney, its steeply-pitched roof (which, as they were to discover, made extending the house downright impossible) and one of the dormer windows. And there was the front garden, sloping gently towards a tennis court where a game of doubles was taking place. Women wearing hats and long white dresses; men dressed in straw boaters and blazers. In the foreground, spectators were seated on a wooden bench, a dog lying obediently at their feet. Elsewhere, children played on a see-saw.

The photograph sold the house as far as Anita was concerned. Here was a mystery that cried out to be solved. Though the current owner loved the house in her own way, she had not loved it enough to unearth its history.

Even an impractical house can tick a number of boxes - a double garage, off-road parking, good-sized gardens front and rear, plus it was on a quiet cul-de-sac less than five minutes' walk from the train station. And so, on their respective drives back to the ground floor flat that was home at the time, each rehearsed arguments why this was the one - despite its appearance of being a money pit. Over a bottle of wine, they transformed flaws into quirks; things in need of repair as opportunities to put their stamp on it. The vendor had been right. Something about the house had spoken to them.

Turning into their road, from the back seat of the taxi, Anita found that her jaw ached with the memory of how she had grinned at Ed.

It turned out that the man who built the house had owned all of the land that made up Chalkdale. Financial difficulties forced him to auction it off, plot by plot. The newer properties, which had arrived in pairs over the better part of two decades, described his reluctance. Sloping link-attached chalets, rendered in white. Mock-Tudor semis, with herringbone brickwork and diamond-cut leaded glass. A hint of Art Deco. Further down, surrounding the narrow cul-de-sac's circular turning point, were retirement bungalows. Anita and Ed had joined an ageing population, many of whom had been the first occupants of the 'new' properties. You moved here, it seemed, and you left in a box. Gradually, since their arrival, those whose next move was to a cemetery were replaced by young families. One elderly neighbour, Edith, recalled a previous steward of their house with great fondness. A retired naval captain who sat in a wicker chair on the porch, smoking his pipe. He kept a lovely garden, but his name had slipped her mind. Never mind, it would come back to her...

"Of course, the house wasn't always painted. I remember when it was just the red brick."

"You do?" Anita enjoyed these snippets. Edith had been a Wren during the war. She'd liked to jive. Been good at it too. Met Glenn Miller once.

"Beautiful, it was. A terrible shame when they whitewashed it. You'll look after it, though."

The pair who owned the house before them had never been liked, she was told. He was something in double glazing. Blocked Edith's view with his high-sided van. It was him who'd crazy paved the drive. There had always been a suspicion hanging over them. And the fact that they sold up and moved away, well that proved it, didn't it? "But you'll stay, I can tell. You're Chalkdale people."

Flanked by post-war semis with tall, hipped roofs that sat further forwards on their plots, the house was slow to reveal itself.

"Anywhere around here will -" As the taxi pulled up

outside what remained of her house, Anita felt utterly unde-fended. Her head swam.

"That'll be five pounds eighty-five, love," the taxi driver said, his eyes reflected back at her in the rear-view mirror.

All Anita could do was stare. Her jaw felt misshapen.

He twisted towards her. "Whenever you're ready."

"Sorry, of course." It was a relief to be able to fumble in her purse for a fiver and two pound coins. "Here you are." She passed them through the sliding window. But her feet didn't seem to want to move. It was as if they knew that her legs weren't up to the job of carrying her.

The cabbie clearly thought Anita was expecting change, but she dismissed his offer of coins. Following the path of her gaze, he blew out his cheeks. "Poor buggers. Know them, do you?"

Anita could feel the length of her windpipe as she spoke. Each bronchus, branching off into bronchioles, choked by soot; speckled with crimson embers. "I'm one of the poor buggers." Reaching blindly for the door handle, she stepped out slowly, clutching her carrier bags. Anita's immediate view was through the posts of the lychgate. Her bitter laugh sliced the air. Wait until Ed saw! The concrete garden path - the one thing they both hated but hadn't got round to changing - had survived, virtually intact. The indentations, designed to give the appearance of stone blockwork, the dips and the cracks, had pooled with black water. *And* we still own a garage, she reminded herself, glancing to the right of the house. That's something, I suppose.

"Listen, I -" At the sound of his voice, she turned to find the taxi driver leaning over the gear stick, speaking through the open passenger window. He looked mortified.

For his sake, she attempted to smile. "It's not a problem. Really."

"I can stick around if you think I'll be any use."

"No, you're alright." How to refer to Ed always posed a challenge. You could hardly call a man in his mid-forties a 'boyfriend', and 'partner' suggested a business relationship. "My other half will be along any minute. In fact, this is probably him now."

"If you're sure." The cabbie looked both doubtful and relieved.

"Yes, here he is," she confirmed.

As soon as the taxi pulled away from the kerb, Ed parked the shiny red hire car in its place. Anita caught sight of his face, the most familiar in her world, and yet there was something *un*familiar about his expression. As he stepped out of the vehicle, jangling a set of keys, she wiped the thought from her mind.

"Sorry, sorry, sorry." Ed skirted the bonnet, the engine clicking as it cooled.

"Why so many apologies?"

He pressed a kiss into Anita's hair. "I wanted to get here before you. I hadn't realised there would be so much paperwork to sign at the hire place."

This visit was intended to be a practice run for the appointment with the loss adjuster. Neither wanted to find themselves overcome in front of a stranger, and both agreed they should prepare a list of questions. She shrugged Ed's concern aside. "If it's any consolation, I only just beat you. This is my taxi."

The driver had slowed on his return journey from the turning circle at the far end of the road, and was looking out of the window - apparently checking that Anita hadn't been mistaken about this being the man she had lived with for fifteen years. Her hands full, Anita nodded and smiled. This small gesture took a disproportionate effort. The makings of a cough gathered force in her chest. She had seen 'before' and 'after' photographs of smokers' lungs. The 'before' a healthy pink; the 'after', charred and blackened.

When she recovered, Ed was frowning, his expression concerned.

"I'm fine," she insisted, trying to stand firm.

"Let's at least put your shopping in the car," Ed said, opening the rear door. Unlike the boot of their Mini, which had always attracted grass cuttings and gravel, this dark grey interior was pristine. "Did you manage to find everything you needed?"

Anita deposited the bags of clothes and toiletries next to Ed's purchases. The truth was that she'd been unable to build up any enthusiasm as she trudged around Kingston. For Ed, shopping was a practical exercise. He emerged from Bentalls having ordered a good suit and carrying bags containing five shirts, three ties, cufflinks and half a dozen pairs of socks (he was particular about those). Then he'd marched into Marks & Spencer looking for underwear, a pack of three t-shirts and an off-the-shelf suit to tide him over. He'd added another pair of jeans (always the same make and fit) to his cache. A quick trip to the chemists for toiletries and Ed announced that he was done and would pick up the hire car while she finished.

Men could never appreciate how difficult it was for women to find a pair of jeans that fitted, let alone the perfect pair of black trousers. Mourning her red silk skirt, her favourite cable-knit lime green jumper, Anita's response to Ed was to turn up her nose.

He slammed the car boot. "Well, at least they won't be borrowed. We'll be able to think about going back to work - for a bit of normality, if nothing else." Ed walked the short distance to the lychgate and stalled. "Can you believe it? The bloody path survived!"

Anita felt in her handbag for her mobile phone, switched to camera function and held it at arm's length. Cataloguing things was what she did. Reduced to the size of the screen, the scene became more manageable.

"*And* the garage."

Set back from the house, it was accessed via a drive that was too narrow for all but the sleekest of cars. Always slightly temperamental, the up-and-over door was ajar. When Anita pushed it higher, it retaliated with a high-pitched screech. Cobwebs and the smell of damp earth greeted her. Ducking her head, she stepped inside to investigate. The remnants of a bird's nest on an old shelving unit among half-used tins of paint; droppings spattered over garden furniture. She cast her gaze about. The garage had become a dumping ground for everything that didn't fit - or that they preferred not to keep - in the house. Included in the unloved hoard were unwanted presents - usually novelty gifts - brought inside for diplomatic reasons when the giver visited. Over time, Anita and Ed had become less certain who had bought what. Friends and family left with the impression that their tastes were considerably more eccentric and kitsch than was actually the case. Anita had rather hoped that looters would have helped themselves. These were not the things you'd choose when starting your life over again! But there was comfort in standing in a structure that was still theirs. Tempted to park herself on one of the garden chairs and take stock, Anita's mood altered. She felt the need to be physically close to Ed.

She found him standing near the spot where she'd left him. He was frowning at the mass of charred timbers, broken materials and glass, and the soup of soot and water that had been their home.

Now that most of what had been solid was derelict, the footprint of the house seemed insubstantial. She captured the image on her mobile phone. "It looks surprisingly small, doesn't it?" she said.

Ed didn't respond. Anita had never felt entitled to all of his thoughts, all of his secrets, and so she allowed him this moment of reflection.

Stepping over the threshold - what had been a tiled step - a powerful stench burned Anita's throat. The house had been their sanctuary. The last one to arrive home from work would always bolt the door on the outside world.

The parquet floor was still awash in places. She placed her feet carefully. Seeing the shapes of familiar things, Anita tried to find niches for them in her memory. All she could compare the process to was playing with her one-year-old goddaughter the previous weekend - less than a week, and yet so much was changed - helping her post plastic shapes into the right shaped holes. "Look at these. They must be the security rods from the front door."

"The locksmith said they were indestructible. It looks like he was right." Coming from behind her, Ed's voice was unusually flat. They seemed to have exchanged roles. She had expected *him* to jolly *her* along.

Anita stooped to examine something made of nondescript metal, remembering the stubborn child's determination to fit a star into a hexagonal hole, bewildered when it refused to cooperate. She dried the metal on the hem of her jumper before she remembered that it was borrowed. Perhaps the thing Anita was looking at wasn't the whole of something. Pointing her phone at the fragment, she took another photo.

It was odd to see what had survived - not only intact, but exactly where it had always been. You expected it of granite worktops and the cast iron burners from the hob. The smoke had blackened every vertical surface. The walls, the chimney breast. Anita likened the smell to the coal tar vaporiser that her mother lit whenever she was suffering from a heavy cold. Her Dad would perch on the edge of her mattress and, as they watched the shadows dance he would recall how, whenever he'd had a chest infection, his mother would wheel his pram down to the gas works so that he could inhale the fumes.

"*Yuk!*"

"It was the same whenever roads were tarred. The first sight of a steamroller and we'd be out there."

But this scent was contaminated. Underlying everything was the damp of the hosepipes.

Still, there were things that had retained their shapes. The dining table - though the chairs hadn't been so lucky. The glass placemats had melted then solidified again; distorted versions of their former selves. Unbelievably, the bookcase seemed to have fared better than the walls. Something inside Anita splintered at the sight of her beloved history books. Her margin notes, the hours of study, the detailed cross-referencing, could never be replicated.

As a curator, you had to set feelings aside. She took a photograph; distanced herself.

She found the copper lightshade over by what had been the French window, now a gaping hole. Identified by its thick metal chain, intact but tarnished, it looked more like a dented dustbin lid. A loud trilling drew her attention. A blackbird on the bird feeder, answering its own question. Anita stepped onto what had previously been a patio. The terracotta pots containing herbs and shrubs had been smashed; the bench where she would sit to drink her morning coffee upturned. But Anita was mesmerised by the view beyond. June was her favourite month. The bottom twelve feet of garden was given over to wildflowers, a wash of poppies, cornflowers and ox-eye daisies. Something about the contrast between the charred battlefield behind her and the rich sea of colour made Anita stand to attention, and then she slowly turned away.

The Buddha's head had fallen from the mantelpiece. It lay peacefully among the dereliction in the raised brick surround of the hearth. Eyes closed, his serene expression was unaltered, the slightest smile curling his lips; one shell-like ear with its elongated lobe; hair twisted in spiralling curls. Anita was ashamed to admit she knew very little about Buddhism. She had bought the hollow silver head because it was a beautiful object. It had seemed like a lucky thing to have in the house.

For a moment, she was back there in the night, barefoot, shaking with cold and shock. Ed whispering, *'It's just stuff,'* as they watched their lives being erased. A chill crept under her skin. Although Anita knew she was more than the sum of everything they'd owned, her armour had been stripped away. Here, with the taste of soot in her mouth, she was forced to admit that, without it, she felt smaller. Less sure of who she was, how she should act. Something of herself or of Ed had been invested in each object. Anita knew the stories behind every one of Ed's childhood relics, each telling a chapter of his life.

She looked to the place above the doorframe where his cricket bat had hung, its ridged side jutting outwards. Anita didn't understand the rules of the game, but had listened to Ed's descriptions of the anatomy of the bat. Made from a wood known as Cricket Bat Willow, she knew it had shoulders and a toe. She knew that a new bat needed to be 'run in', and that this meant hitting every inch of its surface, firstly with a sock-covered mallet, then bare mallet, gradually increasing the force. After at least six hours of painstaking tapping, you did your 'knocking in', hitting an old ball about in the back garden. If the ball left an indentation, you fetched the mallet again. But if you'd done it properly - as Ed had - you could try your hand in the nets. Only if the bat passed the nets was it ready to meet a cricket ball coming from the opposite direction at ninety miles an hour. It was hard to imagine kids these days having the patience.

And, of course, Anita knew the signatures of each member of Ed's team who'd autographed the bat. From the slants, curves and spikes of individual letters, she had painted mental pictures of them. The memory of how Ed would look up at the bat and toast the three team members who were dead was enough to make Anita's lips quiver. A motorbike accident, a heart attack and a suicide.

Now and then, on arriving home, Anita would slot her key into the lock and sense that she would find Ed seated at the dining table oiling the wood, and would find something to busy herself with. Anita always made sure that she included raw linseed oil in Ed's Christmas stocking. It didn't do to run out. In happier moments, Ed would raise his glass towards the bat and recite the names. Anita, who couldn't conjure the names of her own classmates, knew the roll call well enough to be able to correct Ed if, after one glass of wine too many, he skipped one. She knew *FitzWilliams, Graham, Hearty, Humphries* as well as she knew *Pugh, Pugh, Barney, McGrew.*

It pained her to think that, when there'd been seconds to choose, Ed hadn't saved his beloved cricket bat. He had saved cushions.

"How many bloody cushions can two people possibly need?" he used to ask.

He might have rescued something they'd spent hours choosing together, something that told part of their story.

She stooped to right the Buddha's head, thinking, *You were supposed to keep us safe,* shocked when a reply came as clearly as if the words had been spoken: *Ah, but I did. You lived to tell the tale.*

Gripping the head by the ears, she turned it over. It was blackened in places, but Anita knew about restoration. Here was something that could be salvaged. This one thing gave her a spark of hope.

"Ron!" she heard Ed say, and the breath caught in her throat. "We weren't expecting you." There was a pause. "Or were we?"

Sharing none of Ed's surprise, she turned to see her father pulling him into an embrace. It seemed so natural that Dad would show up, at that moment. Like many men of his generation, her father overdressed. He was wearing a collar and tie underneath his jacket.

"I was just passing so I thought I'd drop in." Through what remained of the doorframe, unobserved, Anita gave a secret smile.

"What? You happened to be driving past the end of the road?"

"I honestly didn't know you'd be here. I don't want to get in your way."

"What were you going to do? Turn around and go all the way back to Liverpool without saying hello?"

"It's good to see you, lad..." Though his face was pale, Ron wore an immense look of relief.

Drawing back, Ed glanced down the muddied path towards the lychgate. "Isn't Patti with you?"

"I needed to see for myself, that's all. Silly really. I can barely remember getting myself to Lime Street, but I jumped on the first train to London. Next thing I knew, well, here I am." As he clapped his hands to his sides, Anita's father seemed greyer and shorter, less steady on his feet. Though it must have happened in stages, the shock of discovering that he was old was equal to finding herself standing in a blackened shell that had been her home. "Patti probably thinks I'm in the garden shed. When she finds out I've gone AWOL, she'll be fuming! And the temper on that woman..." After laughing self-deprecatingly, Ron looked about, allowing himself to be vulnerable in his tears; generous with his compassion. "The state of this place... Just look at it." Biting his top lip, slowly shaking his head, he didn't try to reduce their loss to bland words of comfort. Anita liked that her father held nothing back. He sniffed, pulling himself up. "So, how's that daughter of mine?"

Anita shifted, the movement of her feet dislodging a gravel of splintered glass, charcoal and fragments of things she and

Ed had once treasured, grinding it into still smaller particles. Both men turned towards the noise.

"Nita, love!" He opened his arms.

"Dad," Anita said, her eyes filling, her mouth curling upwards. Instead of running towards him and flinging herself into his arms, Anita found that she was rooted to the spot. Her face crumpled.

As arms enfolded her, Anita let her forehead settle on her father's shoulder; the rough fabric of the sports jacket he wore, come summer or winter. Buddha's weight was removed from her hands - "Keep hold of that!" "Don't worry, I will." - and her father shuffled closer still, and for a moment nothing else seemed to matter.

"Come on, now, Tilly Mint. It's alright. I mean, it's not alright, obviously. But it's *going* to be, because you're still in one piece from the look of you. Now then."

There was nothing between father and daughter. He reinforced the indelible ink of her childhood. All of the time that Anita kept her eyes closed and her father's hand cupped the back of her head, she knew that she would be perfectly safe.

CHAPTER FIVE

"That's a pint of bitter for you, Ron, and a white wine for you." Ed placed the drinks on the painted table in front of them. A circle of wood had been cut away, and a polished brass plate with the number eleven had been slotted into the hole it had left behind. "And your food's on its way."

"Aren't you having anything?" Anita glanced up in surprise. Ed's fidgety stance made it obvious that he had no intention of sitting down. Irritation flooded her veins. He had been the one to suggest they all went for a bite to eat at The Sun.

"Actually." He scratched the side of his nose. "I've decided to leave you two on your own to catch up."

Without consulting me, you've changed your mind? They only visited her parents a couple of times a year, while it was only an hour's drive to see Ed's. And yet where were *their* offers of help? She watched Ed thumb the keyboard on his mobile, hoping he hadn't accepted an offer of a drink elsewhere.

"Ron, if you're serious about getting the train from Euston at seven minutes past nine, you'll need to be on the seven forty-five to St Albans. You change at Blackfriars. See?" As Ed crouched down to show Ron the National Rail Enquiries website, Anita felt chastened. She had jumped to the wrong conclusion. "That should give you plenty of time to eat."

"Dad?" Anita asked, embarrassed that they had no spare bed to offer him. Natalie probably wouldn't blink if she took her father back to the house, but that was precisely the point. She didn't want to abuse her friend's generosity - not when she had problems of her own to contend with. It was embarrassing enough that Natalie had insisted on vacating her own bedroom so that Anita and Ed could make use of the en suite.

"I can't expect you to share a bathroom with Reuben," she'd said confidentially as she handed over a bundle of clean towels. "However often I remind him, he hasn't quite learned the art of flushing."

"That sounds like my best bet," Anita's father was saying. "What time will that get me into Lime Street?"

"Just after half-past midnight."

"Gone midnight! I'll be in the doghouse for a week!" His eyes danced with a schoolboy twinkle.

Anita cringed at the sight of sooty hand prints on the lapels of her father's sports jacket. "I don't think you'll be able to hide where you've been."

Ed took control. "How about I phone Patti and tell her we've kidnapped you?"

"Perhaps, if you wouldn't mind. She might bark a bit, but she won't be cross with you."

"I'll wait until I'm outside. It'll be quieter there." The two men looked at each other, lips tight, nodding. Ed's hand shot out. "Good to see you, Ron." Her father took the hand Ed offered in both of his, a grasp rather than a shake, then Ed stooped to kiss the top of Anita's head. "I'll see you back at the bat cave." She watched as he excused himself, sidestepping a couple queuing at the bar.

Ed got as far as the door and then hesitated. "Look out. He's changed his mind," Ron commented. They both waited for his return.

"Scrap that. I'll be back in fifty minutes to give you a lift to the station. That way, I'll be able to promise Patti you'll be on that train."

"Watch out. She'll hold you personally responsible if I'm not!"

"All the way from Liverpool for a couple of hours!" Anita sighed, once they were alone. "Have we ever been to a pub on our own before?"

"It's been a good few years since we've had so much as a private conversation." Ron's pained smile suggested he had seen right through her. "Your Ed's a very thoughtful young man."

She laughed, a single syllable; an attempt to mask her guilt. "He'd be flattered by that description. We're not so young anymore."

"Compared with me, you are!" He reached across the table and took Anita's hand.

Detecting the folded notes, Anita felt her eyebrows pull together. "What's this?"

Ron looked around him at the couples and the groups of drinkers. "Pocket money. Quick, hide it in your purse or they'll all want some."

"But -"

"Behave! I promised your mother I'd see you right. The bank transfer might take a couple of days to land in your account, so -" He shrugged.

It was embarrassing. His being so suddenly white-haired. Her being an adult. The knowledge that refusal wasn't an option. "Thanks, Dad."

"So, how are you, my beautiful girl?"

"Fine." Anita felt her nose prickle. "Until anyone asks, that is!" She stowed the money in her purse and rummaged in her handbag until she found a ragged tissue with a serviceable corner.

"You look completely done in, Tilly Mint."

She indulged a nod. "We lost a whole night's sleep. I'm still catching up." The idea that sleep should be so easy - that you might just lay your head on a pillow and close your eyelids.

"Perhaps you need a little help. Why don't you ask your doctor for something?"

Anita disliked taking medicine unless it was absolutely necessary. She dismissed his suggestion. "I'm fine. Honestly."

Ron made stop signs with his hands. "Far be it from me..."

A display of cheer would be required to stop him from worrying. To stop *both* of her parents from worrying. Because, once her mother had got over the fact that Dad had absconded, she'd sit him down and extract every last detail. "I don't just feel bad for us." Anita's mouth twitched upwards into what was not quite a smile. "I feel as if we've let Mr Cook down."

"Mr Cook?"

"The man who built the house. I must have told you about him."

"Remind me."

Such a simple, familiar phrase coming from her father. *Remind me* was what he used to say when she told him that she'd be late home because she was doing this or that after-school club. Before she read aloud to him. They were also the words he used when she went to him and said, *Remember I need that ten pounds to pay for my history book.* It embarrassed Anita now, her lack of a 'please'. As if she'd been entitled.

"Mr Cook decided to turn the plot into a private pleasure gardens. The idea was that he'd charge an entrance fee, with extra for tennis and taking a boat out on the lake." Anita's mind strayed to the photograph. The one thing she'd really appreciated on their moving-in day was the discovery that the previous owner had left it hanging in the hall. Another thing that had been lost in the fire. Though she might track a copy down at the library, it wouldn't be *their* copy.

A flustered-looking waitress who had done a full circuit of the tables addressed the room. "Any takers? I've got two burgers and chips looking for a home."

Smiling in sympathy, Anita shook her head. Her father was sitting back in his chair, waiting for her to continue. "Mr Cook's problem was that he was one hundred years too late," she resumed. She'd spent hours poring over the land registry records, making meticulous notes. The house hadn't featured until 1906, when the road running alongside the land was first listed. Records from the following year showed the land-scaping of the chalk pit that now formed the far end of the cul-de-sac. "Once the council opened Grove Park in the early twenties, unless they really needed privacy, people wouldn't dream of paying to visit a private pleasure gardens. As takings dropped, Mr Cook was forced to divide up the land. He sold it, plot by plot. The lake was filled in. Builders took over. In the end, the house was all that survived. And now..." Anita shook her head.

Her father let the hand that wasn't curved around his pint glass come to rest on Buddha's topknot, the simple gold band of his wedding ring clinking against its metal. "It seems to me that our friend here had a good grasp of what ails you. Perhaps it was also the cause of Mr Cook's downfall."

"Oh?"

"Buddha said that change is the natural order, and that trying to hold onto things that are changing is one of the major causes of unhappiness. Actually," Ron released his pint and rubbed the palms of his hands together, trying to rid them of soot, "it's something I wish I didn't know so much about."

"In what way?

"I've had some personal experience of losing things. I know how it alters you."

Anita waited, while her father shuffled in his seat. His grip on his pint tightened.

"You'll remember how I told you that my parents' house was bombed during the Blitz."

"Vaguely. You never went into much detail." Perhaps he had, before she became obsessed by more distant history.

"I was only a toddler at the time."

"You were there, in the city? I thought you'd been evacuated."

"No, that wasn't until later. My parents were scared that if they sent me away, they'd never see me again."

"I suppose foster parents got very attached."

"Sometimes it was the children who chose to stay put. They'd been so young, they had no memories of their own parents. And of course, for the older kiddies who were sent overseas, it just wasn't practical to bring them home."

'Usually the mothers went too, but my mother wasn't prepared to lose anyone else, not after she lost her sister."

Anita's brows knotted together. Her father normally changed the subject when there was talk of his Aunty Magda. Even as a child she had sensed there was a hidden subtext. "You'd have thought she'd have wanted to get you away from the bombing," she said.

"You had to be pragmatic, that was the thing - take the view that when your time was up, it was up." A storm cloud passed over her father's eyes. "Whatever the explanation was, my mam always insisted I'd have been too young to remember. Perhaps that's what she told herself in the hope it was true. But some images - they're burnt into your retina." Anita noticed how her father seemed to find it easier not to meet her gaze. Instead, he frowned at the amber contents of his pint glass. "There are things I remember without a doubt. My mother breaking the news that Blackie, the rocking horse in Blackler's children's department, had been lost in the blaze. And the night the match factory went up. You could see the fire from twenty miles away."

The night, full of ungodly sounds: sharp shouts and the rise and fall of screaming sirens, the terrible crackle of flames, the shattering of glass. Anita's throat was dry and tight. Her hand trembled as she lifted her wine glass and sipped. And, in a moment's clarity, she sensed that the reason her father had caught the first train to London was to share this story with her, now that it seemed newly urgent and relevant. She wondered if her father hadn't asked Ed to make himself scarce.

"All those jobs gone too..." He shook his head. "Then there was sitting on the tram, trying to peel back a corner of the cheese netting so that I could see out of the window."

She managed to find the voice to ask, "Was that because of the blackout?"

"No, it was to prevent injuries, in case the glass was blown out. I wasn't daft. I wouldn't get on a tram after dark. Not once I'd been told that the German planes followed the sparks on the overhead trolley. But I remember the blackouts. Trees and lampposts painted with white stripes to stop you walking into them. And I remember the barrage balloon hovering over Cleveland Square. Enormous it was, like something from outer space. But even that didn't stop the bombs."

It seemed extraordinary that Anita hadn't heard these memories before. She swallowed a second time, ambushed by the pain of her throat.

"We were sitting ducks, you see. The Germans headed for the bright lights of Dublin then swung right up the Mersey. Wave after wave of them." Ron glanced up momentarily - perhaps judging whether to go on. Anita held her breath until her father looked back down. "It had been the run-up to Christmas, nineteen forty. Tragedy always seems to hit hardest at Christmas. Whichever cold underground space people crammed themselves into, that was where the Germans dropped their bombs. Air raid shelters, basements, railway arches. After several hours of having my head crushed against my mother's chest, shivering in the dark, we emerged to..." He sighed deeply and shuddered. "Sweet Jesus, it was unimaginable." His head was shaking, a slow denial. "Complete and utter devastation, if you can imagine such a thing." His gaze flickered towards Anita, acknowledging that, newly initiated, she was entitled to this previously locked-away story. "Everything you'd thought of as permanent and safe." He splayed the fingers of one hand. "Gone."

A breath shuddered through Anita, turning into a cough. Grasping one of her hands, her father gave a tight smile. "So we moved. To Bootle, it was. People were generous with what little they had. We collected a few things together in boxes. The Red Cross found me a teddy bear; a raggedy old thing. I didn't stop to think about who it had belonged to: I just grabbed it.

'The Germans followed us. I wondered what they had against me, it felt that personal. I prayed - prayed for them to go away - but honestly, I thought they wouldn't stop until every last one of us was dead."

Even disturbed by the sound of a high-ball tumbler being filled with ice, the moment felt intensely private. Anita understood the depth of anti-German feeling that had pervaded her childhood. It must have been all the more present for her mother, born in the aftermath, a time of brick dust and rubble.

"When I was evacuated, I thought I was being punished for having made such a great big fuss. For some, it was a bit of a jolly, but..." He inhaled whatever was left of the sentence. "You had no idea where you were being sent."

"You went to Wales, didn't you?"

"I was billeted in Merivale with a Mr and Mrs Lloyd. He was a timber merchant, so he owned a pony and trap. I mucked out the pony, that was my job. But, you see, don't you?" His eyes were gentle yet pleading. "I *do* know what you're going through. We lost everything. I had to start over four times in the first five years of my life. In some ways, coming back home was the hardest move of all. I barely remembered how to speak English!"

Unsure how to navigate this new and significant scenery, Anita waited for the moment to settle before saying, "You only ever mentioned being evacuated. I haven't heard you talk about the rest of it before."

Ron shrugged the whole thing away, as if closing a book. His face brightened. "It was a long time ago. Another lifetime."

"Not quite. The war still felt recent when I was growing up. I remember the bomb sites." The streets of her childhood looked too wide because there were no buildings on either side. There had still been piles of rubble. Swathes of waste-land. Windows boarded with corrugated iron.

He took up his pint again and conceded, "The 'bombies'. Of course you would. There wasn't the money to rebuild." Her father's sense of abandonment was etched into the lines of his face. "And that was before most of the docks closed - the 'managed decline' as they now call it. How it's changed, these past few years! Not a week goes by when they're not pouring foundations for some new aircraft hangar. You have to feel for the poor mugs who snapped up converted warehouses, thinking they were paying for river views and now find them-selves sitting on their balconies looking out at a multi-storey car park."

Anita wondered how to steer the conversation back. "It always amazes me..." She was treading dangerously, but some-thing new had opened up between them and she wasn't going to squander the opportunity.

"What?"

"When I look back now, the middle of the sixties doesn't seem so long after the end of the war. You lived through all of that in your own childhood, but you still felt optimistic enough -"

"Table eleven?" The waitress breezed over, inspecting the plates she was carrying at shoulder height. Anita suppressed the urge to say, *Can't you see that you're interrupting?* "Here we are! Sorry for the wait. Who's having the beef and ale pie?"

Ever the dutiful schoolboy, Ron raised one hand. "That's for me, ta very much."

Anita moved the Buddha's head to the corner of the table.

"So you must be the fish and chips." The waitress slid an oval plate in front of Anita. "Anything else I can get you?"

Seeing the ramekin of tomato ketchup on her plate, she said, "No, we're fine," hurriedly, but then relented. "At least I am. What about you, Dad?"

"No, I'm sound."

"Then enjoy!"

Ron rubbed his hands together. "This looks good."

The moment was over. Perhaps it was better that they'd been interrupted. Anita's emotions were erratic; her mind darting all over the place. She had been about to step through a door, ignoring the *No entry* sign.

But, taking up his knife and fork, Ron returned to the question she had hinted at. "You were about to ask why we thought it was the right time to bring a child into the world."

"I was," she said, seeking refuge in her battered cod, wishing for a ramekin of tartare sauce.

"That's what they won the war for - or so we were told." Ron took a mouthful of pie and nodded appreciatively. Thinking that would be the end of it, Anita tried to accept the simple explanation. She was about to test another subject when her father said, "Part of it was living up to expectations. You got married, you had kids - in *that* order! Believe me, I have many regrets, but having *you* was never among them." It felt odd that their hands should be occupied with cutlery. Another time and he might have reached out and stroked Anita's cheek. "If it had been down to me, you wouldn't have been an only child. But your mother..."

Anita's chest tightened. She waited. On a day of revelations, was there more to come?

Ron chuckled. "At first, the ten-year age gap between us worked in my favour. But your mother left me behind. She's far more modern in her thinking than I ever was."

A leap too far for Anita, she retorted, "Mum?"

"You'd be surprised. Especially since she's been on her computer course. She's streets ahead of me." He smiled tenderly, toying with his wedding ring. "I probably shouldn't be telling you this - not that it's anything to be ashamed of, mind." Fork paused mid-air, Ron appeared to be having second thoughts.

"What shouldn't you be telling me?"

"Your mother. After she had you, she had a little of what you call post-natal depression." Even while her father was speaking, synapses were bridged. Anita could finally access the word that had always been on the tip of her tongue. "It was known about, of course, but it wasn't really *talked* about. You were expected to get on with it."

Anita supposed that, in the context of her father's childhood - even her mother's - any hint of ingratitude would have been considered selfish at best, insulting to those who had made sacrifices. Liverpool suffered the highest number of casualties of any city outside London. The fact that the city was far smaller meant that few escaped without losing a loved one.

"There. So now you know everything there is to know."

"And it took less than an hour."

"You don't just need the time. You need the *right* time." Anticipating a thoughtful pause, Anita was taken aback when, having reloaded his fork, her father came straight out with it: "And what about you?"

"What about me?"

"You asked me, so I feel entitled to a question of my own.

Do you ever feel that you're missing out?"

She felt the glare of the spotlight. "By not having children?"

"That's right."

It was startling, this new and sudden openness. Being direct had never been her parents' style. Anita found herself staring into the void. "Yes and no..." It surprised her to find a great ravine. "It's not that I'm unhappy..."

"But?"

She weighed each word. "It's hard at times to reconcile the life I'm living with the life I *thought* I'd be living." Like most girls, Anita had grown up playing mummies and daddies. She had come home after being a flower girl at the age of eight, boasting, *When I get married...* "Right now, I'm glad there's only Ed to think about."

"I don't know." Her father's expression softened, not with pity but with empathy. "Sometimes it helps to have someone else to worry about. To know what you're working so hard for. A reason to haul your arse out of bed each morning. Everything makes that bit more sense when there's a child in the picture." Though she wasn't looking directly at him, Anita was aware of the moment her father's focus shifted. "Speak of the devil. Here's your Ed, come to tell us our time's up."

Having been annoyed he had deserted her three-quarters of an hour earlier, Anita felt a spark of irritation as Ed barged in on this rare moment, crash-landing in the chair beside her. The newfound intimacy with her father might be difficult to reignite.

Completely oblivious, Ed squeezed her knee. "You're alright for another ten minutes. I came to see if you've left me any chips!" He took one from her plate and dipped it in tomato ketchup.

"Dare I ask?" ventured Ron. "How was my good lady wife?"

"Rather you than me. She says you'll be lucky if she doesn't change the locks. But she's going to leave a cold supper for you in the fridge."

"Heart of gold, that woman. I don't know what I did to deserve her."

CHAPTER SIX

Later, in a bed that was not her own, in a house that was not her own, wearing a borrowed t-shirt, Anita lay with her head resting on Ed's shoulder. Her eyes were weeping, though the rest of her was quite still.

"Let's get this straight," he said, his voice soft and close. "You're asking me, *What if the child we don't have had died in the fire?*"

"Yes." For a fleeting moment, it seemed as if he understood her.

"How can I possibly answer that?"

Her lips tightened. She hadn't expected an answer, just an appreciation of why the question might need to be asked.

"And that's what's upsetting you so much. That's *all* that's upsetting you?"

Anita nodded, chewing the corner of the pillow case as if it was a comforter. *Yes.*

Carefully, tenderly, he wiped away a single tear with his index finger. "Have you changed your mind about not wanting children?"

"No!" *Didn't he know her at all?*

"You're not making an awful lot of sense. You realise that, don't you?"

"I know."

But what Anita knew was that a thought - a feeling - given a voice of its own can be transformed into something ridiculous, something belittling. She remained facing Ed for just long enough to leave the impression that he had offered comfort of some sort, then said, "Goodnight." Rough stubble grazed her lips. Turning to face an unfamiliar wall, Anita knew beyond doubt that it was possible to grieve for things that were never yours to own. With no intention of sleeping (how could you contemplate sleep when you couldn't trust the walls of a house - and an unfamiliar one at that - not to smoulder and burst into flames?) Anita stared into the dark, glad of the anonymity it lent her. There was no longer any need to wear a mask.

She couldn't hear the reassuring murmur of the house, settling as its floorboards and central heating pipes contracted. Natalie's house was a 1930's semi. Instead, there was only a dull traffic roar, a constant. And, warmed by heat that radiated from the person Anita often referred to as her *other half,* she felt lonely beyond measure.

CHAPTER SEVEN

"**B**reakers are designed to trip out, but they don't always detect sparks from electrical circuits. That's how most fires start."

The loss adjuster, a man whose name Anita had instantly forgotten, insisted that they wore hard hats. Hers - the smallest of the three - seemed to have been designed for a child. She and Ed refused other protective clothing. The grey of the loss adjuster's workday suit was hidden beneath a white jumpsuit, an oddly inappropriate colour for the job in hand.

The loss adjuster and Ed communed in the hall. There was no room for a third. Normally, Anita might have suggested that they moved to one of the larger spaces, but she'd been worried what she might give away without even opening her mouth. The loss adjuster balanced a clipboard against his chest while Ed, arms folded, asked, "So, you think it was electrical?"

The man sidestepped the question. "That's one for the forensics - *if* your insurers want to go to the expense."

"Do you think they will?"

His mouth did the shrugging for him. "It's difficult to see what would be gained. You've been here how long?"

"Just coming up for fifteen years."

"Then, in a house of this age, in the absence of other

evidence... I'd hedge my bet on it. Unless you've had any rewiring done?"

Anita was standing just inside the doorway of what had been the front room. The ceiling above was all but gone, and yet the springs from the sofa remained. A memory vied with the conversation for her attention and won. Christening the new sofa, her body compressed underneath Ed's, they'd discovered that - unlike their previous three-seater - there would always be an overhang of neck or feet. And so, whilst Ed suggested abandoning the idea, ordering him to sit, Anita had straddled him. *"We had some work done a couple of years back. I couldn't tell you exactly what, but Anita might know. She's in charge of the paperwork."* His neck had curved, taking on the shape of the back of the sofa. Her view as she flexed her thighs was of his Adams apple.

Anita's fingertips pulled at the soft warm skin under her mouth.

"Anita?"

On seeing Ed turn towards her, his reading glasses perched on top of his hardhat, the mirage - so vivid a moment ago - faded to ash. "Hmn?"

"Do you remember anything about the electrical work we had carried out?"

More recently, Anita had entered the living room to find Ed seated on the sofa, lowering his reading glasses so that he could peer over the top of them. They were not younger versions of their parents. They were themselves. Without the first-flush hormones; without the financial worries of their twenties; the career-biased hunger of their thirties. Despite the fact that there was less swinging from chandeliers, Ed remained the only person Anita liked more, the more time she spent with him. And now he was looking at her, expecting something about electrics.

She disguised her sigh. "One of the lights kept on blowing.

The company who fitted the kitchen hadn't earthed it cor-
rectly. It turned out that they'd gone bust, so we played it safe
and had a full inspection. A few other things needed doing. I
think the bill came to a couple of thousand pounds."

Ed seemed satisfied. He turned back to the loss adjuster. "I
know we didn't muck about."

"And this was when?"

"A year ago," she estimated. "I expect I can get a copy of the
paperwork. I know there was a ten-year certificate."

"Might be just as well."

Anita added it to her list, creating a little order in her
newly derailed world.

"Did you use any extension leads or multi-point adaptors?"

The questions were beginning to feel like a test they hadn't
revised for.

"In our bedroom, yes, but not in the spare room."

As Ed shook his head emphatically, Anita wondered if she
would have been so confident.

"Well, I don't see a lot here that can be salvaged."

From her position in the living room, Anita looked
upwards. Everything above - except the patches of sky - was
deepest black. She remembered an auctioneer pointing to a
canvas, explaining how difficult it had been for the sixteenth
century artist to create the impression of shadows on a black
velvet coat, when the fabric was already the darkest colour
in the spectrum. There was shade and texture in the black
above Anita. And, there, at her feet was the paint you'd need
to create it: ground charcoal mixed with water from the firemen's hosepipes, tempered by a recent downpour. It struck
Anita that if what was left of the wardrobe came crashing
down, a plastic hard hat would be about as much use as a
polystyrene cycle helmet.

She excused herself, gripping Ed's arms as she manoeuvred behind him, and entered the dining room. Snatches of

explanations, strings of words followed her. "Methane, volatile organic compounds, formaldehyde." She heard, "Oxides of nitrogen, sulphur dioxide... traces of heavy metals."

Keen to demonstrate his scientific knowledge, the loss adjuster seemed to think he'd found a captive audience in Ed, who was muttering responses, passable imitations of genuine interest. Anita hesitated, wondering if she should go to his rescue, but her mind seemed determined to drift.

"...all give off a range of toxic off-gases, not to mention complex odours."

No, Anita would stick with her list. The clean white pages of the ring-bound pad pleased her.

Opening the lid of the chest, she had stared blankly, unable to think what she was supposed to grab. There was no time for indecision. Her heart racing, she started pulling out cardboard files. Insurance documents, their passports, birth certificates...

Her chest was pounding, her mouth desert dry. This was where Anita had navigated a fog of dense black smoke. How the hell had she managed to breathe? The hangover of the instinct to lower her head persisting, she shot out one hand for support. Expecting the cool smooth surface of the dining table, what Anita touched repulsed her. It was as if she'd reached for a peach and found it rotten. She snatched her hand away and, in doing so, smudged the white of the notepad. Annoyance flared and Anita filled her lungs to find that she was gasping.

She must focus. Look forwards.

"So we can look for somewhere to rent?" Ed was asking.

"Where are you staying at the moment?"

"A friend's putting us up but, to be honest, we're testing her patience."

"By all means, start to make arrangements. The rule of thumb is to look for a similar-sized property, but you'll probably find there's a shortage of two-bedroom houses. No one's going to kick up a stink if you have to go for a small three-bedder."

"What length of lease should we look for?"

"In terms of the rebuild, you'll be looking at the full two years you're covered for -"

"Two years?" Anita heard genuine bewilderment in Ed's voice. There was a stunned pause before he twisted his neck towards her. "Did you hear that, Anita?" He looked winded. "Two years until we get our lives back."

The impression of being in limbo had already descended on Anita. All of their daily rituals - things that were attached to the house - had been swept away. Her recollection of the year they had lived elsewhere had all but evaporated. Everything Anita's father had told her about having to start again - not once, but twice - crystallised. They might manage one move, but two?

Ed's gaze dropped to Anita's notepad and, briefly, the smudged paper seemed to be the thing that was troubling him. But the loss adjuster was demanding his attention.

"It will probably seem as if not much is happening for the first few months. The thing I always tell people is to be realistic."

"So - so we need to look for a long-term let?"

The adjuster shrugged. "You could keep your options open by signing a shorter lease. Living in rented accommodation doesn't suit everyone." Even though doubt was being introduced into the equation, Anita was suddenly alert. The man was tapping the end of his pen against the clipboard. "You might want to go as far as getting planning permission for the rebuild, then sell the land."

"That would be an option?"

Here was a promise of respite; the opening Anita had hardly dared hope for. Until this point, it had felt as if two adults had been settling her future. Now she had questions, questions about possibilities, but the loss adjuster was continuing: "At this stage, everything's an option." *Everything's an option.* Anita wrapped his words around herself like a cashmere cardigan. "Although *if* you decide not to rebuild, payments for rental costs would stop, so you'd need to factor that in." His wince was apologetic, but this inconvenience barely seemed to matter. "Of course, this *is* a big plot." Looking through the house, he was contemplating the back garden. His speech slowed, as if to emphasise the value of the land. "You've got a lot of space to play with. Obviously, your policy won't cover the cost, but you might want to think about putting a larger house on it." It was almost an afterthought.

Ed frowned and blinked - as he often did when something grabbed him. The men turned and stepped out through what had been the tiled porch. As the loss adjuster drew a verbal sketch for Ed, Anita felt as if a door had closed, trapping her inside. "The surrounding houses are larger than yours. I doubt your neighbours would object. You might even be able to fit a pair of semis here. Sell one and put some cash in the bank. That's what I'd do."

"Yes." Ed gave a serious nod. "We might want to think about that."

"Nobody expects something like this to happen, but when it does, you've got to look at the opportunity it gives you. Right?" The loss adjuster turned to face Anita, as if he'd just remembered that this also concerned her. But it was too late. Having given with one hand, he had taken away with the other.

They sat in the hire car - one of the few places that afforded privacy - which was parked outside what remained of their home.

"I don't know why I was expecting the worst." Ed twisted towards Anita. "The loss adjuster didn't seem so bad."

Occasional shouts from children who had yet to be called in for their teas drifted towards them. Bicycle wheels whirring, feet gripping tarmac, a couple of boys tore up and down the middle of the road, fearless in the way only kids who live in cul-de-sacs can be.

Anita concentrated very hard on not tightening her grip on the straps of her handbag as it sat in her lap. She refrained from comment, waiting to see what would come next.

"And he's right. We could do something really exciting with the space."

Anita made herself ask the question: "So you'd want to rebuild?"

"Trying to replace what we had would end up with too many compromises. And I don't know, I kind of like the idea of creating something that's *ours.*" Anita knew how Ed's mind worked. His blueprint was already advancing. He'd stopped buying lottery tickets because, after he'd imagined spending his millions, the thought of not winning was inconceivable. "And don't worry about the money. I know you wanted to live mortgage-free, but I've never understood why you insist we go fifty-fifty on everything. If we were married -"

"Which we're not!" Shocked by her momentary loss of control, Anita was relieved to see that Ed's expression was bemused.

He used his 'reasonable' voice; the one that made it difficult to object: "All I'm *trying* to say is that I don't care about the money. I earn more than you. So what? I've always thought it would be fairer to base our contributions on percentage of salary."

Anita blinked at the unfamiliar dials on the dashboard. She hated being in debt, even to Ed. What she wanted was to be his equal - not part of a mathematical equation. But the reason Anita was sitting so stiffly revolved around more than who was going to pay for what. "Why do we need a bigger house?"

"We don't *need* a bigger house. But think about it. We could have a cinema room, a library… the sort of thing we've seen on *Grand Designs*."

"That sort of thing's fine - for *those* people. But they're not us."

"Which is why we'll find an architect who understands our wish list." Ed was gesticulating, in the way he did when excited.

Anita didn't relish having to trample on his enthusiasm, but what on his wish list represented the two of them? Where was she? The ghost, standing at the dormer window. Anita turned her head and looked out of the passenger window - there was one of the boys, hiding behind their car - away from Ed's open expression; up the concrete garden path they so hated. *Don't cry. Not now.* 'Turning on the taps' was something her mother had accused her of as a child, as if it was something she could control at will, use to her advantage. "The problem is -" *Just phrase it as honestly as you can.* "- I don't want to live in a new house."

Ed's laughter, sharp and disbelieving, jerked her gaze back. "Oh, come on!" he blurted. But she hadn't oversimplified the fact of it. Having stated the truth unemotionally, there was nothing she wanted to add. Anita allowed time for the words to sink in. "Not even one that we've designed ourselves?"

Tight-lipped, she shook her head, staring wordlessly at the windscreen, its harsh angle. Dust had already accumulated in the inaccessible reach of the new dashboard. Worn down with the effort of maintaining a brave face, misery offered a comfort of sorts. Though Anita and Ed rarely swapped harsh words, this was the kind of behaviour that might earn her a half-joking accusation of moodiness tomorrow. And yet it wasn't something she could snap out of.

"Look," Ed said, and she tried not to recoil as the weight of one of his hands came to rest on hers. "I don't think the problem is whether or not the house is new." Ed's voice was gentle. "I understand that you're in mourning. I know *I* am. But having the old house back isn't an option."

He was being very patient, she appreciated that. But Anita also knew her own mind. The outline of the wiper blades blurred.

"The loss adjuster was right. We have to try to see this as an opportunity to leave our mark. You'll be *contributing* to the history of Chalkdale."

He was choosing words that he thought would appeal to her. Only recently she'd described for him how, locking herself in one of the newly-renovated toilet cubicles at Hampton Court, Anita had been ambushed by an urge to leave her mark on the pristine grey walls. It was as though her hand had assumed control. The strength of the desire was surprising. She had never written on toilet walls before, so why now? It wouldn't be permanent: the cubicles were wipe-clean. Hoping to sate the need, she settled on compromise. Inspired by fake graffiti in the Chapel Royal, Anita rummaged in her bag for a biro, wrote *Walter Raleigh* on a sheet of toilet paper, wiped herself, and then flushed it away.

"Think about it." Ed aligned his torso towards her. "We could landscape the garden and reinstate the old name. *Chalkdale Cottage and Private Pleasure Gardens.*"

Anita stared at their conjoined hands. Ed, who was usually able to finish her sentences, simply didn't get it. Moodiness wasn't what was making Anita hold her silence.

"So what you're saying is that you'd want to sell the land with planning permission and look for somewhere else to live?"

She jumped at what felt like the best compromise. "Yes." And here Anita did have the advantage, an argument that went beyond simple gut reaction. "I also think it would be less stressful."

"Less *stressful?*" Ed repeated her words with different emphasis, his hand springing away from hers. It hovered, claw-like, before settling on top of his head. The car rocked as he slumped back in the driver's seat, exasperated. "You *do* remember the nightmare we had finding a house that we both liked?"

The tiller swung away from Anita as she battled with his suggestion. "I wasn't aware that you liked any of the others."

The look that Ed shot at her suggested he thought her naïve.

Anita ran her upper lip through her front teeth. If she was to accept this unwelcome revision, she needed facts. "Which house would *you* have preferred?"

His expression said, *Let's not go there. What's the point?*

Her knees swivelled towards him. "You can't suggest that I've ignored the truth because it didn't suit me and then not tell me the rest."

Ed exhaled noisily, then he spoke without enthusiasm. "The townhouse in Cheam village."

Anita pulsed with resistance.

"It would have been a good investment."

She remembered the modern development, a small mews, close to Nonsuch Park. The walls had been clad in local flint. A double garage took up much of the ground floor. The living room was elevated on the first floor and she remembered a certain feeling of safety. But the fourth bedroom was so small that she'd spun around and commented, "You'd be hard-pushed to fit a single bed in here." And Ed had said, "I'd shelve it. I'd have a reading lamp over here and a big armchair, facing the window."

She had never thought he meant... "But... I don't under-stand. Why didn't you say?"

"I was going to, but then you fell in love with this house and…" He ran one hand through his salt and pepper hair.

"I wanted you to be happy, OK? We both *knew* that buying the cottage was an emotional decision. I don't want to think about how much money we've thrown at it! Property prices have spiralled. If we'd gone for something larger, we could have downsized by now and cashed the profit."

Completely floored by what he was saying, Anita stared through the windscreen. One of the local boys was sitting on the kerb. He spun the pedal of a bike, then inserted a Top Trump card, producing a buzzing noise. "But we both agreed." Even as her narrative began to revise itself, Anita challenged, "We didn't want to pay for rooms we wouldn't be using."

"It's alright for you. I'm the one who's stuck in a job I hate!"

As Anita jolted backwards, the car rocked. Shock dried any remaining tears. This was the job he described as 'money for jam'.

"I'm sorry," Ed said dispassionately, "but you did ask."

Anita back-tracked, grappling to reinstate things that she knew in the places where they belonged. Asking about Ed's day as they sat down to their evening meal; mulling things through over a glass of wine: these rituals were facts. Questions boiled inside her. *How long have you been telling me what you thought I wanted to hear? When did I ask to be treated like a princess?* The idea that Ed had protected her was appalling. Anita intended to tell him so but, seeing Ed's tormented expression, her demands boiled dry. "You're not *stuck,*" she insisted. "In fact you should jack it in tomorrow if that's the way you feel."

"One of us has to have a sensible job."

His bitter tone took Anita aback. "What I do is hardly frivolous!"

Ed's profile assumed that unfamiliar quality Anita had glimpsed once or twice and dismissed as something she had conjured. She felt a separation. Things she thought she knew were rapidly dissolving, other possibilities emerging. Was Ed hinting that he had made *more* sacrifices than she'd realised? That had *never* been part of the deal.

Had he *really* stuck at a job he detested because of her? Anita tried the possibility on for size, but couldn't make it fit. Ed had been working at his firm when she met him - *fifteen years ago!* Having been head-hunted more than once, he'd declined. And when other opportunities cropped up from time to time, he decided against exploring them. Anita had *never* tried to influence him. The whole point was that they had agreed not to overstretch themselves financially. "I know I don't earn as much as you," she said, "but it's hardly a pittance."

"We couldn't *both* live on your salary."

This was why she hated discussing finances. Whatever was said always felt personal, even if that wasn't how it was intended. Anita retaliated: "I'm not suggesting we try to. I'm suggesting you find something that you enjoy doing!"

"I'd have to retrain."

"Not necessarily. You have plenty of skills other companies would be glad of."

"But transferrable to what? It's not a good time to be looking for work. You've seen the unemployment figures."

The conversation seemed to be rapidly heading towards a dead end. There were too many negatives, too many thoughts trying to crowd Anita's head, and the space in the hire car proved too constrictive to contain them. With certainties fracturing, Anita realised she had missed something critical. "But your idea of building something larger depends on you earning the same as you do at the moment. And what about your plans to retire at the age of fifty?" Only four years from now; time had crept up on them.

"At least I'd be able to see the point of busting my gut every day!"

Anita recalled her father's words: *"It helps to have someone else to worry about. Some reason to haul your arse out of bed every morning."* Their present dilemma stemmed - in part, at least - from lacking a purpose that was the equivalent of raising a child. Anita had invested time and energy in her job, their relationship, in creating a home. Never particularly materialistic, she had been happy. And - up until now - she'd believed that Ed was too. But if, as Ed did, you earned more than you needed, and you lived with a partner whose insistence she paid for half of everything meant that - she heard the air leave her nostrils - you couldn't do some of the things you wanted...

Her ability to appreciate Ed's point of view didn't alter the fundamentals. Anita simply couldn't see herself living in a new house. It would be a lie if she said, *I know I'm being unreasonable. I'll think about it.* What had made her relationship with Ed a success was that they were both willing to compromise. They had adopted the rule: *If you're going to make a big fuss, it had better be over something important.* A situation had never arisen before when one couldn't recognise that the other felt more strongly and backed down.

Ed had chosen *this* conversation - timing Anita begrudged - to tell her that he'd compromised when they bought Chalkdale. That he'd done it because her happiness had been more important than a financial investment. If that were true, he had loved her *more* than she'd realised. The question Anita was afraid to voice was, *When did that change?* Or was it simply that, with retirement fifteen years closer, priorities needed to be reassessed? Either way, Ed's silence suggested that it was *her* turn to compromise. He'd done his bit.

But, for Anita, this was no longer simply a conversation about where they would or wouldn't live. Ed implied that she hadn't wanted to see the truth. As far as Anita was concerned, he had deceived her. So much for an equal partnership.

Anita's pounding heart was the metronome she used

to measure the silence. Stalemate expanded until she was compelled to lower her window a little. She angled her head towards the small opening and breathed air tainted with all of those toxic off-gases and protein odours the loss adjuster had been so keen they knew about. She felt nauseous. How did the neighbours live with it?

Eventually, Ed shook his head. He rammed the car key into the ignition and crunched the gears in a way that gave the impression of frustration, but there was violence in the way he threw the car around corners, and no way for Anita to ask him to slow down.

CHAPTER EIGHT

"Oh, Jesus, not another one!"

The first words Anita ever said to him. All Ed had done was to trip over a slack shoelace as he bee-lined towards her. She'd assumed that, like everyone else in the room, he was thoroughly worse for wear, there to make a joke at her expense.

Anita had quickly regretted her offer to help out at a corporate function after several waiting staff had rung in sick. It was being held in the Little Banqueting House, which crouched discreetly behind the hedge of the sunken Pond Garden. The building with its completely over-the-top interior had been designed for William III's private use. As the King became increasingly reclusive, rumours about exactly who and what *entertaining* might entail, grew rife. Less austere than the Palace's great dining halls, it had quickly become one of Anita's favourite spaces. Tonight, she would revise that opinion.

Dressed in a servant's costume that was both historically inaccurate and ill-fitting, Anita had attracted more than her usual share of male attention as she weaved among the pin-striped brigade handing out frosted champagne flutes and salted margarita glasses. Verbally molested, she'd been referred to as a serving wench. At first she'd tried to make a game of it, responding in character, but this seemed to encourage the more raucous men - those who came with an entourage.

Ed moved to a place where there was less danger of being trodden underfoot by leather brogues and stiletto heels, then stooped to tie his shoelaces. "My own fault," he said, clearly ruffled. "Should have stuck to double knots." Unlike the others, he wasn't slurring his words.

"I'm sorry, I thought -" She stepped towards him.

"Don't worry about me. You've got your hands full." Ed picked himself up, sliced his palms together.

She held the tray towards him. "Drink?"

"Not champagne. I'm driving." He came to stand next to Anita, sharing her view of the splendour and those who thought themselves splendid. "Sorry about this lot. I would have rescued you earlier, but you seemed to be giving as good as you got."

"I can't believe I volunteered for this. I'm not even being paid to be insulted." She laughed at the ridiculous situation she'd found herself in.

"How did that happen?"

Anita wasn't sure what it was that made her open up to him, but she found herself confiding: "Everyone else has come down with the flu and I'm... Well, I'm still under probation and a bit too keen, if I'm honest. Instead of making a good impression, I've come dangerously close to getting myself the sack." Five minutes beforehand, Anita had almost acted on the temptation to release a battery of insults - *Oi, softshite!* Instead she'd retreated, seething, to the far end of the room. Positioning herself where, over spiked iron railings, she could enjoy the view of a small strip of Thames and plot her escape from this torture (never mind that her prison was ornate). Forget a boat and a safe passage: Anita could jump the wall, leg it up the tow path, then turn left over the bridge. A train would do it.

Now she threw a final glance in the direction of Hampton Court station before nodding towards the impeccably-dressed crowd: "Your friends are quite a handful." Her dress, loose around the bust, tugged tight under her arms.

"Oh, they're not my friends," he said. "The people you see before you -" he gestured to the blur of tanned faces and whitened teeth, "- are my esteemed colleagues."

Another urgent rise of overenthusiastic laughter grated. She despaired at how little interest they showed in their surroundings. Tonight's event was precisely the kind of social gathering that made Anita yearn for solitude. "I'd assumed corporate entertaining would be a bit more..."

"Sedate?" he suggested. There was a playful quality to his tone.

Head bowed, she smiled to herself. Then, angling her face towards him, she decided that she liked how his dark hair was a little skewiff; the way the stubble emerging to the south of his jawline resembled a corn circle. "A little less like a stag night, anyway." He returned her smile and she looked away in time to see a man steal a covert glance in one of the gilded mirrors for the novelty of seeing himself framed in gold against a backdrop of painted murals. "Why bother shelling out to hire somewhere like this?"

"Ah!" He bunched his mouth with mock regret. "Therein lies a story."

"Go on."

"We weren't welcome back at the venue we chose last year."

"Which was where?"

"A brewery."

She laughed, unsurprised. "So you're notorious?"

"The problem is," Ed mused, "corporate entertaining's been outlawed in the world of financial services."

"Why's that?"

He shrugged. "It's seen as bribery." Above the general din,

someone shouted a greeting. A dozen conversations aborted, heads twisted to see who merited special treatment. Ed looked unimpressed with whomever he saw. "And without clients, well, let's just say that the reason to behave has been removed."

Each carbon-copy alpha male fought to compete with the others, throwing back drinks then reaching for more. It seemed worse somehow that laddish behaviour should take place in this space - ignoring the fact that there was every possibility the banqueting room had been built for bad behaviour.

"Still," Anita said. "I wouldn't *dream* of getting into that sort of state in front of my boss."

It was peculiar, how similar the party-goers looked. Almost without exception (Ed being the misfit), they were in their mid-twenties; stiff-collared shirts, silk ties, exuding the confidence of those who knew they looked good and expected to be admired. Identi-kits. There were few women - intimidating types, dolled up in tight suits, towering heels, immaculate make-up - but those few appeared to mimic the men's behaviour. They had made Anita feel unattractive as they exchanged their empties for full glasses. No please or thank you, as if she wasn't worthy of a glance. Anita was left with the impression that she had been the butt of their mocking laughter.

"See that man over there?" Ed nodded into the sea of cartoon-like, self-congratulatory faces. "Dark hair, royal blue tie. He of the intimidating disposition."

As Anita singled out someone at the centre of a baying group who fitted the description, rage simmered in her chest. The man with the royal blue tie had been the ringleader, enjoying the sound of his voice as he exaggerated the word *wench*. "I had the pleasure earlier. Obnoxious, drunken -" She censored herself. Misfit this man to her right might be, but he was still a client.

"Knob-head?" he suggested. Suppressing laughter, Anita stole an amused sideways glance. He shrugged in a kind of *to hell with it* way. "That's my boss."

"Your *boss?*" That explained why the women were drinking as hard and fast as their male colleagues, trying so hard to impress. The equivalent of children in a classroom shooting their hands into the air, clammering to answer any question they knew the answer to. The silent desperation. *Me, me, me!* "Then there really *is* no reason to behave."

"Work hard, play hard, that's the company ethos. It's frowned on if you don't join in."

Another explosion of insincere laughter bounced off the walls, a pretence of euphoria. "How come you're getting away with it?"

"Designated driver. Plus, I'm not sure I mind being frowned upon." His mouth twitched and he glanced at Anita in a way that brought colour to her cheeks. "Not by this lot, at any rate."

Suddenly, the evening held promise. *Here's where you introduce yourself.* "Anita," she said, determined to look him in the eye and return his smile. It sounded terribly formal. And yet intimate.

"Ed."

Ed. The single syllable resonated. She swallowed. *Say something else. Anything.* "And what is it your company does?"

"Investments. All very dull." His jacket sleeves had ridden up to reveal cufflinks, a skull and crossbones. Chunky and silver. There was a delicacy about his wrists, and she noticed how a small area of cotton had frayed along the well-pressed line where his cuff doubled back. "You start in this business because you have student debts to pay off, then you get sucked in. Here, let me." Ed took a champagne flute from her tray and held it at arm's length in the direction of a colleague's unsteady approach. Anita had been oblivious.

"Cheers, mate. You not having one?" The man dangled an empty glass upside down by its stem.

"I'll take that, shall I?" Ed removed it from harm's way. "No, I pulled the short straw." He shrugged. "I'm driving."

"Unlucky."

"There's always next time."

The drinker merged with the tight crowd and Ed turned back to Anita. "Some of these people start to believe they're worth what they're being paid. But it could all stop tomorrow - in fact, if some people get their way, it probably will." He sighed deeply. "And you? It must be quite something to work in a place like this."

"Most of the time. When I don't have to dress up and smile nicely while being insulted."

"I would never have known." He nodded at her ugly brown costume. "You're a natural."

Anita raised her eyebrows and blinked.

"Pretend I didn't say that." Endearingly flustered, he ran his hand through his hair. "It was supposed to sound more like a compliment than it did. So tell me. What do you do? Most of the time?"

She rearranged her shoulders in the hope that the front of the dress was not gaping as much as she feared. "I'm a curator."

"And what does that involve?"

It was possible to shut out the collision of conversations, the thud of a dirty bass line. "Research, mainly. Usually, you can find me in the library, but I also get involved in helping to organise learning events or sourcing items from auction houses." Hers had been a lifestyle choice, and Anita knew even then that lifestyle choices rarely paid. This job of hers was not nine 'til five - not that she was so naïve as to think there was such a thing. But she could never be accused of having -

"So you haven't sold *your* soul."

Her stomach cartwheeled. *It's not such an unusual turn of phrase*, Anita reminded herself. Ed had simply jumped in before she did. *"No one* could accuse me of that."

"I studied history." Before she could ask where, Ed continued, "It's odd, isn't it?" He moved the knot of his tie from side to side, attempting to loosen it. "Watching from the sidelines, I feel as if I've gate-crashed the wrong party."

"It's very stuffy. I should open a few windows."

"Actually, the reason I came over here was to ask if you know where the non-alcoholic drinks have been hidden."

She scanned the room, passing over Verrio's cherubs and his naked beauties. (Too solid and pale for contemporary tastes.) She drew a blank. "There didn't seem to be a lot of call for them. I'll find you something. Coke? Sparkling water? Don't hold your breath, but we might be able to stretch to a ginger beer."

"Anything, so long as it's got ice in it."

"Don't go anywhere."

He took her tray from her. "Then I might as well make myself useful."

To Anita, it seemed as if a bargain had been struck.

Anita's spirits lifted the moment she stepped down from train to platform and saw the neat row of padlocked bicycles. Here, walking over the bridge, she could breathe. In winter, Hampton Court Palace's chimneys - soft red brickwork with barber-shop spirals - were visible from the crest. On a summer's day like today, when the warm breeze lapped at Anita's legs, trees in full leaf eclipsed her view. She singled out the gigantic false acacia at the Palace's west front; the balls of mistletoe she'd mistaken for crows' nests. Here was England in a nutshell, everything as it should be: river trips; narrow boats and barges moored along the towpath; the old-fashioned ice-cream kiosk still decorated with bunting from the Queen's

Jubilee; heraldic beasts keeping guard at the pillared gateway.

"You never tire of it, do you?"

Twisting her head, she greeted a white-haired colleague dressed in immaculate uniform. Together they took in the sweep of the path, its evenly-spaced concrete posts positioned like sentries.

"Brits travel halfway round the world to see less impressive sights," she said with a sigh. Swayed by what they considered 'exotic', blind to the unicorns, the dragons and the griffins; the history encapsulated in every pockmarked corner stone; the contorted faces of gargoyles; deaf to the stories told by every bricked-in window. All of the detail Anita loved.

"I've missed you," the gate attendant said. "Haven't seen you around these last few days."

"I haven't been here."

"Holiday?"

She suspected he was being kind. "Just a few things to sort out at home." There. She had mentioned 'home' and managed to sound casual. If only she could silence the nagging at the back of her mind. *One of us needs to do something sensible.* Had Ed been trying to suggest that, in order for him to make changes, she *needed to give this up*? Or was it possible that he was envious? After all, his choice of degree had been history. She'd known when she met him that he was a square peg in a round hole.

Determined not to slow her stride - *You're jumping to conclusions* - Anita's feet were accommodating. They knew every uneven surface, from the hollow-sounding ramp in the ticket office, to the cobbles of Base Court and the worn stone slabs of the Tudor kitchen. But, even here, something Anita couldn't pinpoint was amiss. A member of the Family Activities Team nudged her colleague, a message relayed with a series of nods and coughs. Realising that her arrival was being announced, Anita dismissed a wave of irritation. She had posted photos of the burnt-out shell of her house on Facebook to avoid being interrogated. Now she regretted that decision. "Has anyone seen Roz?" she asked.

A guilty look passed between the pair who manned the Tudor Spicery. "Not yet."

What *were* their names? Anita looked from one face to the other but all she could think of was The Spice Girls. It was ridiculous. She'd been for a drink to celebrate one of their birthdays only last week.

Following their gazes, she saw that the food historians were preparing for a school party. Great slabs of beef were being skewered onto twelve-foot lengths of iron. A fire was about to be lit under the spit-rack in Wolsey's roasting kitchen. For a moment Anita felt tempted to laugh at the girls' over-sensitivity - she was fine, after all. But then her own gaze was drawn from the scorch-marks above the great spit, scaling the heights of the heat-charred wall. Strange that she had stood here so often yet never noticed the blistered beams thirty feet above her head.

Her stomach turning to oil, Anita skirted the huge rough wooden table in the centre of the room. She needed an excuse to get out of there. Anything would do.

And she was handed one. "Try the Georgian Apartments. She's supervising the installation of *Secrets of the Royal Bedchamber.*"

"Of course!" Anita had seen the finished costumes on the last day she'd been in before the... before the… She closed her eyes, but all she saw were the pure white ghost-like 'courtiers'.

"Have you seen it yet?"

Someone grabbed hold of her guts and twisted. "No, not in place," she managed. Representations of real people, the figures had been based on Anita's research. Descriptions of height and weight found in diaries and poems. Every pleat and fold precise; hand-punched collars and cuffs giving the appearance of lace. All started to blacken and shrink at the edges, dissolving into flame.

"Steph's team's done an extraordinary job. You'd never know the costumes were made of paper." The voice was muffled. It came to her from a distance, as if she was watching television with the volume turned down low.

"Are you OK, Anita?" Fingers were reaching towards her. She looked at them, trying to snatch her forearm out of their way, all the time moving as if underwater. The human hand was a strange shape when you thought about it. Her eyes trailed the length of the arm. It was attached to one of the girls whose names she couldn't remember. Her face moved in and out of focus. "You look a bit pale." The words were out of sync with her mouth, an echo.

And then, an alarm went off. Anita backed up a few paces, hands clamped over her ears. Mouths moved, but she could no longer make sense of what was being said. The roar and rush of flames was overlaid by a shrill pitch, and Anita crouched low so as not to breathe the toxic fumes. Why did no one else appreciate the need for panic? They'd all practised the drill.

Having stopped what they were doing, the kitchen staff had fixed their eyes on her. Those she stared back at looked embarrassed, exchanging knowing glances with each other.

The only smoke was coming from the great fireplace and here she was, crawling along the cold floor slabs. Concluding that the noise must be inside her skull, Anita self-consciously picked herself up. "I need to get some air. Excuse me."

Her walk became a run. Striking out across Clock Court, where a lone jackdaw delicately picked crumbs from between the cobbles, she was lost at sea, turning about, looking for an archway, an exit, anything. Blood pounding in her ears, her conscious-self divided in two: practical mother and frightened child. 'There!' the mother pointed. 'The Wolsey apartments: run!' Closing the heavy wooden door behind her, she collapsed against it, crumbling inwards.

I'll be caught - caught somewhere I shouldn't be.

You have every right to be here. You work here.

Breathe, Anita demanded of herself. In to the count of four, out to the count of four, until the hammering began to subside.

Though the sheer heart-stopping panic lessened, a residue remained. "For Christ's sake, pull yourself together," she said out loud. Something familiar, that was what she needed. The mother looked about for a distraction. At one end of the room, set against dark wood panelling, hung the painting that had intrigued many art historians: *The Portrait of an Unknown Woman,* as it became known in the twentieth century.

"Do you never tire of theorising?" Roz had voiced the disapproval expected of someone in a senior position. "You know the official explanation."

"If you don't want people to draw comparisons, why hang it opposite a portrait of Queen Elizabeth?"

Because it was the comparison that had continued to taunt Anita. She relied on the fact that it would do so now.

Part of the Royal collection for over 300 years, the painting had previously been displayed with the label *Queen Elizabeth in Fanciful Dress.* And yet Anita was supposed to accept that a case of mistaken identity had occurred. That the frame, inscribed with the name 'Elizabeth' had been recycled.

Anita thought, *If I can just stand here for a few moments and drink in the detail.* She cast her trained eyes over its brushstrokes. Standing in a confident pose, this pale-skinned woman's right hand rested on the head of a stag, a stag which wore a crown. A string of pearls hung from her wrist. The French Ambassador wrote that the Queen's wrists dripped with pearls, but that wasn't to say other women didn't wear similar bracelets. Courtiers rushed to imitate any trend the Queen introduced, even at risk of bankruptcy. The woman's other hand was at her waist. Remembering the hand reaching for her own arm, Anita's heart moved into upper gear. *What else do we know?* She forced her attention.

It was an unusual stance for a woman. If Henry VIII had been painted in this pose, you might say that he was trying to look broader or speak about his sword arm being at the ready. Here, the impression was that the woman was silently seething.

The self that was mother registered that her daughter's breathing had almost returned to normal. As if prepping her daughter before a school test, she demanded, *What else?*

Anita's eyes darted. The woman's face looked heart-shaped, an impression created by her head-dress, described by Horace Walpole as 'something like a Persian', then later, in 1959, compared with the one found in Boissard's woodcarving, 'Virgo Persica'. Anita bridled at how quickly theory was adopted as fact.

What does the woman's face say to you?

It wouldn't suffer fools, and yet it was far from ruthless. There was a delicacy about her flushed cheeks. If she was victorious, victory hadn't won her personal happiness.

What else?

The veil.

What about it?

Photographs taken of the portrait in the late nineteenth century showed the veil monographed with the letter 'R'. *Regina.* But not anymore. It was freely admitted that the painting had been 'extensively rubbed'. Of course, altered art meant nothing in itself - though it usually involved creating something new.

But why would that matter?

The painting had been dated to between 1590 and 1600. By that time, all of Europe was in awe of Elizabeth I. She had become associated with supernatural imagery, Diana the Virgin Huntress. But the woman in the painting was no virgin. She was heavily pregnant. Anita's chest rose and fell once more. She was distracted by what her father had told her about her mother's post-natal depression.

Concentrate. What else do we know about the costume?

There was no surprise that the gown had caused further speculation, covered as it was in Tudor roses. But if the painting was only symbolic, why go to the trouble of altering it? Why paint over the flying birds that George Virtue described in 1725? Why remove the buildings from the background? *Where had Elizabeth been seen that would have damaged her reputation?*

The problem, Anita accepted, was that, in our age of realism, we expect paintings to be literal. A sixteenth century court painter's job was to emphasise power, perpetuate myths. He'd have been punished for painting what he saw.

If the unknown woman *was* Queen Elizabeth, it was true that childlessness made her a target for gossip. But for every whisper that she enjoyed affairs with her favourites, it was put about that she was incapable of normal sexual relations. Perhaps, Anita was reminded as she looked between the face of the unknown woman and the stag, elements of the painting *were* literal. Queen Elizabeth attended several masques. In 1575, her long-term favourite, Robert Dudley, hosted a pageant in her honour. A last-ditch attempt to persuade Elizabeth to marry him or an attempt to subdue Elizabeth's rage after she heard the rumours that his future wife, Lettice Knollys, was already installed at Kenilworth? The Queen's forgiveness came with a high price tag. She killed six deer on one hunt. Perhaps this subversive weeping stag was just one of them. *But why is the animal wearing a crown?*

There was movement behind her, a brisk clipping of heels

on the polished wooden floor.

"Off with her head!" The words echoed around the empty space until Roz came to a standstill. "I thought I might find you here."

Anita felt self-conscious under her manager's gaze.

Having appraised her, apparently finding nothing that required immediate attention, Roz turned to the portrait. "Our unknown woman's not looking very happy today." She pursed those bow-shaped lips that always lent her a look of bemusement. "Go on. What's your latest theory?"

Anita's wild theories were the pretence in this charade. She had concluded some time ago that the portrait was of a queen who'd frequently declared she was married to England, mother to her subjects. But it was a game - *her* game - and Anita was expected to play along. "I'm running with the Diana theme."

Roz nodded. "The virgin goddess."

"Who transformed Acteon into a stag as a punishment for seeing her bathing naked."

"And her hounds tore him to pieces. So who's your stag?"

"Essex. He saw the Queen naked. Or as good as."

Roz sighed, feigning impatience. "We do know Essex entered her bedchamber unannounced after he returned from Ireland, before she was wigged and gowned."

"And Elizabeth threw him to the dogs."

"Deprived of public office. Later executed." Roz raised her eyebrows. "Come to think of it, the dates aren't too far out. And the poetry?"

The sonnet in the bottom right-hand corner of the painting had always plagued Anita. Certain scholars argued it was the work of Edward de Vere, thought by some to be the real William Shakespeare. Anita pulsed with resistance at any suggestion that Elizabeth was betrothed to de Vere. In her opinion, he was a thug. And yet association with an unsuitable man might have been a good enough reason to alter the painting. "I haven't fleshed the whole thing out yet, but he was known to have written poems for the Queen."

"Most male courtiers *bled* poetry. Swearing to lay down your life for your Queen was compulsory." Roz put one finger to her lips, briefly. "I hate to be picky, but who would have commissioned the painting?"

"Essex himself. An apology to the Queen."

Roz nodded slowly. "While all the time he was plotting against her."

"I never said he didn't play a dangerous game."

"So," she swivelled towards Anita, that tidy mass of bright red curls, those concerned smokey-blue eyes. "How are you? You look bloody awful if you don't mind my saying so."

"Go right ahead." The trembling feeling had gone. Only the shame remained.

"You need some colour. Here."

"Please don't be nice," Anita said as Roz removed the bright blue scarf from her own neck and looped it around hers.

"I have no intention of being nice. It would ruin my steely reputation." Roz freed the hair she had trapped under the scarf and looked at the result critically. Frowning, she untied it and tied it in a slightly different way. "Better! At least it gives the impression that you have a little pigment." She assumed the same stern position as the unknown woman, one hand on her hip. But Anita knew her boss of old. She wasn't quite *all woof and no bite,* but they had a seventeen-year history. Roz had always been on her side. "My spies tell me you were acting - and I quote - 'a bit weird'."

"I honestly thought I'd be fine. I *was* fine, right until people started looking at me as if they expected me to break down. And now I'm fine again."

"By 'people', I assume you mean Ruth." So *that* was her name! "She said you acted as if you didn't know who she was."

"My mind blanked out. I honestly don't know what happened." The violent need to escape had left emotional scar tissue. Like Anita's childhood episode of pneumonia, it was something that she imagined would be visible on an X-ray.

"Heart racing? Feeling clammy?"

Anita's mouth fell open.

"I'll tell you, shall I?" Roz bent her knees, trying to get Anita to look her in the eye. "You had a panic attack."

"Please don't send me home." Anita bowed her head, ashamed.

"From what you've told me, that's not an option." Roz sighed, giving the appearance of impatience, then relenting. "But you can't just hide yourself away." She appeared undecided. "How about we grab a coffee, then I set you some research? OK?"

Relief surged through Anita's veins at the thought of tracing a gloved finger over an ancient manuscript, the thrill of the start of the trail. "What did you have in mind?" she asked.

"We're still a bit light on scandal for Bedroom Secrets, so any dirt you can dig up. You know the drill. We want our men mad, bad and devilishly handsome, and our women either wronged virgins or whores."

Is that all we do? Reduce history to gossip? No wonder Ed was scathing.

"Are you with me, Anita?" Roz was clicking her fingers.

"Sorry. Yes." Anita tried to look grateful.

"You don't seem terribly pleased."

"No, something to get my teeth into is exactly what I need."

"I'll let you have the rest of the week. But Anita," Roz shook her head and rolled her eyes. "If you come over all peculiar again, you're not to run and hide yourself away. Come and find me. Alright?"

She made it sound as if there was a moment when Anita could have made a rational choice.

"Alright?" Roz demanded.

There was no option but to give the answer her manager wanted to hear and to try her best to mean it. "Yes."

CHAPTER NINE

"No, you need to stop, Aunty Nita. You have to go back!"

She and her godson Reuben were sitting on the carpet, their backs against the rise of the sofa, his bony knee jabbing her side. Now that she and Ed were installed in Natalie's bedroom, any self-consciousness Reuben had begun to display had evaporated. In fact, he seemed to have taken Natalie's words, *"We have to be very nice to Aunty Nita and Uncle Ed,"* to heart. The fact that Anita had been best friends with Natalie since their student days was immaterial. Having claimed her as *his* friend, Reuben had taken to guarding Anita loyally. What was his was hers.

Coerced into playing a computer game she'd thought would bore her, Anita surprised herself. To be honest, it wasn't the game she found interesting. It was her godson.

"At least he's almost a real person now," Ed had shrugged, when she'd announced she had agreed to babysit.

"It's the least I can do." They had been living under Natalie's roof for the best part of a week. And even though Natalie claimed it was pay-back for all of the small favours she had called on over the years, this kindness seemed disproportionate. "Where else would we have gone?"

"A hotel!" Ed persisted, and then promptly announced

that he had a leaving do to go to after work. Mike someone-or-other. Anita had never been able to keep track of his colleagues. A sideways move, a promotion, lured elsewhere with the promise of a higher bonus, they came and went. Armed with her new knowledge, Anita was even less sure why Ed stayed. Right now, he would be somewhere in Leadenhall Street Market. Probably standing on the cobbles outside the red and gold frontage of the *Lamb Tavern*. Either giving her space or avoiding confrontation. She had thought her future settled. Now it seemed unknowable.

She was determined not to dwell this evening. Here was Reuben, offering distraction. It wasn't possible to watch this smaller but very real person without a degree of fascination. His baggy pyjamas disguised a frame that barely looked substantial enough for the school football pitch. Anita could circle his wrist with her thumb and index finger.

"Go back, Aunty Nita!"

"Why do I need to go back?" Anita had been slow to get to grips with the controls. Her avatar (busty, green-skinned and blonde) had just been building a little forward momentum. Remembering her promise to give Reuben moral guidance, she censored the inclination to swear. "Arghh! How do I reverse?"

"It's that arrow, there. Not that one. The one that points left." Patient to a degree, Reuben could outwit most forty-somethings when it came to his chosen computer game, the one Natalie had trouble prising him away from at mealtimes. To counteract this, Anita got a perverse pleasure out of buying her godson books, Lego and kits to build things with. Proper toys.

Reuben removed his gaze from the vast flat-screen television to demonstrate. He was bright and he knew it. Capable of making you feel as if you were the most important person in his world, he could dish out a pretty good telling off.

"Hands off!" Anita retorted, snatching her handset away from those frighteningly skinny wrists. She'd suffered older playmates who had wanted to take her toys away when she didn't get things right the first time. On the screen, her avatar rotated clumsily. Anita laughed determinedly. "Hah! OK!"

"Now you have to pick the key up." Reuben's mouth was open. A gap-toothed arrangement had replaced his perfect milk teeth. He was going to need braces.

Natalie spoke from the doorway: "I'll be off in five minutes." Her handbag hung open as she checked its contents.

"Bye," Reuben said nonchalantly. Two years ago, after his parents had split up, this announcement would have made him hurl himself at Natalie as if his life depended on it. There would have been a full-scale tantrum, ending with apologetic telephone calls.

"If you're going to behave like a five-year-old, I shall have to treat you like a five-year-old," Natalie had said on one occasion Anita had witnessed.

Unsure what expression was appropriate to adopt when her godson kicked up a stink, Anita had watched his mother march him upstairs. As Reuben craned through the banisters, she saw from the satisfied glint in his eye that he considered he had clawed back a victory. His mother had cancelled her plans. He had her just where he wanted her. Now getting his own way meant something very different.

Anita smiled at Natalie, whose nerves were apparent. "I love that scarf over your jacket," she said.

"Really?" Her friend toyed with its ends.

"Really. You look great."

Natalie tightened the set of her mouth before heading back towards the kitchen. Some tiny detail must have been amiss. Moments later she was back, her left hand clutching the doorframe. "I won't be late," she said.

Anita's skin crawled at what she saw. Her friend had

removed her wedding ring. She felt an illogical desire to protect Reuben from this knowledge. Anita swallowed, smiling up at Natalie. "Don't worry about the time - although you might find me in bed when you get back."

"Have you drunk your hot chocolate, Rubes?"

"Yes," he buffooned, lolling against Anita, a pantomime of a younger child.

Steadying herself, Anita caught sight of her own left hand, fingers splayed on the carpet... No, she wouldn't acknowledge a thought as intimidating as the prospect of starting again - in her mid-forties, alone. She and Ed had agreed to a truce. They wouldn't discuss things *until they were in their own space.* Although she wasn't conscious of sighing, she felt her chest inflate. She couldn't let go of the feeling that Ed was trying to get her to agree to the very thing her gut warned was wrong for her.

"Eight thirty, young man." Natalie was pointing to the face of her watch. "That's forty minutes from now."

"Ooh!"

"It's a school night! And you've already had more than an hour on your computer game, so no mucking Aunty Nita about. Remember: I make her tell me everything."

"She does," Anita told Reuben confidentially, glad to shift her thoughts outwards. "She shines a bright light into my eyes."

"No she doesn't!" Too sophisticated to be had over, her godson's eyes pleaded to be let in on the adult joke.

"Alright, you've got me there." Anita cupped her hand to her mouth and hissed, "She hypnotises me." In the periphery of her vision, Anita saw that Natalie was still watching them from the doorway. "Go, go, go!" she ordered with a wave of her hand. "You'll be late."

"No later than eight thirty!"

"Don't worry about us. We'll be fine. Go and enjoy yourself."

As the slam of the door shook the house, Reuben jumped in with his opening negotiation. "An hour."

Anita knew she should navigate downwards. That was what kids expected. And so she pretended to think long and hard while her avatar skirted the charred wreckage of a building.

"Didn't you hear me?" Reuben demanded.

Anita thumbed the buttons, a movement that had become automatic. "I've decided to ignore you."

"But -"

"You know I'm not allowed to let you stay up later than eight thirty. But if you're really, really lucky, I might forget to look at my watch until nine o'clock."

"Yes!" He punched the air, then pointed to the screen. "Now you have to stop and pick up the key, Aunty Nita."

"Why? What do I need the key for?" She and Ed were to pick up the key for what was to be their home for the next two years on Saturday. An inoffensive cottage, everything neutral, nothing to become attached to. The move would be simple - not like the move to Chalkdale, when the removal men had struggled to fit their bedroom furniture up the bends in the narrow staircase. Now, everything they owned would fit in the boot of the hire car.

"You don't know. That's the whole point." Reuben spoke with authority. Had his voice been deeper - had his wrists not been so very thin - he might have inspired confidence.

Anita tried to take the game seriously. Her godson wanted a worthy opponent. Ed would have been his preferred gaming partner, but Ed was changeable with his affection, rugby-tackling Reuben in the hall one minute, shushing him because he was on an important call the next. *What's* the whole point?" she demanded as her avatar picked the key up.

"You know it's going to come in useful, but you don't know why."

The words flattened Anita.

"That's the whole point," he continued, thinking that she hadn't understood; wanting to make her understand. "You have to collect everything you can because you don't know what you'll need."

Anita's nostrils prickled. Wasn't that what she *had* done? She had thought herself prepared for most eventualities. Glad of the semi-dark, a misshapen lump lodged itself in Anita's throat. Though Natalie claimed her son was sensitive, it would be quite a task to make Reuben understand why she was crying over a stupid computer game. *You soft sod*, she told herself, fighting back a glut of tears.

At Reuben's age, the pockets of Anita's Brownie uniform had been well-stocked. The stub of a pencil, a piece of string too short to be of any use, tissues, a plaster, a two-pence piece for the phone box and a safety pin. Designed for emergencies, the contents of her pockets had only ever come in useful to ward off the stern glare Brown Owl reserved for girls who arrived at meetings ill-prepared for disasters, both natural and man-made. There was a lot to be said for things that made you feel safe.

Virtually nothing was left of the possessions Anita had gathered around her. Just the Buddha's head, a laptop, a passport and her birth certificate. There *was* no guarantee of safety. But her avatar... her avatar had a key and a hammer. And now Anita set her sights on something that looked like a shield.

CHAPTER TEN

A nita was sitting cross-legged on Natalie's bed, working on the spreadsheet she'd been compiling for the insurance claim. She heard the soft thud of the front door. Ed, she assumed, glancing at the alarm clock on the bedside table. She pictured the man she had known for fifteen years sitting on the bottom step, unlacing his shiny black brogues, worrying about waking Reuben. She listened for the deliberate creep of someone trying, but not quite succeeding, to be quiet. A wait of several minutes and there was still no sight of him. He was probably making a coffee. She would go and join him.

Grabbing her new dressing gown from the peg on the back of the door, Anita ventured out onto the landing. All was still, only the white hum of electricity, so she padded downstairs. But instead of Ed, she found Natalie leaning back against the kitchen counter, holding the stem of a wine glass. Her kicked-off shoes had capsized like the *Costa Concordia*.

Anita crossed her arms accusingly, as a mother might when finding a daughter creeping in at all hours. "And what do you think you're doing back so early?"

"Oh." Her friend closed her eyes briefly and shook her head. "It was hopeless. Join me?"

Before she could decline, Natalie had taken another wine

glass out of a head-height cupboard. She seemed in need of consolation. "Go 'ed," Anita said, her Scouse accent deliberate, exaggerated. Natalie opened the fridge, setting bottles clinking. There was a recklessness about the way she poured.

Anita accepted the generous measure, asking, "No good, then?" Her friend had signed up with an internet dating site.

"Do you know," Natalie was equally generous when topping up her own glass. "I'm sure he would have been fine - *if* I'd given him a chance. My homing instinct kicked in by the time the starters arrived."

"Always trust your gut." Anita concealed her relief. She'd tried to make encouraging noises when Natalie had shown her the profile of her date, talking Anita through her process of elimination (no facial tattoos, eyes not too close together, no signs that a previous partner had been cut out of the photograph). But there was no suggestion that he'd been anything other than the best of a bad lot. Natalie deserved better. She deserved someone. Someone like... but it was difficult to imagine her with anyone other than Phil. And Phil had left her.

"What it boils down to is that it's impossible for me to go out and enjoy myself. I'm no good at this. If I wanted some me-time, I'd have preferred to go for a pizza with you." She pulled a face. "Dating sucks."

Anita clinked the edge of the glass that Natalie angled towards hers. "*First* dates suck."

"Always?"

"Pretty much. Don't you remember?" Anita said, though she barely remembered herself.

"Not really. Remind me how anyone ever gets to go on a second date."

"It's the lesser of two evils. Unless you agree to a second date, you have to face another first." A memory ambushed Anita, something that hadn't troubled her consciousness for some time. It had been happening a lot recently, this resurfacing of forgotten things. In her early twenties, she had taken what her forty-something-year-old self would consider a ridiculous risk - a week-long holiday to New York as a second date. With someone Natalie hadn't had the opportunity to vet - thankfully - because, when she did, she hadn't approved. Never go out with a musician! It had ended as these things do - badly - but Anita missed her younger self - the risk-taker. And now the only evidence she'd ever been that person - together with all of her other photographs from the pre-digital days - had gone up in smoke.

Anita followed her friend through the hall. Passing a framed studio portrait of Phil with Reuben sitting in his lap, she wondered how Natalie coped with passing it half a dozen times a day. Perhaps she had trained herself not to see it.

Bent over the sofa, her friend swept items onto the floor - a copy of the *Radio Times*, a remote control, a handful of felt-tipped pens, a plastic helicopter with broken blades. They sat with their feet up, facing each other; positions they'd assumed many times before. "The only reason I put myself through this was because Reuben told me I needed a husband."

Anita felt herself recoil. "Really?"

"He wasn't serious." Natalie wrinkled her nose. "At least, I don't think he was."

"Then what made him say it?"

"I was driving him home from football practice when a light on the dashboard started flashing. I couldn't figure out what the hell it was, so I pulled over. I tried looking it up in the manual but I couldn't find anything that looked remotely like it! So that was Reuben's solution: a new husband."

"Not taking the car to a garage?"

"It was the first time he's ever suggested he might be open to the idea that I might meet someone else."

"And what do you think?"

"On the whole," she tucked stray hair behind her ear, "the garage seems like a safer bet. Anyway, enough self-pity. Did Reuben behave himself for you?"

"He offered to help with my spreadsheet, which was nice."

"Anything to put off going to bed!"

"To be honest, I didn't give him a lot of confidence in my computer skills."

"How *is* the insurance claim coming along?"

"Slowly." Anita shook her head. "I'm working my way room by room, but something always distracts me. This evening I was filling in some blanks about the spare bedroom when I remembered a wicker trunk we kept in a cupboard in the eaves. It was where I stored all my old scrapbooks - the one that had my early drawings of costumes in them. Nothing the loss adjuster would be interested in, but..." Trailing off, she shrugged.

"All those hours you spent!"

"I hadn't looked at them in years, but..." She shook her head, leaving the sentence hanging. It felt as if part of her childhood had been erased. Like the portrait of the unknown woman, small but significant details from Anita's life had been rubbed out. Changes so subtle an inexpert eye might miss them.

By the time she had composed herself, Natalie was nodding at her. "And you and Ed? You can tell me it's none of my business, but I haven't been able to help noticing..."

Anita stared very hard at the wine glass in her hand. It wasn't the first time she'd imagined something she was holding beginning to smoulder. She countered her inclination to let go - before it burst into flames - by clutching the stem.

"Talk to me, Anita."

Managing a tight smile, she forced her gaze upwards. "And there I was, thinking we'd put a cheerful face on things." But Natalie's expression suggested she wouldn't be fobbed off so easily. Intending to gather her thoughts, Anita closed her eyes. Smoke poured out of the walls. There was a glow of orange around the door. Her heart raced. It couldn't happen again; not here, where she was exposed. She snapped them open. "If I say it out loud," her voice quivered, "you're going to think I sound mad."

"You?" Natalie nudged her, only half playfully, with one foot.

"Well, I'll sound like the bad guy, then." The stench was there in Anita's nostrils again, acrid and damp.

"You've just lost your home." Her friend's voice was soft but firm. "And you're under an enormous amount of stress. There *is* no bad guy."

Anita dared herself to glance at what she held in her hand. Just an ordinary wine glass, she reminded herself. Nothing to make your blood pound so violently. "You're right." Her search for an anchor took her back in time. The scene had taken place in their house: the four of them - Phil included - sitting around the dining table. Natalie protesting as Ed piled her plate with too many roast potatoes. He was never happier than when playing host. "Do you remember saying that you couldn't imagine us living anywhere else?"

Looking as if she was about to say no, Natalie seemed to change her mind, nodding. "It was Phil who said it, but I agreed."

"That's the problem." Anita's chest surged. "Neither can I."

"That sounds terribly final."

"I'm struggling to see my way around it." The fire had destroyed part of what Anita had always thought of as her and Ed. The fact that Ed always used the bathroom first, while she padded about barefoot in the next room, going back and forth from fridge to kettle, making porridge and sandwiches, listening to the thin rasp of Ed's razor blade. That wordless but companionable start to the day couldn't be replicated in a house with an upstairs bathroom.

To Anita, her memories of the late nineties, before they moved in together, seemed inaccessible. She remembered three short months of dating: the irresponsibility of Saturdays and Sundays when they only clambered out of creased sheets to phone for takeaways; indulging a secret surge of pleasure when a colleague had asked what she'd done at the weekend and she'd shrugged, "Nothing much." Everything else was a void.

Natalie's brows twitched in a way that suggested she was weighing her words carefully. "*You've* always been all about the *feel* of a place, so my guess is that Ed has come up with a practical solution. And, let's face it, someone has to."

Anita managed a wry smile. "He thinks we should see this as an opportunity to build something bigger."

"*You're* the one who always said that your house was short of a room. Don't deny it!"

"I wasn't going to." Anita tried not to think about the cost, the fact that Ed would have to continue working in a job he hated, but there was no way of *unknowing* what he'd told her - just as there was no way of unknowing that, whilst Ed had once put her happiness first, practicalities now took precedence. "What he has in mind is a Grand Design."

"By which you mean...?"

"Something sleek and modern."

"And you said?"

Handed a cue, Anita shuffled back against the arm of the sofa. "I said that I don't want to live in a new house."

"Oh, Nita!" Sympathy - with just a hint of frustration. "You can't have the old house back. You do know that?"

Tears threatened. "Yes, but most of the value's in the land. We could sell the plot with planning permission and look for something else."

"And you've suggested that to Ed?"

As she nodded, Anita felt a powerful loneliness. "He said that we had enough trouble finding a house we both liked last time. In fact, he more or less admitted he only went along with my choice to make me happy."

"You see, that's so like Ed!"

Anita's dismay at finding Natalie smiling must have been written all over her face.

"What have I said now?"

"Nothing... at least nothing I can..." How could she explain that, by making a single revision to their history, Ed had demolished the foundations of everything Anita thought had been true? In some respects, her shock stemmed from the knowledge that she hadn't even been *aware* of Ed's compromise. "He didn't love the house in the same way I did."

"Oh, he did." Natalie leant forwards and put one hand on Anita's knee. "He just recognises that there's no going back."

"I suppose so." It was a possibility Anita needed to invest in.

"So what's this big idea of his?" Natalie repositioned herself.

"Drawing up a wish list and having an architect design something to fit."

"God, I would absolutely love that! At the top of my list I'd have a window seat looking out over the back garden. One of those really deep ones, piled with cushions. Somewhere to sit and read, or just catch my breath -"

"Natalie!"

"Sorry!" she said, not looking the least bit apologetic. "But imagine it."

Was her enthusiasm a ploy to make Anita look for positives? "You didn't sell this house when you had the choice. You could have started again, somewhere new. Why was that?" As her friend's expression altered, Anita felt guilty for raking up issues that were still raw.

"Too many memories, I suppose. Some of them bad, but, actually, most of them..." Natalie sipped her wine, her long neck moving as she swallowed whatever images had sprung to mind. "Also, for Reuben's sake, I didn't want too much change. Not all at the same time."

Anita wondered if this was what her father had meant when he'd said that it helped to have someone else to think about. "Perhaps that's it. I'm overwhelmed."

"Go easy on yourself. You're grieving."

"For a bloody *house!*" Anita laughed, a single self-deprecating syllable.

"Not just the house," Natalie insisted. "Everything in it and all of the years of your life that it represented."

Gratitude welled from Anita's chest. Natalie understood the very thing Ed refused to acknowledge. The house had been more than bricks and mortar.

"Give yourselves time."

Her friend's use of the plural floored Anita. Natalie was comparing Ed's pain with her own. Had he put her up to this? Had the evening been staged so that this conversation could take place? What was it Natalie had said with such certainty? *He just recognises that there's no going back.* Anita checked herself. Where was this anger coming from? Natalie had come to her rescue. She'd offered them somewhere to stay. As she'd pointed out, there was no bad guy.

Or, Anita pondered, it might still turn out that *she* was the bad guy. What if the electrics hadn't caused the fire? There had been plenty of occasions when she'd left her mobile phone charging overnight. Evidence of her carelessness was a possibility Anita might yet have to face. But not now. "You know the thing that worries me?" She was venturing into new territory. "Ed and I made the decision not to have children. We've never got ourselves into debt. We've both got good jobs. We're in good health."

"What are you saying?"

Anita didn't usually talk about her relationship. She was blurring the lines of previous loyalties. "We haven't had to work through anything this big before."

"But you've had arguments."

Though she pretended to think about it, Anita didn't have to. "Not that I can remember."

"You must have! You've been together for fifteen years."

"He shouted at me once." Just the memory of it made Anita's stomach clench. She drew her knees in closer. "It was over map reading. I sent him the wrong way up the A21."

"And that's *it*? That's the only time he's raised his voice."

She shrugged, knowing full well that it was.

"Wow." Natalie appeared dumbfounded. "I can't begin to imagine that. You actually agree on *everything?*"

Feeling defensive, Anita protested, "Of course we don't *agree*. One of us has to compromise."

"That's what's supposed to happen *after* an argument. One of you makes a tactical apology and the other says, *No, you were right.*"

Power games were precisely what Anita disliked about other people's relationships. The tactical manoeuvres. The constant one-upmanship. You were supposed to be playing for the same team. "So? We cut out the middle man."

"But you never clear the air! That's a lot of tension to have floating about."

It had never struck Anita that arguments might have positive outcomes. "Neither of us likes conflict. We've talked about this. It's because we're both only children. We never rowed with brothers and sisters and made up." But there was a problem, one that Anita hadn't been aware of until that awful scene in the hire car. Feelings *had* been concealed. What if Ed begrudged the decisions he'd taken without her knowing? Out of the blue, the motto *Be Prepared* presented itself. A two-pence piece. A short length of string, its ends unravelling. "We're actually very badly equipped for disasters."

Natalie's eyes clouded. Anita was reminded of the day when her friend had telephoned, unable to get the words out. Anita had said simply, "I'm on my way." She didn't know the details of Natalie's final argument with Phil. The words were immaterial. It was the underlying thing, the thing that couldn't be spoken of. *Whatever feelings I once had for you are gone, and it doesn't matter how we finish this, but this is where it has to stop.* Something that had once glowed golden - she remembered Natalie's face on her wedding day when, having reached the altar, she turned to Anita and handed her the bouquet of yellow rosebuds - had reached its natural end.

But Natalie was leaning towards Anita, offering her sympathy. "And it can't have helped, being here. It's not as if you've had any privacy. Things will be easier, once you're in the rental house."

"I *hope* so. I expect you can't wait to see the back of us."

"Absolutely. The minute you've buggered off and Reuben's dad's collected him for the weekend, I shall be dancing round the house naked. Or doing the hoovering. One or the other."

CHAPTER ELEVEN

"**Y**ou're too far away. Come back to me."

They were lying on body-warmed Egyptian sheets in the rented house. There had been little unpacking to do. With so few clothes between them, Anita hadn't even needed to compete for space in the wardrobe. While she arranged the few outfits she owned - spacing the hangers out so they took up *more* room - Anita had contemplated how little was left to anchor her. Just a job and Ed. Her world had shrunk. *If we were to split up now, there would be no argument about who gets to keep what.*

"How about we crack this open?" Ed startled her out of this appalling and liberating thought. Anita hadn't heard his approach. There were no creaking floorboards in this new house. He was standing in the doorway, holding the neck of a bottle of bubbly and dangling two glasses. Behaving as if they had just arrived at a holiday cottage.

Putting the bottle down on the chest of drawers, Ed walked over to Anita and wrapped his arms around her. "We should celebrate being in our own space again. I know the house doesn't feel like ours yet. But it will do, once we've hung a few things on the walls."

She'd agreed because, caught thinking the unthinkable, she seemed incapable of processing anything else.

Come back to me.

Now, Anita was resting on one side, her head in the crook of her arm. "I can't," she invented an excuse. "I'm watching the bubbles."

In fact, she had been daydreaming about Chalkdale; watching the curtains billow softly in the breeze from the open windows; mesmerised by the shadow-and-light-play of the bright sun and branches from the lilac tree on the parquet floor; turning as she sat at the dining table and seeing great tits pick seeds from the birdfeeder; her spine jolting as the postman let the letterbox clatter shut. Fragments of seemingly insignificant things assumed new meanings. Displaced, Anita wondered, *Do I know who I am without my books and my CDs?* Lying naked, she felt insubstantial, shadow-like. She also felt a growing sense of separateness. Not only from Ed but from her former self.

The warm outline of Ed's hand on her shoulder, the press of his torso against her back, his chin on her shoulder. They were still for a moment, hypnotised by streams of bubbles rising to the surface of the half-full glass on the unremarkable bedside table.

"We can be happy here." Ed pressed his lips against her neck, his gesture surprisingly fierce. "We're about so much more than a house."

Anita could barely reach for his hand with hers. She was supposed to reciprocate, say that she felt the same, but she was *not* the same. How was it possible to have any sense of yourself in a house with smooth plaster walls, painted in various shades of cream; where every angle was a perfect ninety degrees; where hot water travelled noiselessly through pipes? Reactions dulled, it wasn't unpleasant to just let go. For the first time since the night of the fire, Anita felt that if she closed her eyes she might be able to drift. Not necessarily to sleep...

No, she needed to remain on her guard, open to the

possibility that Ed was trying to trick her into saying that her home was wherever he was. This would be taken as agreement to his wish list. And so she turned and kissed him. "I'm going to try the shower out."

He reached out a finger and traced a semicircle under each of her eyes. She felt the stretch of the elastic skin above her cheekbones. Ed's concentrated expression said that he would erase those dark and deep semicircles if he could. Newly self-conscious, she lifted the duvet cover.

She stared into the porthole she had cleared from the fog on the mirror. The outline of the face within the circle was indistinct, its features diminished. Anita touched her face, the reflection touched its face. She turned her face to the side, the reflection turned its face to the side. She smoothed one eyebrow, the porthole fogged. Using the corner of a towel to clear it, she had the sense of alienation, surprised that the reflection moved to her bidding.

Flinching at the touch of hands on her waist, the eyes in the mirror widened and Anita registered how yellowed and bloodshot they were.

"What are you doing?" Ed asked, resting his chin on her shoulder.

She smiled at his reflection, making a joke of it. "Just checking to make sure I'm still me."

"Say 'book.'"

It was an old routine. Ed had expressed surprise when Anita had first told him she came from Liverpool. He'd demanded the proof. She knew what was expected: a *You Say Potato* routine, except that their routine began with 'book'. "Bewk."

"Say 'are you laughing at me?'"

"Are you laffing at me?"

"I'll vouch for you." He turned towards the shower. "You

are Anita Hall. Straightforward. No middle name. First single you ever bought: *Hit Me With Your Rhythm Stick*, and the B-side shocked your mother so much that she banned you from playing it. Favourite album: *Brilliant Trees* by David Sylvian. Favourite film: *Cabaret* - or *Harvey*, depending what mood you're in. Favourite book: currently *Wolf Hall,* subject to frequent changes. Guilty pleasure: *Heat* magazine, which you hide under the cushions -"

His voice was muted by a gush of running water. A shift of focus, she looked at Ed's naked back in the porthole, the creases of his buttocks, as he held his hand under the flow to check the temperature.

He turned towards her before stepping into the shower. "Loves antiques but is shy of vintage. Doesn't like the idea of wearing dead people's clothes. Undertaking a survey of the nation's cafés to locate the UK's best carrot cake..."

It was peculiar to be in a confined space, in such close proximity to another person, someone who had once loved you more than you had realised, and now loved you less, but thought that he was the authority on what was best for you. And yet Anita needed reminding that she was more than an unsmiling passport photo, more than a written record of her place of birth. Ed was the only person who could do this.

She found herself crouching in a corner of the King's Apartments, arms clutching her knees, like Matthew Modine in *Birdy;* confined to a cell, making himself small, his gaze distant with nameless longing, unhinged. It was easy to feel insignificant in the Cartoon Gallery. The architectural grandeur - everything from the room's immense proportions to the mahogany panelling - had been carefully composed to invoke fear and respect. A stage-set for royalty. Kings and Queens swept through, allowing courtiers a passing glimpse before they fell to their knees or curtseyed. Several moments had been lost to Anita; how many, she couldn't begin to estimate. She remembered heat surging to her head, the onset of panic and then...

She dipped her head: she didn't feel very well.

Anita had no memory of the 1986 fire that gutted Sir Christopher Wren's designs, Gibbons's carvings, the great ceiling. But she'd helped guide visitors to the muster station when sirens came screaming from Kingston, Heston, Fulham and Wimbledon as part of a training exercise. Later, wearing thermal imaging equipment, she had rehearsed how valuable artwork might be salvaged.

In her mind, Anita tried to retrace her steps, just as she would when trying to find a set of keys she'd mislaid. This was the South Wing; close to the top-storey grace and favour apartment, home to Lady Daphne Gale. Although newspaper reports claimed that the elderly widow had been incapable of taking care of herself, Lady Gale had lived alone. Neighbours recalled how she would light her way to bed by candle. It was probably one of those naked flames that caused the fire. The fire alarm didn't activate. By chance, a malfunctioning intruder alarm sent residents scurrying from the labyrinth of secret doors and passageways, hinted at by discreet doorbells, brass nameplates. By that time, it was too late for Lady Gale.

Under a cap of her own hands, Anita's head pounded. Somewhere within her, the leaded roof of the three-storey building was crashing down through the gallery below, dragging the priceless ceiling and the wood carvings with it. It was night, and flaming debris was falling. She saw her ghost standing at the dormer window.

Anita staggered to a standing position. Her intention was to add a full stop to the swirling thoughts that had taken her mind hostage when she said, "I can do this." But saying it out loud didn't make it true. The floor beneath her feet no longer felt solid. It seemed to be slanting.

Perhaps Ed was right: she needed to leave her job. Not because it didn't pay well, or was frivolous, but... How could Anita remain in a place where fire had left an undeniable trace? This question scaffolded her fear that rebuilding Chalkdale would be a mistake. It would be tempting fate to live on the site where they'd come so close to disaster.

Following the instructions for a fire drill almost to the letter, Anita hurried out of the Palace without stopping to collect her belongings. She glimpsed the detail on a gold button as she passed a blur of red livery. A left turn across the bridge, she jumped on the first train. When her mobile phone started vibrating and she saw that Roz was trying to reach her, Anita switched it to silent. But she was still clutching the handset when a text arrived: *Car Park Paddy saw you leave. I've covered for you and said you had a doctor's appointment. If you've got any sense you'll take yourself straight there. Call me!* And then, *If you don't reply, I shall have to call Ed.*

A tick danced along the length of Anita's jaw. *Don't call Ed* she typed, feeling helpless.

You won't talk to me. Perhaps you'll talk to him.

Please don't call Ed.

Then get yourself to the doctor's!

Defeated, she keyed a single-word reply: *OK.*

Somehow, Anita found herself in the consulting room, sitting opposite Dr Kernow. On the deep windowsill, among the reference books, the boxes of latex gloves and the tissues, sat framed photographs of the doctor's children. Two boys. Photographs that gave the message *This is me. I'm a person too.*

Dr Kernow switched to smile. "So, I've had confirmation from the hospital that your chest X-rays were clear, which is good news. How have you been feeling otherwise?"

A busy woman, she needed Anita to get to the point so that she could send her on her way within the allotted five-minute time-slot. The elderly patients with wheezing chests and children with bark-like coughs who were crammed into the waiting room preyed on Anita's mind. "I seem to be losing..." As she faltered, the GP looked on questioningly. *My grip on reality. A sense of who I am.* Anita's head had developed a tremor, as if her neck was no longer substantial enough to support it. Speaking the words might make them true. Looking pleadingly about the vicinity of the untidy desk - anywhere but directly into Dr Kernow's eyes - she prayed for rescue.

The undercurrent of impatience dissipated. "You've had an awful lot to deal with. Has anything specific happened that I should know about? Any symptoms?"

"Everything," Anita said, discovering that by concentrating on a spot on the coarse surface of one of the carpet tiles - a spot Dr Kernow frowned at to see if it was of significance - she was able to speak, if not fluently, then well enough to make herself understood. Her mouth twitched. "I don't know what to do. I don't know what's real and what's inside my head. I'm beginning to doubt people I should be able to trust. I'm having panic attacks, my heart's been racing..."

And then it struck Anita: she didn't need to find the words. All the evidence she needed was on her mobile phone. She could just show Dr Kernow. Her hand shook as she flicked.

"What is this I'm looking at?"

"It's what's left of my house." This and this and this.

The GP nodded, her face grim. "It's not surprising you're having difficulty processing the information, let alone deciding how best to move forwards. But, because you've had palpitations, I'll just take a listen to your chest and check your blood pressure. OK?"

Dr Kernow applied the cold bell of the stethoscope to Anita's skin, saying, "Deep breath."

The simple, deliberate act brought it home to Anita that

she hadn't been breathing normally. "And out." She felt the cold pressure move three times, and then the GP sat back in her chair.

"Nothing obvious to worry about. Tell me, when have these panic attacks been happening? Have there been any patterns?"

She nodded. "At work."

"And are you sleeping?"

A memory of flames and the shadows of flames. The liquid roar. Joan of Arc. The shake of her head, uncontrolled. Anita put one hand to her neck to steady it. "I don't feel safe enough to sleep."

"Then it's important that we help you to feel safe. Roll up your sleeve for me." Anita resisted the idea that the world might ever feel safe again. How could it? The deflated cushion of the equipment used to measure blood pressure was velcroed in place, like the armbands she'd worn when learning to swim. As the air pumped it tight, a vein in Anita's arm began to pulse.

"Perfectly normal. Although sleep isn't the whole answer, you'll feel one hundred per cent better after a couple of good nights' rest. I'm going to give you a prescription for sleeping tablets. Just a few days' worth. They'll help get you back into your normal routine, then I'd like to see you again and talk about where we go from there. I don't want to start you on anti-depressants at the same time as sleeping tablets, but we might also think about some counselling to help you over the hump. It's not just about talking through what's going on, although that's important. We can teach you coping mechanisms for dealing with anxiety attacks. Obviously, it's a problem that the attacks seem to be triggered by something in your place of work." Dr Kernow frowned. "I think I have to recommend that you take some time away from there. Get some perspective."

Gratitude washed over Anita. She was being granted permission to absent herself from her own life.

"Is there anywhere you can go for a few days?"

"How was work?" Ed topped up her wine glass.

"Fine." Anita's knife and fork hesitated, mid-air. She shouldn't drink too much if she intended to take a sleeping pill. "Although I'm thinking of taking a few days off and visiting my parents."

"Want me to come?"

"No," Anita said as lightly as possible. "I want to thank them for the money, and... well, Dad was so sweet coming down like that. I should spend time alone with them."

"I'm glad you said that. Not that I wouldn't want to go. It's just that now's not a good time, work-wise."

Anita monitored Ed's expression, but it was unreadable. Loathing his job didn't appear to have lessened his commitment. Or had he expected her to have forgotten what he'd said? In which case, shouldn't Ed say so?

"Do you want to take the car?"

"I don't want to leave you stranded. Besides," she lapsed into childhood vernacular, "the train's dead easy."

"When are you thinking of going?"

She hadn't made up her mind until that moment. "Tomorrow."

"And Roz is happy with that?"

Anita smiled, amazed that Ed was unable to see that, though she still looked like herself on the outside, her internal organs, her skeletal structure - every cell of her being - were in the process of rearranging themselves. "Actually, it was Roz who suggested I take a few days off. You don't mind that I'll be leaving you to deal with the loss adjuster?"

"You read his email. Now that we've submitted your spreadsheet, it's over to them. Although obviously, at some point..."

"I know. We have to make some important decisions."

"No rush."

Her father answered the phone saying, "Keep your hair on!"

"Dad!" Anita said with some relief. She was sitting on the single bed in the spare room for privacy.

"Tilly Mint! I'd assumed it was going to be someone trying to sell me car insurance. How's the new house? Have you settled in?"

"It's fine." The smooth plaster of a bare wall mocked her. "All very magnolia."

"Ah, one of those!" he commiserated. "Your mother's upstairs on the computer. Shall I fetch her?"

"Actually, it was you I was after."

"That sounds like trouble. Should I be worried?"

"Not unless you don't want a visitor. I was thinking of coming to visit for a few days. But the last thing I want is for Mum to start cleaning the house from top to bottom. I thought it might be safer to surprise her."

"Especially given how bad her chest's been recently!"

"Is it worse?"

"It certainly hasn't got any better, let's put it that way. When's this happening, then?"

"Tomorrow."

"Tomorrow! Then I'd better have a bath."

CHAPTER TWELVE

Locating her reserved seat in carriage A, the so-called 'quiet carriage', Anita felt her stomach drop. A large man dressed in a baseball cap and shorts was overflowing from the window seat into hers. He was speaking loudly into his mobile phone, one bare knee jolting up and down, like a drummer denied a drum kit.

"Excuse me," she ventured.

He glanced at the orange and white ticket she was holding and grudgingly moved the offending knee an inch or two. By the time Anita had folded down her table, it had crept back. Aware that exhaustion was making her intolerant - that in all probability this wasn't a deliberate display of masculinity - Anita swallowed the caustic comment that threatened to erupt. After removing a book, she stowed her case on the overhead rack and sat, aligning her body towards the aisle. Though she found herself apologising repeatedly to passengers who were boarding, the man to her left seemed oblivious.

Even after he ended his phone call, one of his hands was in perpetual motion, typing on an invisible keyboard. When it paused, his knee started up again. A nervous energy rose off him, making it impossible for Anita to relax. When the train stopped at the next station, she took the opportunity to move.

Travelling backwards, Anita's copy of *A Girl is a Half-formed*

Thing lay open in her lap. It was the book everyone had told her she *should* be reading - the one that was winning all of this year's big awards - but she'd lost the appetite for translating its fragmented sentences. What she really needed was something comfortingly familiar. Instead her mind wandered to Natalie's advice: not too much change, not all at once. A pang for Reuben and the changes he'd have to face when his mother decided she *was* ready for a relationship; brief, like the rapidly changing scenery. Telegraph wires strung between poles in fields of unkempt grass which moved like waves. A sudden river, and then it was gone. Some half-remembered thing. Something she had promised Natalie she would do.

The white plastic back of the seat was reflected in the glass, and the cellophane from her hoisin duck wrap vibrated gently on the fold-down table. Staring out of the window strained Anita's heavy-lidded eyes, and yet she looked. With no need to keep up a pretence for others, Anita could admit that she was completely wrung out. Strange, that this thought should be comforting.

England sped past. She let it wash over her. A blur of construction sites, industrial parks and factories gave way to green hedge and gossamer cloud. A field of brown cows sitting down; she raised her eyes skywards for signs of rain. A field of Friesians standing.

After the announcement for each stop was made, Anita repeated the name of the place to herself, trying to picture herself living there. Obscurity appealed. To start again where no one knew you - or your parents. No one to act the innocent, asking, 'Was that your Anita I saw?' knowing full well it was and that her mother would be appalled. *Our Anita in New York? Don't be soft.* Perhaps starting again with next to nothing wasn't impossible. She had left home with a rucksack on her back once before. There had been something empowering about heading out into the world, alone and self-sufficient.

But that was the Anita who'd taken risks - the New York on a second date Anita.

A sad little station coffee kiosk, its grille padlocked down. A man sitting alone, blue plastic seating, not even bothering to look up at the train. An elderly man; his only distinguishing features - glasses and a flat cap - a disguise. Perhaps the station platform was as good a place as any to do the crossword. But who was he? Didn't he have a home to go to?

Everywhere, it seemed, buildings were rising out of wasteland. Offices to let. Flats for sale. Metal frames, like oversized Meccano sets. They struck Anita as obscene; the process of change relentless. A man in an orange hi-vis suit, supervising as a small square of tarmac was rolled. A job that required standing about watching others work. She couldn't imagine living where everything felt new and temporary. Perhaps the next stop. There was no urgency. Anita allowed her lids to close and she dozed.

Once, she woke with skyscrapers imprinted on her retinas. Anita had felt at home in New York, Liverpool's big brother, colour to its monochrome. And, of course, everything had been hormone-heightened, rose-tinted, new. Anita idly applied lip salve. She would just look him up on Facebook. Chances were, Anita wouldn't be able to find him - or if she did, she wouldn't recognise him. A footwear designer at Adidas. No, that wouldn't be him. She scrolled on: too young, too young, American, retired. *See more of the same name.* No profile photo. Public figure - whatever that meant. Works at film industry. Picture of a pot-bellied pig. Hopeless! But wait: there - that was the name of his high school. And here was his wife. Anita blinked. Ex-wife. Far easier to get a feel for what was going on in his life by clicking through her profile. She looked nice, the sort of person Anita could imagine being friends with. Should she message him? Anita had no idea what greeting she might send after a gap of over twenty years.

Hi! Just stumbled across your details... She would send a friend request and see if he accepted. Leave it at that.

Wait: here was what appeared to be a selfie taken by his *daughter.* Though it was illogical, Anita was taken aback. He had told her repeatedly that there were better things to do with your life than having children. Although she'd said nothing at the time, this was one of the things that had made Anita feel as if they were in tune with each other. Scrutinising the picture, she struggled to find any resemblance between the teenage girl and the image of the man in his mid-twenties that she carried inside her head. And what was this? A football-playing son. *Two* children. It was foolish, this need of hers to recapture something that was obviously long gone. So much had happened. But there was no *retract friend request* button, so that was that.

To distract herself, Anita texted Natalie, thanking her once again for putting up with them (a suitable pun) and telling her where she'd be for the next few days. *Hug Reuben for me.* Then she had no excuse not to contact Roz. This was the difficult one. On any other day, Roz was both a friend and her boss, but Anita had taken leave without notice. It was inexcusable. Anita's typing was hesitant, as if her thumbs resisted the words. *Roz, you were completely right. I had another meltdown. I am getting help. My GP suggested I get away, so I'm on my way to my parents'. I'm so sorry to let you down without notice. I don't know what else I can say except that I'll contact you in a couple of days' time.* There were other words - better words - but the important thing was to send something. Facts sat heavily, undigested, as the train moved forwards. Roz would have no option but to react as her boss.

Someone was glaring at her. A woman. The *no mobile phones* rule didn't apply to texting. Besides, plenty of other pulsing electronic equipment was on display. For the last twenty minutes, one woman had punctuated the comings and goings of the carriage with tuneless bursts. Presumably she was under the impression that her headphones not only filled her ears with music, but filtered out any sound she produced. Still, Anita made a pantomime of putting her phone away.

Finally, they crossed the wrought iron expanse of Runcorn Bridge - her first glimpse of the life-blood of her home city, the Mersey. Leaning forwards to see the flat gun-grey ribbon of water, something primal happened; a response in her veins. Snaking through familiar sandstone cuttings, she relished being back within the landscape of her childhood; embraced the prospect of feeling grounded; the friendliness of the people; their humour; their 'Who the bloody hell d'you think you are?' attitude.

The city's reaction to the arrival of a bright yellow Japanese sculpture, the so-called Superlambanana, was typical. "Are you having a laugh?" was the universal outcry. And yet, when it disappeared from Wapping, the cry of "Oi! Who's nicked our lambanana?" could be heard all the way from Chester Zoo. Because, even though they hated it, Liverpool had adopted it as its own. Besides, being such an eyesore, it had become an excellent landmark when you needed to give directions to cabbies.

This unlocking of Anita's memories set a slide show in motion: sitting on the front step of her Nana's Walton terrace while the adults congregated in the tiny front room, smoking so many ciggies that the ceiling needed repainting every year. The Pier Head, the Albert Dock; a skyline dominated by the Three Graces and, above, by two cathedrals competing for the souls of sinners; and everything that fell in between - narrow Mathew Street, home to the Cavern and Eric's; her own spiritual home, the Walker Art Gallery. Would she still be able to feel it? Or, like some of the people in her slide show, was she seeing the ghost of a place that only existed in her mind.

She grabbed the handrail, lifted her case, stepped over the gulf between train and platform. With the soles of her shoes planted firmly, Anita hesitated. But there, behind the barrier at the far end of the platform, was a white-haired man looking enormously pleased with himself. He held up a homemade sign: *Cab for Tilly Mint*. The gap between adulthood and childhood narrowed. Anita wasn't sure whether to laugh or cry, but her mouth stretched wide, and her feet strode forwards, her wheeled case trundling behind her.

"Back of a packet of cornflakes?" she asked, nodding at the sign.

With an expression of mock-horror, her father turned it slowly to reveal the familiar red logo on a background of blue. "Shreddies. Do you want a lift or shall I see if I can get myself another fare?"

She shrugged. "Don't mind if I do," and then she laughed and hurled herself into his arms.

"You soft lass. As good as it is to see you, you'd better back off. Someone will think we're in one of those adverts for families."

"I think the adverts are supposed to be for train tickets." She stood back; drank in her surroundings. Rather than looking like a poor relative, the station forecourt wasn't so different from the forecourt at Euston. Digital this and that. The usual shops. It didn't seem so long ago when she'd caught the Friday night train home for the weekend and there had only been a ticket office and a W H Smith's. Mind you, in those days *Fuck Off All Cockneys* had been sprayed on the tunnel walls. Scousers weren't shy in their opinion of southerners, and as for someone who would choose the south... But in those days, Anita had been able to switch from Emma Thompson to Cilla whenever it suited her.

"How did you know which train I was on?" she asked

"Very little gets past me."

"Ed phoned and told you!"

"He might have done. Or it might have been Mr Branson himself. Shall I take that case of yours?"

"No, you're alright." It was easy, slipping into the role of the child. "There's only the one."

"You don't think I'd have offered otherwise? Come 'ed. Let's get you home so your mother can give us both what for."

She paused on the steps, high above the traffic roar.

"All present and correct?" her father asked.

It was all still there. St George's Hall, its concert halls and law courts, Prince Albert high on his horse; to Anita's right, the Walker Art Gallery, the Central Library and the Empire. "Just as I left it," she said.

CHAPTER THIRTEEN

P atti's hands were curved over the computer keyboard when the ringing of the doorbell stilled them. They splayed slightly, her disturbed train of thought soon to be lost altogether. "Oh, you're joking," she said out loud. "What now?" Although, in truth, since Ron was out on one of his missions of mercy, it had been a quiet morning. She heaved herself up from the desk, squeezed around the side, drew back the lace nets (they could do with a wash) and peered down. There was no one on the front path, looking as if they might be selling redemption or dishcloths. Whichever devil it was must have let themselves into the porch. It was like a greenhouse in there at this time of year. She'd better rescue them before they suffocated. Patti turned the key in the window lock and opened the glass an inch or two.

"You'll have to hang on a minute. I'm upstairs, in the office." It had a pleasingly important sound. Patti's realm was the house, and the office was where she did her thinking. In fact, leaving the house these days, her reaction on finding that the city and all of its streets were functioning perfectly well without her was surprise. With one final glare at the unfinished sentence on the screen, Patti tightened her mouth, and then released an exasperated *Ah!* "The good stuff doesn't get away. If it was meant to be, it'll come back to you."

Her feet landed heavily on the treads of the stairs. She came down sideways on, right foot first, nervous until it found its hold. Then the left came to meet it, far surer of itself. More haste, less speed, as they say. The halfway landing, a glance at the oval of frosted glass gave little away. The top of a head. Brown hair, if she was forced to guess. The muffle of a voice. Nothing much to go by.

Then, just as she was almost there - she might have known it! - the sound of a key turning in the lock. The door swung inwards.

Dear God! She clapped one hand to her chest.

An expectant expression, not unlike the fit-to-burst face of the little girl who used to hide in the cupboard under the stairs, patiently awaiting discovery. And yet, a grown woman, with a smile that quivered and crows' feet. An undeniably adult daughter, infused with a new fragility. Dark crescents like bruises under her eyes. And standing to one side of Anita was Ron, complicit in whatever roguishness was afoot.

"Honest to God, the pair of you!" Patti said once she realised they expected her to speak. She took a few paces forwards, gathered Anita to her shoulder and held her there, self-conscious as always when physical contact was demanded.

Anita's soft breath tickled her ear. "Sorry, Mum. I know how you hate surprises."

"I should have known something was up when your father hoovered the living room last night." She glared over Anita's shoulder at her husband, whose card she had marked. Ron had the grace to look sheepish. "But to tell the truth, it's good to see some proof that you're still in one piece." In fact, there had been two hours of frenzied activity when Ron had roared through the house like a hurricane, nothing safe that wasn't nailed down. Clutter had accumulated over the years, and Patti was more than willing to admit it was time for a clear-out, but Ron could be indiscriminate. Suddenly, everything had to go. Although he hadn't said as much, Patti's impression was that he'd been looking for something specific. It had become urgent that he track it down, even though it was more than likely he hadn't seen it for years, and entirely possible that it had fallen victim to one of his previous clear-outs. She'd heard him rummaging around in the loft, stomping overhead, going up and down that dreadful rickety metal ladder (she wished he'd get round to replacing it), covering himself - and everything else - in dust.

"I hoped that Dad would have told you that," Anita said.

She rolled her eyes. "Your father!"

An impish expression rounding his features, Ron slapped one of his wrists.

"As well you might! First, I'm frantic about our Anita here, and then you go and do one of your disappearing acts!" She stood aside. "Well, get yourself inside, love." The initial shock having subsided, Patti studied Anita, recognising a broken soul who needed feeding up when she saw one. "I'll put the kettle on. Then I'd better work out if I've got anything that I can stretch to feed the three of us." She hadn't got any of Anita's favourites in the house. No Earl Grey tea or slimline tonic. Patti usually liked to lay out a nice welcoming buffet with all the picky bits. In fact, she had let supplies get a bit low - and she hadn't inherited her mother's knack of making a silk purse out of a sow's ear. Truth be told, Patti had been a bit slack on the cooking front of late, passing ready meals off as new recipes. But she'd been busy, creating.

"Don't worry." Looking especially smug, Ron held up a plain white plastic bag. "I made a stop at Grimmond's and he had some very nice fillet steak, so I'll be cooking my specialty tonight."

Raising her eyebrows, Patti was undecided whether to be put out that Ron was planning to take over her kitchen, or relax and enjoy her daughter's company.

"In fact, why don't the two of you put your feet up while I make a start on the posh tatties."

Patti looked wide-eyed at her daughter. "Who am I to argue? Of all the -" She swiped a couple of pairs of Ron's Y-fronts from the radiator in the hall, where she'd hung them to dry. Trust Ron to have missed them when he was tidying up.

"So," she said, throwing the underwear after her husband into the kitchen, and ushering her daughter over to one of the armchairs. "Where are you up to with the house?"

The corners of Anita's mouth twitched in a way that made Patti question if rushing in had been insensitive. "We're waiting to hear if the insurers are happy with the loss adjuster's opinion about what started the fire."

"And what was his verdict?" She could hear Ron's cheerful whistling; the clink of mugs being brought down from the cupboard. She hoped he'd pick a few of the newer ones.

"Electrical, so he thinks, but we've been warned that the insurers might want to get a forensic report."

"From what your father told me," Patti levered herself into the matching armchair, "it doesn't sound as if there's much left for anyone to inspect!"

Anita delved into her handbag for her mobile phone. Patti felt more than a little put out as her daughter thumbed the touchscreen. They had only just sat down and already Anita was distracted by people who she'd no doubt seen far more recently than Easter. But then, without warning, Anita thrust the device towards her. "Here. See for yourself. These are the photos I took."

"Sweet Jesus." Confronted with such stark evidence, Patti's disbelief was released in a half-whisper; part prayer, part exclamation. *This* was her daughter's reality.

"Just flick the screen sideways," Anita said.

Patti glanced at Anita who was leaning forwards. The heels of her hands were pressed against her eyes, almost as if she couldn't bear to see. Patti's inclination was to look away, as she might when confronted with a news report of a warzone, feeling that the photos were too invasive, too personal. But Ron had made his pilgrimage. This was the least she could do. It was almost impossible to take in, the extent of the devastation. Patti wasn't even sure what she was looking at in some of the shots. And to think her first thought had been for the christening robe!

Anita was clearly trying to suppress a yawn. "We'll probably never be sure how it began."

"But the insurance will cover everything, won't it?"

"We're waiting on formalities, as I understand it. But until the insurers agree, we can't do anything with the site. To be honest, I'm glad to have a bit of breathing space."

"Oh?"

"There are lots of decisions to make about how we rebuild - or if we rebuild at all." Anita removed her hands and shook her head. Now that her poor bloodshot eyes were revealed, they darted from her graduation photograph to one of Ron's gardening magazines. *What wasn't she saying?* "We're not quite on the same page yet."

"You and the loss adjuster?"

Looking as if she was in two minds, Anita exhaled loudly and then relented. "Actually, Mum, it's me and Ed. What he wants would mean taking out a mortgage again, and I like living mortgage-free." She seemed to be struggling to shape the words. "To be honest, I thought we both did."

Patti, not privy to the details of her daughter's financial arrangements, held her tongue. It was difficult to know what might cause offence.

"It puts pressure on me to earn more money."

Looking just above her daughter's shoulder, Patti was unexpectedly distracted. Ron had filled a rose vase with home-grown sweet peas. A mix called *Magda* - the one he always chose in honour of his mother's sister. The blooms cascaded onto the mantel: a combination of violets and pale blues. Patti's lips pulled apart. She hadn't been aware they were out yet. Was it really that long since she'd ventured down to the bottom of the garden?

"...which I can't do in the job I'm in."

Offered this cue, Patti snapped back. Anita's work was a safe subject, one they often discussed. "But you love your job! And I don't expect Lucy Worsley's is up for grabs." Patti refused to miss a single television programme the chief curator presented. It was the closest she came to understanding what Anita's job involved. Over time, she'd come to admire Lucy's unusual quality; someone whose trademark hairclip singled her out as slightly old-fashioned, and yet her eyes always had that saucy glint.

"And Roz won't be going anywhere either. Why would anyone give up their dream job?"

Unsure what any of this meant as far as the rebuilding of the house was concerned, Patti made what she hoped would be interpreted as a sympathetic sound.

"But it's not just the money, Mum. It's *what* Ed wants to build." Anita's voice rose in a painful crescendo until it peaked. "And please don't say that I can't have the old house back, because I realise that!"

Patti's mouth pinched, but the remorse that flooded Anita's eyes suggested her daughter regretted her tone of voice, if not the words themselves.

"I'm sorry." Sitting with her shoulders hunched forwards, she seemed to be swamped by the armchair. Almost childlike.

"No, you're alright." Patti frowned and massaged the soft skin above her mouth, feeling it give beneath her thumb. "You *could* have the old house back," she ventured, picking her way carefully over eggshell. "Not the bricks themselves, but I'm sure that, with your background, you could source parquet flooring and cast iron fire places. Plenty of places specialise in that sort of thing. There's a huge salvage yard over at Nantwich - although I think they call it *reclaimed* materials these days."

Anita sat back and exhaled sharply, as if laughter had caught in her throat. "Why didn't I think of that? I probably have contacts I could use."

Patti felt validated. The first thing to pop into her head (to her mind, the obvious solution) had proven useful. Looking at her fragile daughter, a little window opened. It was as if she was able to extend an arm through it and, by stretching all the way to her fingertips, she could almost touch that unreachable thing.

"Thank you, Mum." Anita seemed to have perked up. "I thought a bit of perspective might be a good thing."

"We could take a drive over the other side of the water if you like. Go hunting for doorknockers and find a nice pub to have lunch in while we're at it." But her daughter's attention had drifted, her expression set in new determination. "Your father must have forgotten about the tea," Patti said, determined to combat how deflated she felt. She *had* been useful. "I'll chivvy him along."

Ron had buttered a small rectangular ovenware dish. Next to it stood a pint of double cream. The garlic clove was peeled and chopped. Her husband always liked to have his tools at the ready. On the opposite work surface, the teabags had made it as far as the mugs. He was busily slicing potatoes with the mandolin. Patti flicked the switch of the kettle, which purred into action.

"It's just boiled." Ron looked over his shoulder, as if surprised to see her there.

The sight of his fingertips coming so close to the blade made Patti wince. "Concentrate on what you're doing! The last thing we need is a trip to A & E." After replacing a chipped mug (demoted to a 'gardening mug') with a newer one, she turned and hissed over the sound of steam. "Did Anita say how long she'd be staying?"

"I didn't ask. How long does she normally stay? A couple of days?"

It was impossible to think that Ron wouldn't have noticed the bags like bruises under his daughter's eyes. The pair were so in tune with each other they didn't need to exchange words. "I don't get the impression that this *is* 'normally'."

"It makes no odds to me." Ron gave chase as a transparent slice of potato escaped. He pressed another peeled half against the blade. "It's not as if I have any social engagements to cancel. You?"

"No. No plans. I just wish you hadn't sprung this on me."

"Anita asked me not to tell you. She doesn't want anyone making a big fuss."

"I rather think it's my job to make a fuss of her. That's what mothers are for." She lowered her voice even further. "I've just seen the photos of their house."

"Hmm."

Patti knew that she would feel even more foolish saying that she'd had no idea. Ron had tried to explain, but he'd been worn out by his long and unusually emotional day. And she'd been short with him.

Mistaking her silence for annoyance, Ron gave a harsh whisper of his own. "She didn't want to put you to any trouble."

"I would have liked to change the sheets."

"I checked the spare room. They hadn't been slept in."

Fresh out of objections, Patti returned to the tea-making, picking up the kettle. And then her heart stopped. She remembered the boxes that the delivery man had hauled up to the spare room. It would hardly have been reasonable to expect him to tackle the rickety metal ladder to the loft.

"If you really want to know how long she's thinking of staying, why don't you ask?"

She looked at the handle of the kettle, looked at her hand, and realised there was something she should be doing. The tea. Patti poured the water. "You don't ask someone who's just arrived when they're thinking of leaving, you div!"

"Don't you?" Ron's voice was jaunty, the rhythm from the potato slicer steady.

"No!"

"That'll explain why so few visitors come back and see us a second time."

As Patti reached the living room doorway, a tray balanced in her hands, Anita jumped up to clear a space on the coffee table and to reposition two coasters.

Patti picked her words carefully. "Do you have any plans while you're here?"

"Nothing special. I thought I might pick up some clothes. Other than that, I'll probably just sit in the garden and read if the weather's nice."

"There's no one you'd like to see? Friends?"

Anita shook her head and the corners of her mouth pulled downwards. "There's no one I keep in touch with these days. Just you and Dad."

Probably just a couple of days, then.

"I might go to Crosby beach to see the Gormley sculptures."

"Lovely," Patti said, though when Ron had taken her that time, she'd been utterly overwhelmed. The one hundred identical figures - cast from the artist's naked body, or so she'd read - seemed desolate. Some of them up to their necks in water, some covered in clams. She'd trudged behind Ron, who had marvelled out loud, turning his attention to each of the iron men, pointing out how differently they were weathering. Its scale had precisely the opposite effect on Patti, emphasising her insignificance. She had felt as if she were walking on quicksand, and doubted that Ron would notice when her head disappeared beneath the surface.

The carpet pile hissed reluctantly as Anita opened the door to the bedroom that had been hers from the moment she outgrew the cot-room until she left home. Her immediate view was a pile of boxes stacked against the wall. Arrive unannounced and this was the welcome you got. They were a new addition since her last visit with Ed. How long ago was that? Her overriding memory was of trudging round Ness Botanic Gardens, feigning enthusiasm at the few snowdrops and crocuses that had dared show their heads in defiance of such a bitter wind. Taking refuge in the café as soon as was polite, hands thawing on mugs, they had tripped over each other to agree when her mother said that it was beautiful in summer.

"Of course, it's nothing compared with Kew," Patti added, and there wasn't much you could say in response to that. Ed had tactfully pointed out that the Kew experience was marred by the roar of jumbo jets, and from there he marched the conversation onwards to Boris Johnson's proposals for a new London City airport.

"I've never managed to get your mother on a plane."

"You've never flown?" Ed asked Patti.

She'd been defensive. "I've never seen the need."

"Scared stiff," Ron mouthed.

For a long time, when Anita visited at weekends, the room had reflected her parents' expectation that she couldn't possibly survive on her own in the big smoke. They were distrustful of a city they barely knew; a city of rogue politicians, knife-wielding youths and corrupt Fleet Street reporters who perpetuated appalling lies while claiming to speak for the people. It wouldn't be long before she'd be back, in need of home-cooked stew with dumplings.

Now more of a storage space, it was a stale-aired room you simply closed the door on and forgot about. It was silly really to think of it as 'hers', not when Anita's 'London years' outnumbered the years she'd lived at home - if a place abandoned over twenty-five years ago could be called 'home'. Although the anniversary had passed unnoticed, the scales of Anita's lifespan had tipped ten years ago.

Anita had once thought the room large. Being allocated the 'big bedroom' was effectively her first promotion in life. Her single bed had been replaced with a double, to accommodate guests who came to stay - though she doubted this was a frequent occurrence. Navigating the small space at the end of the bed on her quest to open a window, Anita noted that furniture had been shunted together. Space for a new, but already overflowing, bookshelf. A folded ironing board jammed between the chest of drawers and the wardrobe.

Fuelled by a lungful of air, exhaustion made its claim. *Take the weight off.* Anita perched on the edge of the mattress. *Lie yourself down. That's better.* She registered slight discomfort. A small lump under the duvet.

Something was tucked up in bed, head resting on the pillow - the way that she'd once arranged her dolls and teddies. Smiling crookedly, Anita picked whatever it was up. Something coarse and matted. Here was the pull in her blood she'd hoped for. Barely daring to believe, tears crammed into her eyes. What Anita held in her hands was a relic - possibly the only one to have survived intact. One of her first toys, handstitched by her mother, Iris had wide-spaced button eyes, an unevenly shaped face, and an x-shaped mouth. She was short armed, and wore trousers that looked like cowboys' chaps, complete with felt braces. This 2D teddy had accompanied her to the 'big bedroom', carried her into childhood.

A soft click.

"Knock, knock!"

She scooted her legs around, swiped her palms quickly over both cheeks and looked up in wonder as her father's face appeared around the door. "Where..?" Anita fumbled for other words, but it seemed that was all she was capable of saying.

On her way to check that there were clean towels in the bathroom - something Patti was willing to bet wouldn't have crossed Ron's mind - she hesitated at the sound of voices coming from the guest bedroom.

"Up in the loft. I didn't know for sure, but I thought I'd have a rummage around. In fact, I brought a few bits and bobs down with me." Another piece of missing jigsaw. That's what Ron had been up to last night! Standing stock still, salivating at the comforting smell of creamy potatoes, Patti listened for a cue - the moment when she could give the impression she hadn't been eavesdropping.

"All of those boxes?"

"No! That little lot are your mother's. There's just the two boxes."

A rush of fabric conditioner and line drying, Patti lifted a pile of neat white squares out of the linen cupboard, a careful movement, as if they were fragile. Not wanting to contaminate the clean laundry with garlic, she risked clicking the door shut.

"What's inside them?"

"Photograph albums. A few clothes. I thought you might like to see if there's anything in there you want. I had a feeling -"

"Thank you, Dad."

Hearing her daughter's words swell with gratitude, Patti felt excluded. Her husband and daughter had such a natural way with each other. Anita's first word had been *Dadda*. Patti had been the one to teach it to her, exaggerating the two syllables whenever Ron entered a room, not realising how it would pain her when *Mamma* didn't follow for several months. But now, when her daughter needed her, she had failed once again. It was Ron who'd instinctively known that Anita needed to reconnect, without any fuss, with few words. But he was giving away the souvenirs Patti thought of as *hers* to give. What little she had salvaged from the clothes Anita grew out of, baby things that might have been sold second-hand, precious things only a mother would keep.

"What do you want me to do with them?" Patti had asked, hands on hips, admiring the cache she had spread out on the table.

Her twenty-one-year-old daughter had barely given the carefully grouped items a glance. "Chuck them, I suppose," she shrugged.

There had been no point in feeling rebuffed. You couldn't combat confidence like Anita's, least of all warn her it wouldn't last. Always so sure, she never imagined the possibility that something might come along and shatter all her certainties. Patti had shuddered as she'd overheard her daughter singing in her bedroom at the top of her voice: lyrics that told of insanity and despair and suicide and bombs; fascism and floods and shipbuilding and drug-taking; yearning and loneliness; teenage pregnancy and infidelity. Packaged as three-minute pop songs, presented in such a way that stripped meaning from lyrics - at least, to those who had yet to experience what the world would throw at them.

But Patti had experienced her own personal war. Sensing that these seemingly inconsequential things might yet prove useful, she had quietly packed them away for when that time came. And, now that it had arrived, Ron had stolen her thunder. Marooned on the landing, Patti toyed with the idea of bursting through the door, giving the impression that she hadn't known the pair of them were locked together in their own world.

"Don't thank me, thank your mam. She saved these things. If

it had been down to me, I would have chucked them years ago."

Thrown off balance, Patti took an involuntary step backwards, her foot locating the one creaky floorboard on the landing.

"Talk of the devil!" Ron raised his voice. "Is that you creeping about, Patti?"

"I thought I'd bring Anita some clean towels." Patti sidled self-consciously into view, the bundle in front of her validating what she'd said. She swallowed at the sight of the cardboard boxes - four, one on top of the other. Her throat constricted. Some of the words she had typed; all those unspoken and unspeakable things! They must see her fear. But there they were, father and daughter seated side by side, one of Ron's hands squeezing Anita's knee; Anita giving a weak smile and holding up a small scrap of felt and condensed fur.

"You kept Iris!" Disbelief choked her grown-up daughter's words.

"Won't you look at that!" Patti abandoned the towels on top of the stack (she felt more comfortable now that it was shrouded). "I'd completely forgotten. My mother made that for you."

"I thought you made it!"

"No. No." Patti plumped her new short hair, choosing what she hoped was a bright expression. "I'm afraid I wasn't well for a while after you were born. Your Nana made Iris for you while she sat with me."

"But I can remember -" Anita narrowed her eyes, trying to pinpoint some distant thing. "I remember you..." Then she nodded with certainty. "Sewing her eyes on!"

"Repairs!" Ron reached out one hand.

"Oh, she wouldn't be able to remember that." Patti dismissed her husband as if swatting a wasp away, and then smiled crookedly at Anita. "You chewed Iris's eyes while you were teething. One of them came loose. I was terrified you'd choke on it, so I sewed them on tighter to make sure they wouldn't come off."

Anita blinked. She seemed to be looking inwards, time travelling. "I can remember lying on my side in my cot, watching you."

"You *remember* that?" Patti leant on the towel-softened stack of boxes for support. "You weren't even walking at the time."

"It must be my first memory." Anita laughed, curiosity altering her features. "Although if you'd asked me five minutes ago, I would have given you a different answer."

Patti was overwhelmed by a feeling of inclusion. It wasn't often that she felt as if she'd arrived at a place where she truly belonged - but what was in the boxes had the potential to ruin it all. Why oh why had she written something so self-indulgent? The writing itself wasn't the problem. That had been therapy. But, told that *what* she'd written was worthy, flattered into vanity, she'd been persuaded to self-publish. Others who were compelled to write truths sealed them in time capsules, locked them in trunks, awaiting discovery after their deaths. The decision to hush up or make the details public left to the sons and daughters who stumbled across them. She looked at Anita and knew what her daughter's choice would be. She would burn it. And it would be the right choice.

One day when Ron was out, Patti would convince one of the lads who had paved the drive to take the books to the dump in their van.

"Well," said Ron, having satisfied himself that the three plates were piled with more than they could possibly eat. "Patti, love," he widened his eyes at her, "aren't you going to tell Anita your news?"

Never one to draw attention to herself, Patti attempted to divert him. "Oh, it's not a big deal." She cut into her steak to examine it: just the right shade of pink in the middle. Good. She was going to enjoy this.

Undeterred, Ron turned to their daughter. "Your mother," he indicated with a nod of his head, "has joined the 'blogging community'. I have got that right, haven't I?"

"Has she?" Anita was staring at Patti in a way that made her check that sauce wasn't dripping down her chin.

"I can never get her off that computer these days, never mind get a look in myself. Pass me the horseradish when you've finished, love."

Handing the jar over, Patti was appalled to find two pairs of expectant eyes fixed on her, her husband's bright with encouragement. The knowledge that her hobby was worthy of discussion over dinner came as something of a surprise. And yet, it seemed daft to shy away from the reaction of her nearest and dearest when she happily swapped opinions with complete strangers. "You remember that computer evening class I took a while ago?" she ventured. "Well, I thought I'd have a play around on the internet and see what all the fuss was about. And I found a discussion forum -"

"Hear that?" Ron elbowed Anita. *"Discussion forum.* She's up to speed with all the lingo."

She could see what Ron was doing. He was steering the focus away from Anita. But there was also pride in his voice. Until this moment, it hadn't crossed Patti's mind that her husband might actually be *proud* of her. "It was a thread about people who'd been evacuated from Liverpool during the last war, and so I thought I'd share a few family stories." *My mother went for an interview at the Kardomah Café in the Derby Square area and got the job. But, when she arrived dressed in her best togs to start work the next day, all she found was a pile of rubble.* "Almost immediately, half a dozen replies popped up. One of them triggered something else, so I just carried on from there." A few lines of text. Enter. A few more.

And then that one thing she'd posted. *Measuring what size socks you needed by wrapping them around your fist. If the toe and heel met, that was your size.* Replies - replies from as far away as Canada and New Zealand! And so Patti started to peel back the layers. *In the playground, daring each other to swing higher, so that you could see into the top storey of the police station and pull faces at the bobbies, who'd stick out their tongues if they saw you.* Memories she had no idea she'd stored away. And who'd have thought that all these people were out there? *There was no pocket money so I joined the church choir, because it paid 7/6d (about 41p) a month, which wasn't bad for singing like a scalded cat at someone's wedding.* Some of them lonely, like her; taking part in a discussion for hours on end. *I would take stray dogs I found on old bomb sites home with me, only to be given what for and told to take them back to wherever I'd found them.* Joining the conversation when they got home from work, asking, 'What have I missed?' *Both of us would bunk off school, then spend the day going back and forth on the ferry to Birkenhead. We hid in the toilets when the boat docked and we never got caught!* "Before I knew it, the person who ran the site got in touch and asked if I would help curate it."

"So now we have two curators in the family," Ron cut in, grinning.

Patti was quick to put him straight. "It's nothing like Anita's work! I just compile other people's stories."

Enough to intrigue Anita, she said, "That sounds *exactly* like my job."

"Oh, I'm sure what I do isn't nearly as complicated. I just vet the stories, tidy them up a little. And, if I find that other people have started threads about the same subject or mention the same location, I put them in touch with each other. It's very organic."

Patti had been about to tell her daughter how much she

had enjoyed Anita's blog about graffiti at Hampton Court Palace. The fact that people throughout history have always felt the need to leave their mark. How older markings aren't seen as vandalism, but make us wonder about the people who scratched the stone. She had found herself perfectly in tune with its tone, thinking about what her own legacy would be. But she felt a stab of jealousy as her daughter deferred to Ron. "Have you submitted your story, Dad?"

"Your mother doesn't want me poking my nose in. This is *her* thing." He smiled briefly at Patti, then reached across and tapped Anita's wine glass. "Anyway, how's your Merlot? Your Ed told me you can't go wrong with Chilean."

Anita sipped and raised her eyebrows approvingly. "Very nice. But I'm serious, Dad, you should. Journalism's your background."

Ron made a dismissive noise at the back of his throat. "Births, marriages and deaths. It was hardly journalism!"

"You're far too modest, Ron," Patti felt compelled to say. "You did your fair share of reporting."

"You see! Mum wouldn't mind, would you, Mum?"

Patti opened her mouth without really knowing how she was going to reply. In fact, she felt relieved when Anita, who was helping herself to more glazed carrots, went on, "You know, Mum, it's fantastic that you're preserving these stories. We know far too much about kings and queens. The things that happen to ordinary people - that's the real history."

Ron cut in. "Tell her about the other one, Patti." For a moment she felt the onset of panic. "Your own blog."

While recovering her wits, Patti feigned a smile. "I've started a book blog with a lady I met through a discussion on the other site." This was her baby. "We review anything, just as long as it's set in Liverpool. Beryl Bainbridge, Maureen Lee, Helen Forrester -"

"The Liver Bird Book Blog," Ron was gesticulating, a broccoli floret pronged on his fork. She'd spent half of

Anita's childhood trying to teach her table manners, when it appeared she'd copied most of them from her father. "These days, if your mam's not on the computer, she's got her nose stuck in a book. She's a pretty mean reviewer. If they get the detail wrong..." Ron blew out his cheeks and chuckled.

"I never say that the author's wrong!" Patti was keen to correct him. "I say that *so-and-so was there at the time and that's not how she remembers it.* And I add a little quote. Of course, once you've published your mission statement," Patti felt the heat rise to her neck, self-conscious at the sound of such a grand title, "you get sent all sorts."

Anita stilled her glass. "People send you books to review?"

Patti found that she was able to ignore a small drop of red wine that had made its way onto the white tablecloth. "Do they!" She took up her own wine glass and sipped enthusiastically.

"*Boxes* of the things we've got upstairs!" Patti frowned at Ron, who was now using his knife to indicate. "You'll find half of them stacked in your bedroom, I'm afraid."

Patti leant towards her daughter. "Some of them take me right outside my comfort zone, I can tell you. Sci-fi, memoirs - what they call '*grim*oirs' these days - exposés."

"How can you give something a fair review when you know it's not your thing?"

"Oh, we haven't set ourselves up as experts." Patti waved the question away. "There are hundreds of book bloggers out there already."

Anita was frowning. "I don't understand. If it's not for book reviews -"

"It's how well the author captures the *locality* that we're interested in. Our audience is made up of people who are trying to discover their roots. Or re-discover them, I suppose. We marry up the memories with the storytelling. Compare them side by side."

"That's fantastic, Mum!" Anita gave a sharp laugh. "In

fact, I'm amazed we don't do something similar at the Palace. Hilary Mantel, Phillipa Gregory..."

It was good to know you still had it in you to impress your grown-up daughter. "Well, it keeps me busy while your father's in the garden."

"No, honestly, Mum. It's amazing, what you're doing."

"But it's not the same as writing a book, is it?" As soon as the words were out Patti, regretted them. Why on earth...? She hurriedly deferred to Ron. "Or a newspaper column."

Busy chewing a mouthful of steak, he reacted with a curt *hmn*.

Patti had never really wanted *anything* to go out under her name, not even the blog. She'd assumed it would be possible to hide behind a domain name, but oh no! The minute you were on-line, people expected you to have a profile. *"You do not owe the truth to every pertinent enquirer.* That's 'nosy parker' to you and me." The most sensible piece of advice she'd ever been given. *"You* decide how much to give away. No one else." Empowered by her college tutor's words, Patti had applied them liberally. Lying was against her nature, but holding back - both on opinions and the truth - seemed sensible. In this day and age you didn't know when you'd log onto a computer and find your own words ambushed by quote marks - miles away from the context you'd given them.

"The steak was perfect, Dad." Anita laid down her knife and fork and sat back in her chair. "Lots of books start life as blogs, Mum. More than you'd think."

Her heart thumping, Patti said, "Is that right?", praying she'd succeeded in sounding as if she was ignorant of such things.

CHAPTER FOURTEEN

Supervised by Iris, Anita laid her treasure trove on top of the floral duvet cover. Her father was right: there really *were* two curators in the family. Her mother had packed the souvenirs of her childhood away with care. Categorising them, she had used money bags for small items, padded envelopes for larger ones. Here, a pair of tiny knitted bootees, the type you rarely see these days. (Blue being her favourite colour, Anita didn't question why they were that colour for a girl.) Old school reports in exercise books with green covers, passed from teacher to teacher; criticism written in slanting ink. *Her handwriting shows little sign of improvement. Distinctly wilful. Thinks she knows best.* Supposedly character-building! Acerbic and razor sharp, comments that, had one crept onto Reuben's report, Natalie would have stormed the school gates demanding an explanation. Memories stirred. Mrs Lord, whose accuracy with a blackboard rubber was legendary. A nameless echo: "If I hear one more sniff, *all* of you will be staying behind." Mrs Wilson, who made any boy who dared enter her classroom with shoulder-length hair tie it in bunches and kept a variety of decorated bands (rumoured to have been parted from their owners during humiliating nit checks) in the drawers of her desk for that purpose. These days, you'd call it bullying. A smile caught Anita unawares.

The memory of a defiant boy who refused point blank to cut his hair. He took his seat in front of Mrs Wilson, having let Lizzie plait and crown it with a jewelled Alice band.

The appearance of her former best friend was an unwelcome intrusion. Patti kept up with Lizzie's mother, Geraldine. Though Anita occasionally asked after her old classmate, nobody was under the illusion that this was out of anything other than politeness. Anita's age, with a grown-up daughter - who was now a mother herself - and three teenage boys. What could they possibly have to say to each other?

Anita used the opportunity to take stock of her haul. *You're approaching this all wrong*, she chided herself. *Imagine you're a research subject.*

She unfolded the top of the next money bag. Here was the medal she'd been given for her First Holy Communion. A chalice, grapes surrounding its stem, and a host. Zinc, Anita suspected. She remembered biting it. There! Close to the edge, were the indentations her milk teeth had left. "Hoping for silver?" her father had teased - although the truth was that she'd been hoping for chocolate. A white plastic rosary, made to resemble mother of pearl. Running the smooth oval beads through her fingers - ten beads, a gap and then a single bead - Anita could almost hear the monotonous drone of Hail Marys, all meaning lost with repetition. The rosary beads had been married up with dressing-up jewellery and a silver coin cast to honour the Queen's Jubilee.

Anita unfolded another bag and drew from it the yellow cross-over tie from her Brownie uniform. She unfolded it, revealing a number of badges snipped from her dress, quashing her inclination to pull at the remaining brown cotton threads. History too, they must be left intact. The Promise Badge showing an elfin man within a trefoil. The Artist Badge, depicted by a pencil. The Book Lover Badge, that one was obvious. A saucepan she presumed was for cooking - though her mother would have scalped Anita if she'd found her alone in the kitchen. A badge that resembled a road sign warning drivers that children were crossing - something to do with road safety? A wheelbarrow. She suspected she had claimed her Gardener's Badge for helping her father, something Anita had only ever done under duress. In the race to get to ten, no Brownie had been above exaggeration.

Anita pulled thank you letters from a packet. Here was her childish handwriting, so much neater than the adult scrawl that replaced it. She used a pen so rarely these days. Shuffling through them, she was amazed that she could actually recall biting her bottom lip in concentration, the paper angled in front of her, tracing the shape of each letter. *Thank you for the one pound. Mummy hasn't given it to me as she doesn't have change. I hope she will soon.* The letters and cards must have been recovered after the people they were addressed to had died.

With these few forgotten belongings, Anita began stitching together a patchwork childhood. She reacquainted herself with the contents of photograph albums. Damaged streets - the Luftwaffe's legacy. A terrace, one or two houses seeming intact at first glance. On closer inspection, Anita saw that an upstairs bedroom was filled with debris from the roof. Next door, the structure of the bay window was solid, whilst the upper floor was missing. The next house along had had its frontage blown away, although its side wall and the line of the roof - if not the roof itself - was apparent, and then... a gap where number 43 should have been. Any occupants who'd had the misfortune to be at home would have been buried under that debris. Was this one of the houses her father had spoken about, reduced to rubble? Or had his experience ignited an interest in other demolished houses? Devastation that happened twenty years before Anita was born had cast a shadow over her childhood. Great wastelands of hollowed-out ground served as playgrounds, derelict buildings known as 'bombies', no money even to demolish what had been damaged. There was a kind of forced cheer; insistence that she should be grateful that she was born in peacetime, when there was no rationing and when you wouldn't be woken in the early hours by the scream of an air raid siren.

Tired of being lectured about these things, Anita had once shot back, "I didn't ask to be born!" Her mother's look had frozen in shock and she had turned and ran upstairs before she got a good slap.

Now, twenty years seemed such a brief time. How raw memories must have been! Perhaps, rather than criticising as she'd supposed, her parents had been warning her not to take everything for granted; to recognise the golden moments for what they were.

Her mind switched briefly to Ed and a recent walking holiday in the Lake District. They had climbed Helvellyn from Grisedale Tarn and were sitting on the broad moon-like expanse just shy of the summit, backs resting against their rucksacks, basking in the layered landscape. "I could look at that view forever," she'd said. *"You* can," he'd replied. "It'll be bloody freezing in an hour or two."

The reality you held in your hands might at any moment be snatched away. She should phone Ed. Touch base.

She shuffled more loose black and white photographs, the sky bleached white. If there was a balcony, women would be gossiping on it; children sitting, dangling their legs.

Anita opened another photograph album, tucked a straying photo back into its corners. Her mother as a young girl, slim to the point of being skinny, her hair curled. Wearing a knee-length skirt, she was clinging to a lamppost which played host to a sign. 'Play Street: vehicles prohibited sunrise to sunset'.

She paused again at a picture of an athletic young boy

(a boy her mother hadn't yet met), wearing only swimming trunks. His arms outstretched, he was preparing to dive into the steaming water of the Leeds and Liverpool Canal. Anita recognised the backdrop as the place where hot water discharged from the Tate & Lyle factory - the so-called 'scaldies'. Despite her pleas, Anita had never been allowed to swim there. There had been 'accidents', her mother keenly pointed out, but no matter how foreboding Patti's tone, these warnings had the opposite effect to the one that was intended. Anita had whined *Pleeease!* in the way little girls do when trying to wear parents down.

Never a strong swimmer, Patti had exploded, "No means no, young lady! And don't you dare go behind my back and ask your father."

Feeling hard done by, Anita had sulked, suggesting to her adult self that she wasn't above playing one of her parents off against the other. She glanced in the direction of the dressing table to study her reflection: *Show me the seven-year-old.* Wilful, manipulative and, it seemed, a sneak. It wasn't altogether pleasant, this reconstructed image.

And then, looking breathtakingly young - barely out of childhood in her mother's case - her parents on their wedding day. Her father's hair quiffed, her mother's short and still curled. Anita stared hard into their faces, searching for... perhaps something that had never been there. She knew their story. They had met only fourteen days earlier. The formidable Roscoes and the approachable Halls had called a family meeting ("Like *High Noon*," her father had laughed), only to find that they were unified. Both sets of parents were dead against the marriage.

"But what's the alternative?" Mrs Hall demanded. Mrs Roscoe's nostrils flared as she contemplated possibilities, liking none that sprang to mind. And so it was settled. They did not give their blessing but neither would they stand in the couple's way.

Growing up, Anita had thought it a romance of fairy tale proportions, wallowing in the prestige of being the daughter of parents who had fallen in love at first sight.

"We showed them, didn't we?" her father would ask her mother when he recited the story, but Patti shuffled awkwardly in her seat, as if she might have sided with the parents if pressed.

Dissatisfied, Anita turned the thick cardboard pages impatiently. She wanted evidence that her reality had been shaken before, and that she'd come through to the other side, intact. And so she bypassed the familiar baby photos; pausing briefly at her christening photos, the robe that had gone up in smoke; the toddler who, pulling at an adult hand, seemed so sure of herself.

It was a seven-year-old who made Anita stop. A miniature bride dressed in a white knee-length dress with lace detailing, her hair covered by a short veil, her fringe cut straight across her forehead. Patti had sat her on the kitchen worktop the night before, using a wooden rule as a guide. The seven-year-old's hands were steepled so piously that Anita could almost feel the crease at her wrists. White sandals had been bought specially. Informed that there wouldn't be another occasion that demanded such extravagance, she had worn them until her toes curled over the soles. But it was the girl's unsmiling face that fixed Anita. Absentmindedly, she picked up the cheap medallion threaded on soft blue wool and held it to her lips. She had just received her First Holy Communion, closing those large brown eyes demurely and offering her tongue, as she would when the doctor demanded she say, *Aaah*.

The nun tasked with preparing Anita's class for the day had dismissed a complaint that one boy didn't understand how the transformation of the host took place, snapping, "This isn't science, Brian!" Every other child shrank into their seats, glad they hadn't stuck up their hands. "It is not for you to *understand* one of the greatest mysteries of the Church. It's enough that you *believe* Jesus *wants* to come to you." And, heightening expectations further, she used the phrase 'world-shaking' to describe what would happen.

Everything from the moment the altar boy rang the small silver bell came as a bitter disappointment. Anita had returned to her pew, the host on her tongue, thinking how fortunate it was they were required to kneel. You wouldn't want to fall over when the earthquake began. While waiting to be transformed, she prayed as devoutly as she knew how but, although she'd followed the instructions precisely ("Let the host dissolve, *don't* on any account chew!") her world didn't shake. She felt precisely the same as she always had (except that, having skipped breakfast, she was starving hungry). All her classmates exchanged smiles, as if they'd been let in on a big secret. Anita was alone. She'd been shut out.

But, as she had processed out of the church, her parents and grandparents - the formidable Roscoes and the approachable Halls - greeted her as if she'd done something incredibly clever. The day was to be one of gifts and celebrations. Not wanting to spoil it, Anita tried to convince herself that an unblessed host must have made it into the chalice. She'd been given a dud. Next Sunday would be different.

But it wasn't, and neither was the next. Still untransformed, Anita no longer believed that the world was going to shake, and if she didn't believe in this - the reason Catholic martyrs had been burnt at the stake - what use did she have for the rest?

This weekly charade became the great pretence of Anita's childhood. In time she stopped minding and indulged in people-watching. Plus, Anita was able to enjoy feeling smug when a child was hauled up to the front of the class and singled out for the terrible sin of skipping Holy Mass.

One Sunday, when Anita would have been in her early teens, Patti had demanded she explain her reluctance to go to church. Before she could stop herself, the truth overflowed in a moment's hormone-induced carelessness.

"Hallelujah!" Her father said from behind his copy of Saturday's *Echo*, the newspaper he worked on five days a week. "Perhaps now we can all stop wasting our time."

Patti flattened her hands, pushed back her chair and left the table without a single word. Anita stared at the place where her mother's hands had been, stunned by her father's unexpected reaction. Ron rustled the page lower and winked. "Give her time. It's me she's upset with, not you."

"Why did you never say anything before?" she asked, wide-eyed.

"Your mother's always known how I feel," he snapped, and then, aware he might have appeared inconsistent, added, "The war finished it for me. Not there and then. You needed to believe that God was on your side just to get through it. But looking back..."

The effort of digesting this dried Anita's mouth. She tried what her father had said on for size. It certainly explained why he always seemed to struggle to remember the words to prayers. He had been selective about the parts he joined in with.

But Ron wasn't finished. Setting aside his newspaper, he leaned towards Anita. "There were lots of reasons. Because I thought I was going for your sake. Because it's easier to keep the peace than stand up and be counted. Because it would upset my mother to hear I'd stopped going - no doubt it still will. But if *you've* been brave enough to speak your mind, then you deserve my support."

Still reeling from this revelation, Anita felt mortified when her mother appeared in the doorway, dressed in her Sunday best and announced, "Well, I'm off." Her expression was pinched. No doubt she was imagining the humiliating inquisition she would face. *On your own, Patti?* Not one but *two* family members unaccounted for? "If you're not going to keep me company, the least you can do is peel the spuds."

Patti continued to take herself off to mass, standing tall in an otherwise empty pew, always putting a little extra in the collection plate. Compensation, you might say. It was a habit she stuck to until both of Anita's grandmothers were dead and buried.

With her new appreciation of the importance of rituals, Anita felt a sadness - an urge to seek out her mother - but Patti wasn't to be found in the kitchen.

"I told you," said her father, who was kneeling at the edge of a flowerbed, sieving soil. He shook the sieve vigorously from side to side. The way the stones bounced on top reminded Anita of pastry-making. "She'll be upstairs in the office tapping away on that computer of hers. Most days I don't see her until lunchtime."

"I didn't realise. The door was closed."

"That's her equivalent of a Do Not Disturb sign. Did you find anything interesting in the boxes from the loft?"

She hugged herself. "I did, thank you. Things I'd forgotten existed."

He made an appreciative noise, but seemed to be preoccupied.

"I think I'll go for a walk."

"Good idea. Get some good old-fashioned Mersey air into your lungs. I might do the same thing myself in a bit."

"I can wait for you if you like."

"No, I'm not quite done here yet. What shall I tell your mother? Will you be back for your lunch?"

"You're alright. I'll grab something when I'm out. I might make a day of it. Maybe do some shopping."

Her father was grinning up at her. "What?" she asked.

"You've gone native. Ed'll have to teach you how to speak like Helena Bonham Carter all over again."

Patti frowned on hearing the front door slam. She slid back her chair and pushed down on her desk to lever her bulk out of the seat. Anita was at the end of the path, closing the gate behind her. Even dressed casually, she had a purposeful look about her. Patti glanced at the bottom right-hand corner of her screen. It was gone eleven (Lord, she hadn't even been aware of the time). This might be the best opportunity she would get.

She walked the length of the landing, entering the guest bedroom. Surprising how quickly she'd started to think of the room as Anita's again. Her daughter had clearly made a start on sorting through the boxes Ron had brought down from the loft. Items were spread out on top of the duvet cover (in her original groupings, she noticed with a spark of pride). But that wasn't why Patti was there. Contemplating the remaining pile of boxes - untouched - she sighed deeply. There was no way she'd be able to manage on her own.

Pulling the net curtain aside, Patti saw her husband on his knees, concentrating on a task that, to her, seemed quite unnecessary - although he would quote Monty Don at her if she questioned him. His ears appeared to be free of the headphones he sometimes wore. She pushed open the window and shouted: "Ron!"

He stopped sieving soil. "What's up?"

"Was that our Anita leaving the house?"

He sat back on his heels. "She's taken herself off for a walk."

"But it'll be lunchtime in an hour or so."

"I got the impression she wants to do her own thing."

Distracted briefly by thoughts of the spread she had planned to lay out in the dining room, Patti hoisted herself back on track. "Could you spare me a moment? I need some help lifting a few things."

"Right now?" he asked, sounding less than keen.

"Yes, Ron, now!" Then she pulled the window to before he had time to argue.

While waiting for her husband to make an appearance, Patti began to rearrange the bookcase, cramming more volumes onto its shelves. Idling, she raised her eyebrows. *The H-bomb Girl* had a cover like the opening credits of a Bond film. Give her a Beryl Bainbridge or a Maureen Lee any day of the week!

Ron entered the room, asking, "What's so urgent that it couldn't wait?" Immediately, he propped himself up on the pile of boxes.

"I thought we could take the opportunity while Anita's out to clear a bit more space. It can't be very relaxing for her, surrounded on all sides."

"Righto." He looked about. "What do you suggest?"

"Those boxes will either have to go under the bed or on top of the wardrobe."

Ron knelt on one knee and lifted the valance. He pulled at the drawer in the divan base, finding it full of linen. "We might get one box on top of the wardrobe, but not a lot more. What's in them all, anyway?"

Patti may have hesitated a little too long. "It's only four boxes, Ron."

He made his hands into stop signs. "I stand corrected. So? What's in the *four boxes*?"

"Books."

"Your blog must be even more popular than I thought it was!" He grabbed hold of both sides of the box that topped the pile and heaved it towards his chest, then tried to get a hold underneath.

"Don't hurt yourself," Patti cautioned. Ron was a man whose physical exertions were always accompanied by sounds that suggested he was in agony.

"Can you move that chair over here so's I can stand on it," he asked, nodding and shuffling sideways. But when it came to trying to step onto the chair with both hands full, Patti could see he was going to struggle.

"It's no good," Ron said, carefully sliding the box back on top of the pile, the veins on his forehead raised with the effort.

"Well, never mind," Patti sighed. *The boxes are sealed,* she calmed herself. There was no reason why Anita should open them. She just would have felt more comfortable knowing they were out of harm's way. But before Patti had the presence of mind to tell her husband not to bother, Ron had removed a pair of secateurs from his gardening belt and started snipping the perforated seal. All Patti could do was watch, feeling every cut as if it were inside her. As her world spun ever more slowly, Ron twisted his head to glance at her, looking chuffed with himself. "If at first you don't succeed..."

This was not how she had planned one of her life's more significant moments. Because what had she really achieved? Her career had been cut short by marriage before it even got off the ground. She had hardly distinguished herself as a mother, let alone a homemaker. The book hadn't seemed real until this moment, and now she couldn't bear for it to be another disappointment. As Ron discarded the protective layer of scrunched brown paper on the carpet, Patti's stomach fluttered. She was impatient to see how the jacket cover she had sketched for the designer looked. And she realised that she wanted so much more. Having heard pride colour Ron's voice recently, Patti longed to hear it again.

Grabbing handfuls of paperbacks - *her* paperbacks - Ron began piling them on the floor. He then opened the wardrobe door and said what was obvious to them both. "We should have checked in here first! There's room for at least half of them, I reckon."

Just as he did when digging, Ron got a rhythm going. The books clunked against the wooden back panel. Patti couldn't think of a single legitimate excuse to ask him to stop stacking the books in the bottom of the wardrobe, their spines facing out. While he was looking the other way, Patti lifted one of the paperbacks from the box. The idea that you could push a few buttons and *this* would be the end result. The feel of it, in her hands, the width, the weight. The cover smooth and cool under her thumbs. *A book!* Her lips began to tremble. Tearful wasn't how she'd imagined she would feel at the culmination of so many months' hard work.

"Hang about," Ron said.

It had taken him longer to notice than she'd imagined it would. "What's that?" Patti blinked and then, secreting the book behind her back, she feigned innocence.

With hands on his hips, her husband looked into the box, puzzled. "They're all the same."

"Yes," Patti said, without a clue where she was going with this.

"All four boxes?" He angled his head to look at her.

"That's right." Patti swallowed, clutching her copy. "The author donated them. She thought we could sell them and use the proceeds to fund the website. Sylvia and I are planning a car boot sale."

"Car Bootle, that's the one you want." Advice dispensed, Ron continued, and Patti was able to breathe once more. "There must be at least a couple of hundred here. It seems very generous." He was taking more of an interest now, turning one of the books over, frowning.

"She's not bothered about money. She just wants people to read what she's written."

As he cast his eyes over the blurb - the hundred or so words Patti had agonised about - her stomach cartwheeled. Part of her wanted to blurt out *Do you think people will be interested?* But, without his knowing, this was Ron's story. Anita's too. The fact remained that Patti hadn't asked their permission. What right had she to write down the truth about her life, when it concerned the lives of others?

"If she's so keen for people to read what she's written," Ron scoffed, twisting his wrist so that he could read the spine and then the front cover. "Why hasn't she owned up to it?"

Patti hadn't felt that she could take full credit for the book. As her fingers had danced, the words that appeared on the screen ambushed her. Had she really been holding *all that* inside? "What's that?" she asked, her voice a pitch too high.

"She hasn't put her name on the cover."

Clearing her throat, Patti attempted to sound authoritative. "Ah, didn't she? She said she was thinking of publishing anonymously."

"Why wouldn't you put your name to a book you've written? Unless it's no good, that is."

As Ron scoffed, Patti's jaw tightened defensively. "There are lots of reasons I can think of. She might be too well known in another profession, for starters."

"Then she should have used a pseudonym!"

"What, like J K Rowling? It didn't take long for people to find her out." It wouldn't do to appear to know too much. Deliberately softening her voice, Patti shrugged. "Besides, I think it's nice to be a little mysterious."

Chuckling, Ron resumed his stacking duties.

"What now?" she asked.

"It's someone we know, isn't it?"

"I'm not saying!"

"I knew it! And you're not going to tell me because she's sworn you to secrecy."

"Something like that." Patti watched the pile in the bottom of the wardrobe grow. Anita would see the books the minute she opened the door. She'd wonder why they were there now when they hadn't been earlier. She'd... Was she panicking over nothing? Perhaps something in plain view would prove less of a temptation. Ron had held handfuls of the books and had yet to open the front cover.

Patti did a poor job of convincing herself. At length, a gravelly voice seemed to arrive of its own accord. "I think that's enough now."

"You're probably right," Ron conceded, straightening up. "Anita won't have room to hang her coat if I carry on."

He stepped up onto the chair.

"What are you doing now?" she asked.

"Piling the rest on top of the wardrobe. Keep them coming."

It made it worse somehow that Patti was involved in the process. And yet she couldn't help marvelling. *After all this time, these are my books.*

"Don't worry," her husband said as he climbed back down. "I'll get it out of you."

Patti mimed zipping her mouth closed.

"You've already let slip that the author's a *she*. Well, if you've no further use for me, I might head out for a spot of fresh air myself. Build up an appetite for lunch."

And before she thought to turn around and ask him if there wasn't enough fresh air in the garden for his liking, he was saying "Walkies!" to that invisible dog of his.

The water was a churning mass that changed hue when clouds passed over its expanse. Just being by the river felt cleansing. It hadn't always been like this. The Mersey of Anita's childhood had been dubbed Britain's Filthiest River, little more than an extension of the sewers. It was said that, if you fell in, you'd die of poisoning before you drowned. Thirty years ago, people would have scoffed, "Are you having a laugh?" at the suggestion that people would be willing to pay good money for a waterside property. But now - now the prospect looked increasingly attractive.

Anita cringed inwardly as Ed's name flashed up on the screen of her vibrating mobile. "Hello you," she said, a cheerful if guilt-ridden greeting.

"Are you on your own?" Ed would be on his lunch break. Anita could tell from the sound of his voice that he was walking. The grinding traffic noises suggested he was at street level. In her mind, she placed him in Eastcheap, just outside Pret a Manger.

"I'm on my own, yes. Down by the waterfront." Anita stopped in front of chain railings, standing on stone cobbles. Recent years had seen the import of a tradition. Just as Parisians inscribed messages to their lovers on padlocks, tossing the keys into the Seine, so too had Liverpool's melting-pot of city dwellers. She toyed with a metallic purple box, a keyhole at its centre and ventured, "Is everything alright?" Reading what was written there, Anita's insides shrank with embarrassment, as if her hairdresser had caught her reading sex tips in a magazine.

"Roz just called. She asked me how you were."

Feeling her facial muscles tense, she dropped the padlock. "Ah."

"Don't be cross with *her*. She's worried sick about you." In the pause, Anita could hear a faint siren. "And so am I, now that I've spoken to her. You didn't tell me Anita! And I shouldn't have had to find out like that."

"No, you shouldn't have," she conceded, imagining Ed rubbing his fingertips over the razor-cut hairs on the back of his neck. "I've been struggling to make sense of things. I just needed to get away."

"So it *wasn't* Roz's suggestion that you took a few days' off?"

"It was the doctor's." Anita imagined she was confirming what Ed had already guessed.

His tone suggested not. "The doctor's?"

"I've been having panic attacks."

"When?" He exhaled the word.

"At work, mainly."

She heard the shock of breath leave Ed's mouth as clearly as if he'd been standing next to her.

"I'm stressed, that's all - and I know you are too. That's why I didn't feel I could say anything."

"Since when did we stop telling each other everything?" The question jarred. What Ed had told her in anger - about his job, about the house - had been like discovering that the black and white Liverpool of her memories was now gaudy with colour. "Did the doctor prescribe anything for you?"

Wind-whipped hair obscured her vision. The weather was changing. "Sleeping tablets. But she wants me to go back to see her when I get home." *Home.* A word that no longer had any context. Neither here nor there, and nowhere in between.

His tone softened. "Are they working?"

"I slept right through last night. But things feel, I don't know... simpler here."

"Without me piling the pressure on!"

Anita didn't want to discuss this, divided by distance. "You know that's not what I meant." But what had she meant? Buffeted by the river breeze, things that were happening two hundred and fifty miles away no longer felt overwhelming. In fact, they seemed to have little to do with her. "I feel like a child here. All of my decisions are made for me. What I eat, when I'm going to eat it, whether there's enough hot water for me to have a bath. A few more days and I'll be going stir crazy but, for now, it's what I need." That was only partly true. Anita walked into a room to hear the tails of abandoned sentences and, when she left the room, hushed conversations were resumed.

"I know, I know." He sounded deflated. She imagined him scratching at the corner of one eye. "So," Ed said, changing the subject. "What else have you been doing?"

"My dad brought down all of my stuff from the loft. Everything I left behind, though I'd forgotten most of it existed. I'm working my way through, looking at old photograph albums."

"Maybe I should try that. It sounds therapeutic."

"Did your parents hang on to much of your stuff?"

"I've no idea."

"You should ask them."

"Perhaps I will. Listen. When are you planning on coming home?"

The summons Anita had been waiting for. Trying to keep her voice light, she said, "I think I might stay for the weekend. I didn't book a return ticket."

There was a pause.

She thought about what she had just said. "Ed? Are you still there?"

"I don't like the house without you. There's hardly anything there that belongs to you." There was a pause. "It looks as if you've moved out."

With his tone suggesting that the possibility had crossed his mind, Anita cut him short: "Ed." But what next? She knew she had caused him pain, but Anita remembered that her seven-year-old self had been capable of deception. Keeping up a pretence was part of her toolbox.

"What?"

Her mood was lower than it had been for the past couple of days. "I left Liverpool for a reason."

"It's not the same place that you left. There's no shortage of money now."

"No, there isn't." She sighed distractedly, turning towards the sweeping green curve of the Echo Arena. She didn't object when new steel and glass peaks pierced London's skyline. That city hadn't been the backdrop to her childhood. The Thames didn't flow in her bloodstream. But it wasn't right to desert a city that had been managed into decline, only to return after those who had never stopped believing brought it back from the brink. "I don't belong here. Not any longer." She attempted to brighten her voice; "If it's any consolation, I'll be bringing more home with me than I packed."

"Shopping?"

"The thought *had* crossed my mind." A cormorant bobbed by, carried on the current.

"Listen. For what it's worth, if you'd told me you were struggling, I'd have suggested you visit your parents. In fact, I would have driven you there myself."

Anita tucked wind-blown hair behind her ear. Having her decision ratified wasn't what she wanted. At the same time, Ed wasn't *one of the bad guys*. Even angered, she could hear how much he cared. And yet he *was* a large part of what she'd wanted to get away from. How could Anita go home before she figured out what that meant?

"Are you still there? Anita?"

"I forgot that you couldn't see me," she fibbed. "I was nodding."

"What shall I tell Roz? Or do *you* want to call her?"

"I suppose I should call." But that would mean more awkward questions. The doctor had told Anita that she needed coping mechanisms; help to fend off future panic attacks. Here, in the open air, distraction techniques sounded so over the top, but put her back in the Tudor kitchen...

"I'll tell her that she shouldn't expect to see you until next week at the earliest."

"Thank you."

"Should I buy something for Sunday dinner?"

"Yes." Anita found herself nodding again, smiling. "That would be nice."

"Any special requests?"

"You choose."

"I'd better head back to work before they send out a search party. But you're to call me, OK?"

"OK," she relented. She almost said that she had meant to, but the obvious response would have been, *What stopped you?* Another question she didn't have the answer to.

"Oh, I almost forget. Natalie called to remind you about Reuben's birthday on Saturday. Obviously, you're not going to be able to make it."

Shit! Anita clenched her eyes shut. "I *knew* there was something I'd forgotten!"

"Was there a present or something? I could drop it round there."

"There was," she said, waiting for what she had said to sink in. Like everything else, it was gone. *How could something this important have slipped her mind?*

"Right. Well, I don't mind picking something up. Reuben dropped a few unsubtle hints while we were staying there. I've got the general idea."

Did it matter if her godson ended up with a computer game for once? Anita asked herself. "The real problem is that I promised to help with the food for his party."

"Right." Ed's voice was flat.

She sighed, furious with herself. "I'll have to come home."

"No, don't do that. I'm not doing anything on Saturday afternoon."

"It's a children's birthday party, Ed. Do you have any idea how loud it will be? You'll hate it."

"I was thinking of offering to go round and make a few sandwiches, not staying for the whole thing."

"In that case, thank you. That would be really kind of you."

Wandering in the direction of the Pier Head, it struck Anita how limited her view was. The Three Graces - cathedrals to the heyday of shipping - were obscured by the angular white lines of the Museum of Liverpool. Regeneration was the word on everyone's lips. The problem was that nobody seemed to know when to stop. Backed by a blue sky, the docklands resembled an architect's portfolio showing what was possible, but shouldn't necessarily be attempted.

Reminded that she had yet to set foot inside the museum (her father's review had been scathing; he'd called it an 'aircraft hangar'), Anita's walk assumed a new purpose. She rather liked the atrium. Flooded with natural light, the corkscrew staircase reflected the spiral painted on the floor below. One hand on the smooth rail, Anita felt her way upwards. The space seemed to have been created to showcase the cityscape - here was the view of the Three Graces she'd missed. The Royal Liver Building topped with the Liver Birds, the palatial Cunard Building and the domed Port of Liverpool building. She remembered the shining Portland stone fighting to emerge as layers of soot and smog were blasted away.

The displays seemed almost secondary; a triumph of making something out of not very much. The merit was in the graphics, the touchscreen monitors, arrangements that enticed you to their centres like a maze.

A whole section dedicated to Liverpool writers. *I was a woman, I was Liverpudlian and I could write.* Shy of people's reactions when they heard that she wrote, Romana Barrack went under the name Carla Lane. *The Liver Birds, Bread* and *Butterflies:* the trio of television programmes Anita had grown up with. She smiled, picturing Wendy Craig scattering cornflakes all over the kitchen as if they were rose petals, a housewife's *Fantasia* gone mad.

Next to *The Liver Birds* was Beryl Bainbridge. Seated at her desk, her chin resting on one hand, she peered out of the black and white photograph from deeply soulful eyes, her expression curious rather than critical.

Willy Russell, Alan Bleasdale, Clive Barker, Lynda La Plante... And poets too: Roger McGough, Adrian Henri, Brian Patten. Her mother was right: Liverpool had a strong tradition of literature, its focus the people. *Her* people. But what right did Anita have to claim she was one of them when she'd spent years disguising her accent?

That guilty thought led her to the first floor, a display about the Liverpool overhead railway, 'The first and fastest electric railway in the world'. Watching a jumpy black and white film, the camera shake made Anita feel seasick. Belonging to the dim and distant past, the so-called 'dockers' umbrella' had never seemed real to Anita. It had been a childhood story that sat on her bookshelf alongside *Black Beauty* and *The Secret Garden* before this footage of its journey - to places with familiar names - made it concrete.

And then, about to board a restored carriage, Anita froze. Her father was sitting on one of its slatted benches, praying hands tucked neatly between his knees. Keeping guard, a pair of rather obvious waxworks made it possible for a lonely figure to feel that he wasn't quite so alone. His lips were moving and his faraway expression informed Anita that she was witnessing a starkly private moment. Announcing herself would have been like waking a sleepwalker.

Backing away, Anita watched with curiosity. There had been hints of a connection between her father and the overhead railway, something half-told. She wondered how often he sat there, in the same seat, talking to an unseen person (quite often, she imagined). The phrase *an unknown woman* came to mind. A person who had died before 1956, the year the film's commentator had confirmed was when the railway closed. This wasn't Ron's *Brief Encounter*. He wouldn't have met Patti by then. The date might have been even earlier, the retired man masking a sensitive young boy. The unknown woman of Anita's imagination wasn't a magnificent goddess, but an ordinary lady, dressed in a raincoat, tan tights, sensible court shoes. Her hair would be permed, her face free of make-up, her expression attentive, open.

It was peculiar for Anita to see her father in a moment's

quiet contemplation. Gone was the self-deprecation, the wrist-slapping, the wisecracks. What if this secretive self was closer to the truth; the rest a mask? While standing to one side, glowing with discovery, all at once Anita sensed that she was being watched. She glanced over her shoulder, half expecting to see her mother. Her eyes darted towards a pillar. Perhaps even Ed - though logic told her he was officed in a steel and glass tower in the City. Feeling foolish, she turned back to her father, still-sitting, lips moving.

Some stories should remain secret. This one would never be featured on her mother's blog because *even she didn't know*. No wonder he'd steered the dinner-table conversation towards wine! So Anita quietly removed herself, taking the long way back to the corkscrew staircase. And though she no longer felt in the mood for shopping, she took herself off to Liverpool One and dragged her heels around John Lewis, giving her father plenty of time to get home before her.

"Anyway," said Ron. "That's you bang up to date, or as near as dammit. I'd best think about getting back before Patti misses me." Shifting his gaze - slowly does it - he let the carriage come in to focus. Ron realised that his lower back was killing him. "That's the problem with bending over flowerbeds followed by a long spell of sitting." No matter, it was just him and the waxworks. He nodded to the one in the brown overalls - just as he'd done on his first visit, quite put out when it didn't respond. "You won't mind if I do a few limbering up exercises, will you?"

Ron linked his fingers and, pushing his palms away from him, heard his left elbow click. Then he raised his linked hands above his head, which forced him to sit upright. Reaching his left arm a little, and then his right, he found himself in a familiar pose: a position from which a twelve-year-old boy might dive into factory-warmed waters sparkling in the late afternoon sunlight. He imagined surfacing just in time to see Sandra Wright clambering onto the bank, her bare back lightly freckled, her swimming costume riding up to reveal the curve of one delectable buttock. Five years earlier, she had shouted, "Oi, Ron," flashed her knickers at him and ran off, expecting him to give chase. He'd played it cool because, even then, he knew that if he waited she'd be back with more. Now she glared.

"Still flashing me?" he grinned.

"Still ogling?" she'd replied.

Remember that, Aunty Magda, remember that? Because that was the thing about his aunt. There was nothing he couldn't say to her. She never judged.

There was something transportative about living in the same city all of your life; walking around familiar geography, knee-deep in the history of the place. And superimposed over a street map carried both inside and outside his head (the then and the now), were the milestones of his own life. Now he was older - with less to look forward to, he supposed - Ron spent a great deal of time in the past. In a single half hour, he might be a child crying in a damp cellar, clasped to his mother's chest; a child of five sitting on the clean-swept step of his grandmother's terraced house, while the adults crammed themselves into the front parlour, discussing things that didn't concern him. He might be a school-leaver, discovering the pleasure of smoking illicit ciggies on park benches (illicit because he'd bought them with coins dropped into his cap while he pretended to be collecting for the Sailors' Home).

Once, an office worker stopped and asked for a light. Before Ron could reach for his matches, she scooped back her hair, and bent down to touch the end of her cigarette to his, her blouse falling open as the embers flared. A quick *thank you*, smoke coiling in his face and him left with a grin that made his jaw ache all afternoon.

Passing Queen Square, he might be a boy weaving through the fruit and vegetable market, snaring himself a crisp apple when no one was looking.

He might be a lad of fifteen (though, with his first paid job, he thought himself a man), the pads of his fingers permanently ink-stained, parcel string cutting off his circulation as he hauled bundles up from the print rooms where the giant presses roared, sending reams of paper flying, ready to be cut and folded. Everything a great hurry, accompanied by hollering and the sound of running feet. From there, the papers would be rushed to station forecourts, newsstands and corner shops. Taking his father's advice, he kept one eye on the job he wanted: the spectacle-wearing writers, banging out copy in smoke-filled offices, untended cigarettes dripping from the corners of mouths. Writing impressed girls. Become one, and he might get a date - that was his thinking. "Yes, Sir!" he shouted on cue, talking a good line; making sure he was in the right place when errands needed to be run. And when they said, "I think we might have something for a bright lad like you," his chest swelled with anticipation.

They put him on the obituaries column. Four years of writing about dead people and where to send the flowers. Not famous people. Just ordinary, everyday deaths. *Not like you, Aunty Madga. Thankfully.*

Ron liked weekdays in the museum. There were few tourists to get in his way - what tourists would find to interest them here, he didn't know! They'd be milling round The Beatles Story, in raptures over the little round glasses that sat on top of the white piano. Ron had ventured down into what had once been damp cellars - the place where slaves used to be held, they said - but his appetite for nostalgia vanished once he'd read enough to convince him that a story he'd been repeating for years was false. For the life of him, he couldn't remember who'd told him it in the first place. How many people had elbowed their friends and said, "We've got a right one here"? Or perhaps they mistook it for the bluster Ron was known for, back in the day. It wasn't that he hadn't been in the thick of the action; experienced the cocktail of body odour, cigarettes and cheap perfume at the Cavern Club's lunchtime sessions. Crushed next to someone you might never see again, or backed into a curved wall (where he'd scratched his name between other names), a glass of coke in hand. The band only inches away, he remembered Ringo drumming for Rory Storm and the Hurricanes; remembered the cries of 'Bring back Pete.' Emerging, crickets in his ears, surprised to find it was still daylight. For a while, he'd tried convincing the *Echo* to allow him to write a column about the music that was coming out of Liverpool, but they couldn't see the potential. Frustrated, he complained to Bill Harry about it over coffee one evening at the Jacaranda; how his boss was unable to grasp that young people with money to burn wanted their own music, their own style, their own scene. Ron had lacked the nerve to go it alone. It was Bill who appointed himself the *voice of youth.* His magazine, *Mersey Beat*, sold out of its first print run. If Ron had one regret, it was that he hadn't done enough to make the *Echo* see sense.

Gripping the edge of the bench, he took a moment to appreciate the workmanship. The metal rivets and the way the legs of the utilitarian benches had been shaped like the legs of dining room chairs. Then he stood. Turned. "Oh, and Aunty Magda, I'm not quite sure when I'll be back to see you. Things are a bit topsy-turvy at home. Not the best of circumstances. Still. It's not often I get to spend a bit of time with our Anita. What's that?" He paused and chuckled. "No, it doesn't matter how old they are. You never stop worrying."

CHAPTER FIFTEEN

"There you are!" Patti rushed to greet Anita, who was closing the front door behind her. She carried a John Lewis bag over each shoulder. The large cardboard types with ribbons for handles, reserved for people who spent a small fortune. "Did you buy yourself something nice?"

"A few things, actually. I had the services of a personal shopper." Anita seemed to have perked up a little. "Apparently I've been wearing the wrong-shaped clothes for years."

"Rubbish. You always look very smart." Patti racked her brains for a reason to keep her daughter downstairs. "Have you eaten? I can make you something if you're hungry."

"I'm fine. I stopped for coffee and a muffin."

Aware that she was trailing Anita a little too closely, Patti remarked, "You'll probably notice -" her breathing slowing her down, hauling herself upwards "- we had a little tidy -" she straggled behind on the stairs. "Made a bit more room for you."

Anita stepped lightly. "Mum, I really don't want to put you to any trouble."

"Yes, well the downside is -" Anita had reached the small landing "- there's less hanging space in the wardrobe." It struck Patti that it might be best if Anita was the one who suggested that the books were in her way.

"I'm sure I'll be fine. I really don't need much room."

"Just some books." Patti found herself answering a question that hadn't been asked. She heard herself laugh. "You'll probably notice, they're all the same. Yes." She could feel the circuit of every breath in her lungs. "A local author." Better stick to the story she had fed Ron. Anita was reaching for the bedroom door handle. "She's donated them so that we can raise a bit of money for the website."

"All this talk of books reminds me." Her daughter hesitated, turned. "I'm not sure Dad would approve but I went to the new museum."

"He'd like to see the architect shot!"

"So you haven't been yet?"

"Your father won't hear of it. Boycotting it is his idea of a protest." Patti's stomach was churning. She regretted eating the sausage rolls that had been left over from lunch.

"There's a whole section on Liverpool authors. I'd forgotten just how many there are."

Back to the subject: "I doubt you'll find this one in there. Maybe one day." Patti could feel the slow trickle of a single bead of perspiration, all the way from her forehead and down the side of her face.

"I wouldn't have paid much attention if it hadn't been for your blog. People focus on Liverpool's music scene, but there's so much more."

Patti hovered in the doorway, watching Anita put the shopping bags on the bed. "I haven't read it yet. The book, that is. I couldn't tell you if it's any good." She was rambling. She really needed to stop spouting nonsense before she went too far.

Anita was removing small parcels and laying them out. "She can't expect to jump to the top of your reading list - even if she *is* a friend."

"Oh, she's not a friend." Patti thought she should take the initiative and open the door of the wardrobe. Show she had nothing to hide. "Shall we see if there's room for your new clothes? You don't want them getting creased." A small thrill coursed through Patti's veins at the sight of the neat stacks Ron had created. Were all those books really *hers*?

As Anita ripped into the neat squares of pale pink tissue, Patti unhooked the first of the spare hangers, holding it in readiness. *Christ, what would Anita make of the title?* "Oh, I like this," she said of a silky turquoise blouse, loose at the top but tapered at the hem.

"It's a 'capsule wardrobe' apparently." Anita looked sceptical. "The maximum number of outfits from the minimum number of clothes. I don't feel as if any of them are very *me*. To be honest, I couldn't find the energy to argue."

"Perhaps there needs to be a *new* you." Patti squared the shoulders carefully on the hanger. "Things have changed."

"It's one hell of a before and after!" Anita shifted her weight from foot to foot. The nervous energy in the room seemed to be infectious. "Maybe we could just move a few of those books out of the way," she said, and before Patti had the presence of mind to stop her, Anita reached past and picked up a stack. She paid no attention to the books themselves. They were simply an inconvenience. "There's no need to call Dad. Where do you think they should go?"

Patti felt her heartbeat accelerate. "I was thinking of the loft. Your father can -" But there was no telling her daughter. It had always been the same.

She was very efficient. That was the thing about Anita. She soon had the wardrobe empty, its contents piled in the middle of the landing under the loft hatch. Patti steadied the rickety ladder as it creaked under her daughter's weight. "Alright, love?" she asked, angling her head backwards, trying to see into the dark.

"I think so."

Even standing at the foot of the ladder made Patti queasy. "If I remember rightly, the light switch is on the left, just -"

"Got it!" The slats inside the roof were revealed in a yellow glow. "Now we can see what we're doing."

As Patti went to step onto the bottom rung, one hand occupied by books, Anita stopped her: "Don't come up, Mum. The ladder won't take both of us. I'll come down a couple of steps and you can hand them to me." She avoided using the word 'weight' as she always did. Patti's size was never spoken of - but it was there in the concern in Anita's voice.

Bending repeatedly to pick up two books in each hand was much more of a workout than Patti usually got. She could feel the strain of her clothes, the swell of her stomach against her thighs. But it seemed to her that energy flowed between her and the books. Not an electric shock, more of a pleasing surge.

"This box is full." Anita lowered her foot onto the ladder once more. "We must be nearly done."

Patti had no desire to stop. "Just a few more." In fact, it struck her that she could just keep going. Anita wouldn't know. And so she carried on, like a thief. Handful after greedy handful.

CHAPTER SIXTEEN

Feeling an urge to be near her father, Anita took the book she was reading down to the back garden. She shook out a beach towel and laid it on the grass. Ron was kneeling on a small foam mat, not far from where he'd been when she had spoken to him the day before.

"That's coming along nicely," she said. The slow, methodical work involved a sieve the size of a drum and a lot of sideways shaking. The only evidence of progress was a small cairn of medium-sized stones.

"Gardening's like decorating. If you don't put preparation in, you can't expect the results." His voice was breathy. "I think your mother gets a bit impatient with me, to be honest."

"She seems to have plenty to busy herself with."

Anita lay on her front in the sweet-smelling grass. It was good to feel connected to the earth. The buzz and crawl of insects, the occasional dragging and dredging of a plane as it churned up the clouds and the constant of her father's low-level activity. Once, a small stone bounced off her thigh, and her father cheered, "Goal!"

"Oi, watch it!" she retorted.

The backs of her skinny jeans heated, an uncomfortable second skin. But these things were enough. Enough, it seemed, to send her drifting into a place of listlessness. She heard movement, which she mistook for the rustle of silk, and faraway voices. Voices that sounded a little like her parents trying not to disturb her.

"Let her just rest a while."

"She'll end up with one half of her face sunburnt."

"I'd rather that than we wake her. She's lost a lot of sleep."

A cool shadow passed over the skin of Anita's face. Later she would discover that a makeshift parasol had been set up, an effect achieved by pegging a sheet onto the washing line. It was easy to let her parents go on thinking she was sleeping. She used to pretend on long car journeys, so that she could enjoy the feeling of being carried inside the house and put to bed. The comfort of relinquishing control.

Ron had forewarning that the doorbell was about to ring. He had come in from the garden and was making his way between the kitchen and the foot of the stairs when he heard the familiar swish of someone sliding the porch door open. Competing voices followed, none of them particularly enamoured, giving the impression that some of the party were here under duress. It occurred to Ron that he might still have time to dart upstairs and lock himself in the bathroom, but that would be cowardly. Someone else would have to deal with the visitors and he didn't want that someone to be Anita. The only other option was to enjoy the element of surprise and ambush them before they had the chance to put their happy faces on.

Bracing himself for boredom, he whipped the door open, to find Geraldine frozen, her index finger extended in readiness to make contact with the doorbell. Behind her stood a large woman with far too much cleavage on display. A second glance had him thinking, *Sweet Jesus, it can't be!* But what other explanation was there? It must be Geraldine's Lizzie, and, with her, a motley assemblage of teenagers who had sprung up to replace the toddlers in Ron's memory.

"I thought I heard voices," he said. "To what do we owe the honour? It can't be Christmas already."

"Ron! You'll be the death of me!" Geraldine recovered herself sufficiently to slap his chest playfully. Then, as if she'd given a silent command, the troops surged past him. "We thought we'd come and pay our respects to your Anita."

"Pay your respects? She's not royalty." This was his second choice of words. His first had been that she wasn't dead, but he seemed to remember something about Geraldine's husband being unwell, and Ron wasn't confident that he was up to speed with the latest. "In fact, I think she's having a kip right now."

With hands on the teenagers' shoulders, Geraldine said, "Boys, you remember Ron, don't you?"

It was clear from the studied way they avoided eye contact that they lacked the inclination to rack their memories.

Put in his place in his own home! Ron stepped outside to slide the porch door to, which earned him the rebuke, "Off out then, are you?" from Lizzie. To be honest, it wasn't the worst idea he'd heard all day. He made a second attempt to reconcile the vision in front of him with the small girl in pigtails. Ron had never been able to push the swings high enough or spin the roundabout fast enough for Lizzie's liking. When she shrieked, the noise went clean through you, and you'd have pushed or spun anything to get away from it.

He raised an index finger, affirmation that he knew Lizzie was joking, and closed the door, trapping himself inside with the rest of them.

Wedged against his own front door, Ron was about to open his mouth to say, "Go on through," when it became apparent that Geraldine didn't need an invitation. She was busy devising a seating plan. He was rather glad when Patti appeared in the kitchen doorway to relieve him of the need for any other social niceties.

JANE DAVIS

"Were you expecting Geraldine and her clan?" he hissed.

From the roll of Patti's eyes, he could see she wasn't any happier about the prospect of entertaining uninvited guests than he was. "I called to say that I wouldn't be able to go over to hers," she whispered. "How was I to know it would be translated as an invitation for the entire family?"

Ron gripped his wife's arm in empathy and turned to face the occupants of the living room.

"At least you have those leftover sausage rolls and the pizza to offer them."

"No, that all went."

"Oh."

They'd done a good job of making themselves at home. "I'll just put the kettle on, then I'll wake Sleeping Beauty. Unless any of the youngsters would prefer a cold drink?" Ron aimed his last comment at the teenage contingency slumped on the sofa, arms folded and legs jutting out in front of them.

One of them shot him a *why should I care?* look. Accepting the offer of a drink, whether it was tea or Coca-Cola, was only going to prolong his agony. He had important business to get back to on a Saturday afternoon. Visiting his nan was one thing, but being dragged round to see a friend of hers - one he could scarcely remember - was another. Ron commiserated. His own needs weren't urgent - so long as they cleared off home before *Final Score*.

About to mention to the boys that he had a few cans of Cains bitter, he hesitated, unsure of the protocol. Offering beer to teenagers in front of their mother was rather like offering sweets to youngsters. You never knew quite what the reaction was going to be. "I'll tell you what," he said. "I'll make a pot of tea, then you can make your minds up."

Filling the kettle, he looked out into the garden and saw that Anita was still lying on that old beach towel, her book pages-down, her sunglasses abandoned, one arm extended over the top of her head. Waking his sleeping daughter wasn't something he'd had to do for many years. Patti had often delegated this task to him when their daughter was a teenager and hadn't shown her face by eleven a.m. - the dividing line between catching up on sleep after a late night and laziness as far as his wife was concerned. At about ten forty-five, as Patti would start to check her watch with increasing impatience, he would fold his copy of the *Echo*, saying, "I think I'll just see what our Anita's up to."

Ron squirmed inwardly. In his opinion, waking an adult should be approached with caution - not to mention someone who so clearly had a lot of catching up to do. He stepped outside. A sculptor might have placed Anita more prettily, but the furled fingers of the hand that strayed over her head looked so delicate. He had balanced his hands on his knees, when Anita said, "I heard."

She had yet to open her eyes. "Did you hear *who* it is?"

"Gerry. I'd know that laugh anywhere."

"Plus four."

"Four." She let out a groan. "Mum's cronies?"

"Lizzie and her three youngest. And I don't think you can blame your mother, love." His attempt at a joke. "Not when you're the reason she knows Geraldine in the first place."

Anita pretended to sob. "Do they know I'm here?"

He felt embarrassed to be saying this: "It's you they've come to see."

Now Anita was up on one elbow. "She's come to gloat. That's what Gerry does."

"Gloat?" He was taken aback.

"Gerry pretends to be Mum's friend, but she arrives dressed in her *World's Best Nan* t-shirt and rubs her up the wrong way. It's her way of saying, 'Your daughter may have got the job in London, but look what *mine* did.'"

"From what little I saw of those lads, there's not one who's worth boasting about." Although, admittedly, Ron quite liked the boy who'd shown a bit of a spark. Come to think of it, there was a familiar look about him. Perhaps he'd just fill a tray with a few cans of beer and a few of coke. Then no one could accuse him of giving alcohol to underage teens. Patti's face appeared framed by the kitchen window and she came to the back door to beckon impatiently.

"Come on," he sighed. "The sooner we go inside, the sooner we get this over with."

Anita was rousing herself, pushing herself up as if performing a press-up. "That's what you said when you took me to the dentist for my first filling," she sulked.

Compared with this, a filling might be relatively pain-free. He waited until she was on her feet. It wouldn't help to point out that the towel had left an impression on the side of her face. To Ron, it was incredibly endearing. "It's a multi-purpose saying."

She narrowed her eyes. "It took me forever to trust you again."

Even with the indentations in her skin, a little slippage of mascara and her hair slightly skewiff, his daughter was quite beautiful. In fact, Ron observed, this was probably the point in her life when she would look the most beautiful, caught off-guard, all of her slight imperfections combining. Except perhaps that day when she was about three, and he'd taken her for a walk to get her out of Patti's hair. The pavements slick after a recent downpour, Anita had insisted on stopping at every dripping downpipe to sing *Incy Wincy Spider*. The hem of her cotton dress soaked through as she crouched to make her hands climb upwards. And he'd let her, his ray of sunshine, stunned by her radiance.

Now, he smiled. Anita had the unexpected look of his aunt about her. Ron found himself quite overcome; having to turn away and pretend he had something in his eye. In the periphery of his blurred vision, he saw Anita deposit the book and her sunglasses on the kitchen worktop.

He growled, "I see your mother's already taken the tea things through," whipping open the fridge, and extracting cans. "Which leaves me in charge of fizzy pop." He felt in need of a stiff drink. Beer would do, even if no one else was interested.

"You'd better give me one of those." Anita swiped one of the cans of bitter off the worktop before it had even made it as far as the tray. It hissed as she opened it.

Surprised by his daughter's choice of drink - he'd never known her to drink beer - Ron asked, "Dutch courage?"

She winced as she swallowed. "I can't even remember when I last saw Lizzie."

"You had some kind of a falling out, didn't you?" Ron's question prompted an open-mouthed glare from his daughter. And then he remembered: it had been over a boy. Jason. Oh, blimey, it was that same boy who was the father of Lizzie's four!

As the penny dropped, so too did his jaw. Anita nodded: *Remember it now, do you?*

Jason Adams! He'd had him pegged from the moment he saw him sitting on their sofa. It was difficult for Ron to say exactly why he recoiled. Jason and Anita had only been watching television, but the boy's arm was arced around Anita's shoulder, laying claim to his daughter. Ron had thrust one hand into his trouser pocket to prevent it from pointing to the door, while the words *Get out of my house!* crowded his chest, attempting to force their way into his throat.

"Alright, Mr Hall?" Jason had chirped as he noticed him standing there, but it was the undercurrent, you see. He might as well have said, 'I'm here to stay, and there isn't a damned thing you can do about it.' And Anita had twisted her head and said, "Hello, Dad," looking so happy.

The slow boil of fury. Ron had battled to contain it as he waited for the thing to burn itself out. At the breakfast table each day, Ron monitored his daughter's face carefully for signs of change. A father doesn't miss a thing like that.

He'd let Patti dole out the sympathy after the breakup. Shushed out of the way, it was all Ron could do to stop himself from running victory laps around the back garden. That was the one time he could recall when Patti hadn't complained about the hours Anita spent cooped up in her bedroom. "Let her be," she'd chided, while she cooked tasty morsels to tempt her daughter. Food was Patti's answer in times of crises. "Try to eat a little cheese on toast, love. I'll leave it on a tray outside your door. You come and get it when you're feeling up to it."

"I thought one of the lads looked familiar. Oh, love, I'm sorry..." Thunderstruck, he felt like an executioner preparing to parade the accused in front of a blood-hungry crowd. *Go and gawp at Anita. She's feeling a bit fragile and is home for some TLC.* But she was already walking away from him, into the hall. All he could do was bring up the rear, chastising himself.

Ron's head jerked as he heard Geraldine's cry of "Anita! Come over here and let us take a look at you, love," sickening emotion instilled in every syllable. So much for women's intuition. Pity was the last thing his daughter needed!

He arrived in time to see Geraldine hugging Anita, splaying her fingers as if the garish nail varnish she had painted herself with was still drying. This sort of overdone familiarity made Ron deeply uncomfortable. "At least you're still here. You're alive, sweetheart. You've come back to us."

From the way that Anita went limp in Geraldine's arms, he pondered, *I bet she barely feels it.*

Lizzie had reluctantly craned herself to her feet, and she offered a subdued, "Hiya," apologising unnecessarily for the absence of her daughter, whose youngest had tonsillitis.

Ordinarily, this might have passed Ron by, but now the words seemed designed to point out that she was the matriarch of her own clan. A grandmother - imagine! It seemed almost indecent, at Lizzie's age.

Anita faced the sofa, a sterling effort. "So, if I remember rightly, it's Barry, John-Joe and Benji, but I don't know for the life of me which one of you is which."

"I'm Ben," the boy with the attitude spoke up, nodding sideways. "But no one's called him John-Joe since he was five."

Attempting diplomacy, Geraldine jumped in. The kind of smile that barely concealed criticism. "Well, it's been a long time since Anita's seen you."

Ben pointed to the tray. "Can I 'ave that last beer?"

There was one of those extended pauses, when Geraldine's nostrils flared. She threw her daughter a cautionary glance. Sour-faced women, both of them. Ron found himself on the receiving end of one of Patti's withering looks. *Now why would you want to go putting temptation in his way?*

"What about a shandy?" Anita suggested, and there was a noticeable thaw. "Bring that tinny through to the kitchen and I'll find some lemonade."

Good on you, Ron chuckled inwardly, as Ben hopped up from the sofa. His daughter had learned that trick from him. You poured the beer into a glass and added a dash of lemonade (he could hear Anita asking Ben to take the lid off the two-litre bottle, because she always struggled). No one was any the wiser. Ron had always taken the view that saying no was futile. A blank refusal gave kids cause to go behind your back. Better to say, 'just the one'. At least now Anita would have one of them on her side.

Once the drinks were dispensed, Ron was redundant, small talk not being his area of expertise. Even the women appeared to struggle after medical opinions had been exchanged about the poorly granddaughter. Most of the subjects of Patti and

Geraldine's gossip were off-limits seeing as they were sat in the room. Lizzie punctuated the silence by picking on the three lads. "Sit up straight," "'Aven't you got anything to say for yourselves?" to which the one Ron thought was called John retorted, "It was nutt'n, Mum. End of." The broadest of all of them, his Scouse accent neatly fitted Dave Allen's description: half Irish, a quarter Welsh and a quarter phlegm.

"Go on!" Geraldine, prompted, her voice nervous with laughter. "Tell them what you did,"

"Honest to God, you're doin' my 'ead in."

Ron had to stop himself from cheering, *Good on you, lad, you tell her.* But Anita perched on the arm of the sofa and managed to extract from Ben that he was in the Army Cadets and was a bit partial to Cheryl Cole. "Only with the sound turned down, like. I prefer Jake Bugg if you're actually talking about music."

And though Ron had never heard of him, Anita clearly knew who he was on about.

Ben's monosyllabic brothers were deeply involved in their electronic devices. Something that would have been considered rude just a few years ago, but now Ron was supposed to accept that he was behind the times with his manners as well as with technology. Good beer would have been wasted on those two.

He was rather proud of how Anita coped, even though she'd done nothing except gravitate towards the lad with the most life in him and divert the conversation away from herself. She seemed to have rediscovered some of her sparkle. In fact, sit her next to a teenager and the years fell away. Ben was indulging in a little flirtation. Ron could tell his behaviour was making Lizzie, whose folded arms further emphasised her cleavage, deeply uncomfortable. All that attention from an attractive woman must have proved too much to resist.

Watching his daughter, Ron remembered things he hadn't

shared with anyone else about her teenage years. Covering for her that time she'd been caught bunking off. It was by chance that he'd arrived home just in time to intercept the call from the school secretary. Clattering downstairs in an attempt to get there first, Anita froze halfway, listening as he claimed to have kept her at home, muttering something about a family emergency. He had particularly enjoyed the moment his daughter's eyes lit up like an old-fashioned cash register, as if *he* was the one who was breaking the rules. *But Mum would have...* On the day in question Ron hadn't felt up to the confinement of the office. He had decided not to go back to work after an interview had finished earlier than scheduled. So, in a way, he'd been bunking off too.

He recalled the time when he'd waited in the car to pick her up after a party. In those days, while smoking was still socially acceptable, fathers who didn't want to embarrass their kids spent a great deal of time waiting in cars, the radio on, ciggies dangling. It had been a pleasant way to spend the odd half hour. He'd seen her emerge, arm in arm with a girl, stumbling slightly, heads together, giggling. He'd stubbed out his cigarette in the ashtray. And, it being rather obvious that Anita was a little worse for wear, he'd asked, "Did you have a nice time?"

She'd come right out with it: "I just kissed a boy," which was unexpected, to say the least.

Ron felt as if someone had reached into his chest and grabbed hold of his heart as he watched Anita strap herself into the car seat and hug herself. He was unable to prevent himself from saying, "I hope it was just kissing!"

"Dad!" she'd squealed, as if he'd underestimated her. "I'm hardly going to risk getting pregnant, am I?"

He had no idea that this was the sort of thing a teenage daughter might say to her father. Sex was one of those excruciating mother-daughter things he'd hoped to avoid. "Aren't you?" In his experience, rather a lot of girls had.

"I want to go to uni, don't I?"

And so he'd always seen her plans to study as a good thing, squirrelling away a little money each month for when the time came. Forewarned, this knowledge had enabled him to rejoice in Anita's O-level results in a way that Patti never had. Because, even though he knew that a degree would probably take her away from Liverpool, they kept Anita's teenage years on the straight and narrow.

His policy had always been not to report back to Patti. His wife would only have demanded answers to the questions she'd have asked in his place. And because this much became apparent to Anita, she would share extraordinary facts about her life, and Ron thought how useful some of her insights would have been to him as a teenager. As parents went, it was Patti who'd had the raw deal, coping with the blood-stained sheets, the hormonal outbursts and the revision fatigue. She'd never seen the late-night sparkle. Ron, on the other hand, had received rare glimpses into the workings of his daughter's soul. Conversations that could only ever be had driving through deserted streets shortly after midnight. Her triumphs and heartaches, both large and small. Her attempts at expressing the fear that she might be unlovable. *What, you? You div.* That a wrong choice might set her life on a disastrous course. *There are such things as second chances.* That she might not meet the person she was supposed to spend the rest of her life with. *Well, either you believe in fate or you don't.* What if I get homesick? *Then come home. We've no plans to rent out your room. Not yet, at least.*

He'd given her scope to let off steam on a Saturday night because, time and time again, Anita had proved that her grades wouldn't suffer. Until Jason's arrival, nothing had threatened her plans to go to university.

'Gobby, swagger, proud, cheeky' - the profile of a typical

Scouser, according to a sign Ron had read in the Museum of Liverpool. Anita had been so smitten that, for a few tortuous weeks, Jason seemed to have the potential to undo her hard work. All of that course work, those long hours of revision. It was terrible to watch the way her eyes trailed after him as he left the room. And, because Ron hadn't confided in Patti, he endured the anguish alone.

Ron wondered if Anita saw Jason as she looked at Ben, crossing one leg towards him. And, if she did, was there a part of her in which the betrayal would always be raw, or did what had seemed catastrophic at the time now seem trivial?

Pleasantly relaxed by the beer, Ron turned to Lizzie - who was occupying his favourite armchair - with affection. Not only had she taken Jason off his daughter's hands, but she had confirmed that Ron's fears had been well-founded: Lizzie was the person Anita might have become. And it wasn't that Lizzie had nothing to show for it. It was just that those things would have made his Anita thoroughly miserable.

Of course, it had been sheer hell watching his daughter having her heart trampled on by such an unworthy scumbag, but if Jason had had his way... Even now, his can of Cains compressed, his hand determined to make a fist.

In the natural order of events, Patti and Geraldine couldn't have remained friends while their daughters were battling it out. But the next thing Ron had heard was that Lizzie had fallen pregnant, and Patti (who whispered to Ron in the dark about Anita's narrow escape) played the Good Samaritan, counselling an inconsolable Geraldine. Gratitude washed over Ron. If it had been his Anita, she would never have spread her wings, never met Ed - now there was a good man, the sort you could rely on to take care of your daughter. Although this latest chapter was challenge enough to test any relationship, no doubt about it. And they weren't out of the woods yet, by any means.

Patti fretted, but fretting was a mother's job. She used to routinely wake Ron in the early hours to ask his opinion about what he thought young people wanted these days. But young people want what they have always wanted. And that is to *be* wanted. To be accepted. To be loved. To be desired. Not to be like their parents. To find a place they belong, a place to call their own. To feel part of something bigger, wider, broader than themselves. To leave their mark on the world.

And tomorrow Anita was going home again. She'd only been back for a few days, but to Ron, it would feel as if she was leaving home for the first time, just as it always did. That bittersweet blend of immense pride and having your heart ripped out of your chest. And so, for today, he would feast his eyes and remember that he had been blessed.

CHAPTER SEVENTEEN

Anita flung herself down on the bed, undecided whether to laugh, cry or breathe a sigh of relief. What the hell had Lizzie been trying to prove, parading her family in front of her? That she'd been *entitled?* That the fact that Lizzie was still with Jason after all these years meant that she'd been *right* to do what she'd done?

It could so easily have been her. For all of Anita's lofty ideals, all of the times she'd told her dad, "I wouldn't be so stupid," she'd been exactly that stupid. And so, at the same time as having to endure the humiliation of her best friend stealing her boyfriend - hanging off his arm when Anita passed them at the bus stop, having people stare and gossip about her behind her back - she'd had to wait. Everywhere she looked there seemed to be pregnant women. Women pushing prams and pushchairs down Church Street. Madonna was singing, 'Papa don't preach'. Even Michelle from *EastEnders* was pregnant.

Her period had never been late before. For five agonising days, her mind had wandered: she would fight for Jason; he'd have to marry her now; Christ, how the hell would she break the news to her dad? He'd storm round there and punch his lights out.

One day, when both of her parents were out, Anita went

to the medicine cupboard, standing on the kitchen surface as she used to when she stole marzipan as a child. She took out a bottle of aspirin and gulped them back, one by one, cringing with each bitter swallow. She'd counted to twenty-eight when panic sent her rushing to the bathroom. Two fingers down her throat and violent retching produced a chalky trail. Sitting on the rough carpet tiles by the side of the toilet, Anita clutched her knees to her chest sobbing tears of terror at what she might have done - and at what the alternative was. Two children with the same father, and not three weeks to separate them in age.

Then, the sight of blood on her knickers. And, there, more proof on a square of toilet paper! Deep red redemption.

This was madness. It had all happened years ago. Being in Liverpool - being there without Ed - was making her disappear into her past. She'd seen a chip wrapper blown on a stiff breeze, and cries of *Support the Miners!* had echoed at her. While shopping, she'd walked past Ted Baker, on the corner where Probe Records used to have its door. Stood on the spot where thousands boarded ships with one-way tickets to America. But how could resurrected things feel so raw? Anita thought she'd insulated herself against them. Was this drifting backwards because she now had so few reminders of who she'd become? Her anchor was gone.

And why the hell did Ben have to be the one to answer her? The one who looked so like... *Say his name. It won't kill you.* Jason.

What was the point in choosing not to have children when the Lizzies of this world happily stepped in and took your quota? Anita pinched her nostrils. Self-pity wasn't what she needed. She craved a friendly voice, a distraction. With a shaking hand, she reached for her mobile phone.

"Hello," a chirpy response. A voice fuelled by Tizer, chocolate fingers and Fizzy Fish. Reuben.

She made her voice deliberately stern. "Have I reached the birthday boy?"

"Who is this?"

And she began to sing. *"Happy birthday to you. Happy birthday to you. I saw a fat monkey -"*

He feigned boredom. "Aunty Nita."

"And I thought it was you. How did you guess?"

"You're the only one who's not here."

That stung. "I'm really sorry I missed your party. Did you have a good time?"

"It was wicked."

"Who's that on the phone, Rubes?"

"It's only Aunty Nita."

Anita jerked the phone away from her ear.

"Remember to say thank you for the present."

"Oh, yeah. Thank you for the present."

"I was wondering if Ed had been round to see you."

She had been about to ask if it was something he had wanted when her godson said, "He's a really bad dancer."

She felt an illogical jealousy. "Ed stayed for your party?"

"Yeah! Do you want to speak to him? I can get him if you want. He's helping Mum clear up."

"No - but I'd like a quick word with her."

"Mum!"

"Do you think you could warn me the next time you're going to shout in my ear? That's twice you've deafened me."

He laughed again. "Are you going to come round to play the new computer game when you get back?"

"Definitely. I need the practice."

"OK, bye. Things to do."

And, as quick as that, he was gone. There was dead space before Natalie said, "Hi Anita."

"I have to say, your son's phone manner is getting very businesslike. He doesn't mess around."

"He's growing up so fast, it's terrifying. Double figures, can you believe it? How's Liverpool?"

"Good. Mainly."

"Mainly?"

"Long story. Just came face to face with someone I would have preferred not to see. I think I'm ready to come home."

"Ed will be pleased to have you back. I'm not sure how I would have managed without him today."

"Listen, I'm so sorry. I completely forgot. My head's all over the place."

"Don't worry about it. You've not been well." Was that the explanation Ed had given? Anita wasn't sure how she felt about being stamped with the word *fragile*. "Not everyone would think to send someone in their place. It wasn't the same as having you here, obviously. I had to ask him to cut the sandwiches into fours, that sort of thing. But at least Ed knew his way around the kitchen, and it's been... I dunno. It's been nice having a man around. To get the lids off the bottles of coke, if nothing else."

"No Phil?" she asked. Reuben had said that *she* was the only one who wasn't there. Up until this point Anita had imagined the men cracking open bottles of beer, ignoring the age restriction on the trampoline and outdoing themselves in the silly dancing stakes.

"No. No Phil." Natalie's tone didn't invite sympathy or questions.

"Well," Anita forced herself to say, "You should reward yourselves with a glass or two of wine."

"That's exactly what we're doing. Ed brought a very nice bottle of sauvignon blanc with him."

It wasn't as if he needed permission, but knowing Ed was having a drink with her best friend felt odd. Odd that Anita was not there to... the word that came to mind was *chaperone*. She swallowed. "Well, I should probably go and peel some potatoes for dinner," she said. "Before I'm accused of skiving."

"Anita, did Reuben mention his dad?"

"No. No he didn't."

"Maybe he didn't expect him to turn up." Natalie gave a bitter laugh. "He's smarter than I am!"

Anita knew that this *not expecting* would haunt her friend. "You obviously gave him a really good birthday."

"Yes, I did." She sounded satisfied. Proud, even. "Hey, we should grab a coffee next week. Catch up properly."

"I'd like that."

For several moments after the call ended Anita stared hard at her mobile, imagining Reuben putting on a brave face so that Natalie would think she'd done enough. In some ways, she felt that Phil had betrayed them all, acting the part not only of a husband and father, but also of one of their closest friends. Perhaps she was being too hard. Attending his son's party would have been painful - maybe *too* painful. Being back in the house he was still paying for, with his ex-wife and his ten-year-old son, playing the role that was expected - and in public, too. It didn't matter who'd ended the relationship. As today had proven, emotions could still ambush you unexpectedly. Perhaps Reuben would have seen Natalie and Phil being civil towards each other and read more into it. Maybe Phil had spared them the *I don't want Dad to go. It's not fair.* But still, a nameless nagging started up at the back of her mind. "Stupid," she dismissed it, putting the phone down on the bedside table.

Potatoes.

CHAPTER EIGHTEEN

"That's everything in the car," her father said, stepping back into the house. "Your five-minute warning starts from," he glanced at his wrist, the sign that they should synchronise watches. "Now!"

"I'll just make sure I haven't done my usual trick and left something upstairs."

Anita scanned the bathroom for stray cosmetics. Then she tackled her old bedroom, deciding there was time to strip the bed: the pillowcases, the duvet cover and the fitted sheet. Returning from a trip across the landing to the linen basket, observing how bare the mattress looked, she repositioned the pillows and the duvet. An unnecessary check of all of the drawers then, closing the wardrobe doors, she caught sight of the title on the spines of the books that were neatly stacked on top. *An Unknown Woman.* Surprising that she hadn't noticed it before now. This was evidence of just how distracted she'd been.

The street on the front cover was comfortingly familiar. A faded background, a girl holding an adult hand - presumably her mother's - the woman herself out of shot. *A Girl is a Half-formed Thing* had been heavy going. Something lighter, something set in the geography of her childhood, might be the antidote.

"*Anita!*"

"Coming." She stowed the book in her handbag. Her mother would hardly miss one.

"I'd begun to think you'd nipped out the back while I wasn't looking," her father quipped as she appeared at the top of the staircase.

Patti was on sentry duty by the front door, ready to make her habitual inspection. "Let's take a look at you." It didn't matter if you were six or forty-six, you had to pass her test of how a respectable person should look when going out into the world.

Anita was leaving again. Confused at wanting to go, knowing that, in a few days, when she least expected it, she would experience a searing homesickness. Added to the complex mix was the knowledge that she no longer had anywhere to call home. She stood up straight, arms by her sides as her mother circled, satisfying herself that there were no labels on display, no bra straps showing.

"Won't you come to the station with us, Patti?" Dad issued his usual invitation, with the predictable reply.

"There's no point in us both going. I'll make a start on the tidying."

Anita took this as her cue to kiss her mother's cheek. Patti tightened her mouth and nodded. "Don't be a stranger."

Insulated from the city, inside her father's Mondeo, Anita caught a brief glimpse of the Museum of Liverpool, where she'd stumbled across him. Could she refer to it in such a way that he would know his secret - whatever it was - would remain safe? But he was singing along to one of his beloved skiffle CDs and Anita squandered the moment, casually enquiring about his plans for the rest of the day. And then they were pulling into a parking space at the drop-off point, and he was trying to press a fold of notes on her.

"Put that away, Dad," she said, embarrassed.

"Don't be daft. What am I going to spend it on?"

Anita didn't want their last few moments together to be tarnished by disagreement, and she was old enough to understand that this was not about giving or receiving, but about her father's need to feel useful. Reluctantly, she took his money.

Hands freed, he held both of hers and they sat smiling at each other.

"I almost forgot," he broke the silence. "There's something in the glovebox for you." Anita raised her eyebrows, pushed the button and let the door fall open. "I overheard you and your mother talking. And, well, I'll shut up. You'll see what it is soon enough." Her father looked both excited and self-conscious as she reached for the plastic bag that had been neatly folded back on itself.

Inside was a brass doorknob. Spherical, and with circles etched around it, even before Anita looked, the feel of it in her hand was familiar. She had a vision of Ed reaching for the doorknob of the spare room, and jerking his hand away; shaking it as if he wanted to be rid of it. She just about managed to get the words out: "Thanks, Dad."

"Don't feel you have to build a house around it. You could always put it in a sock and use it as a weapon."

She wasn't even on the train yet and Anita was heading back to where she'd started. She wrapped the doorknob up again and forced a smile. "I'll bear that in mind."

Anita hadn't bothered to reserve a seat. She sought out a table, where she thought she'd be less likely to feel hemmed in. But, like cinema goers, passengers congregated around the few customers who'd got there first. Two women gossiping in American accents sidled into the seats next to Anita's. When they realised that their knees were almost touching, one shuffled closer. She opened a hardback copy of *The Goldfinch* and announced, "I'm going to read," perhaps a suggestion that her friend quieten down a little.

The other woman hefted her feet onto the seat, almost as if she was admiring her gold flip-flops and manicured nails. The woman who was reading was stealthier. She balanced the soles of both jewel-encrusted sandals on the edge of the seat, ready for a quick retreat. Irritation tightened Anita's chest. You expected this of teenagers, not middle-aged women. She sipped from her water bottle and repositioned it so that the notice requesting that passengers please refrain from putting their feet on the seats was in plain view. The women didn't react - and yet they clearly knew the rules, as was demonstrated when a member of the catering team wheeled the shivering drinks trolley up the aisle.

While the train pulled out of Lime Street Station, Anita told herself, *How they behave is none of your business.* She reached into her bag for the book she had taken from the top of the wardrobe. The word 'stolen' didn't enter her mind. Flicking through to the first chapter, it occurred to her - fleetingly - that it might be pleasant to put her feet up. Then, just as she was about to begin reading, the small window above her head slammed shut, causing a dramatic pressure change in her ears.

CHAPTER NINETEEN

*I*f family myths were to be believed, it all began when my mother, Clementina (never called anything other than Clemmie, unless her father was dishing out a roasting), tripped on the way up the aisle of St Xavier's. As a child, I heard elderly female relatives hiss behind cupped hands that the fall had been a bad omen - although, it was probably nothing more than the combination of high heels, a hem that could have done with another inch taking off it, and the double brandy Clemmie had downed to quell her pre-wedding nerves.

Perhaps that was why the author had sought her mother out. Two coincidences: her grandmother's name and tripping on the way up the aisle.

She hadn't dared let go of her bouquet, so she didn't break her fall, avoiding a fractured wrist. In fact, Clemmie was lucky, suffering little more than bruised pride, a grazed chin and a swollen tongue from where she'd bitten it. Though there were audible gasps - though relatives jostled uncharitably in their pews for a better view - the incident itself was only witnessed by those with aisle seats. Clemmie's father - my grandfather - was confined to a wheelchair by then, so all he could do was cry out, "Mind yourself!" as he watched his daughter topple.

Using one finger as a bookmark, Anita checked the cover for the name of the author. She checked the spine. *An*

Unknown Woman. Was that the title of the book or a reference to its author? A new cause of unease crept over her - and it had nothing to do with being penned in by the legs of the two women to her left.

He couldn't have helped her to her feet if he'd wanted to: it was the groom - my father - who deserted his post in the front pew to offer a hand. Over quickly, the incident would have been forgotten had my grandfather not had the ill-grace to joke about it in his speech, acting out the part of shouting after her: "Mind yourself! Quite the most useless advice I've ever given my lovely daughter" (though it was debatable whether that was true).

By the time I was six, I had heard various renditions of the story, but my mother would scoff and say, "The devious gossip! She wasn't even there," and, "You'd think we were living in the dark ages," and, on the subject of bad omens, "Well, I'm still here, aren't I?"

I hadn't even guessed at the form my mother's bad luck had taken until some months after I held my own daughter in my arms for the first time.

Who was this writer who wished to remain anonymous and refused to name her main character?

After the initial panic of finding I was pregnant so soon after the wedding (it was just as well I'd insisted on a wedding ring first), I was overjoyed when everybody said from the way I was carrying it that the baby would be a boy.

"A boy!" Ray had said, as if we'd won the pools, making me feel as if I had done something special and clever, not something half the general population got up to on a Saturday night. The truth was that I barely knew my husband. We had met and married within fourteen days.

Anita felt winded. There was longer any room for doubt. The unknown author and the unknown woman were one and the same.

Flattered by Ray's proposal, buoyed up by his confidence,

his certainty, I didn't suffer a single doubt until the eve of our wedding. Then, I was plagued by the possibility that I was going through with it to spite my parents, Clemmie especially, who was vocal with her opinion that I should wait at least a year and see how I felt. But I'd had that roller-coaster feeling. It was too late to announce that I had changed my mind.

Did her father know? Anita had very little idea about the secrets her parents shared and the things they kept to themselves. If not, what a way to discover that your wife would have backed out if she had thought she wouldn't lose face!

I resigned from my secretarial job, because it was expected of me. As soon as you knew you were expecting, the general consensus was that you were taking up a job that rightfully belonged to someone else, no matter how well qualified you were or how long you'd trained. Ray never faltered, never expressed concern about money. He brought me flowers, massaged my feet and set about decorating the spare room.

But that overwhelming rush of emotion I had been led to expect didn't materialise when the midwife turned to hand the child to me.

"It's a little girl," the woman (a formidable but kindly presence), announced.

My reaction was to recoil, heels scuffing the blood-stained sheets. "No, that's not my baby. My baby's a boy." But the woman placed the child in my unwilling arms, moulding them into a cradle, and all I could do was look down, appalled. I couldn't help it: I thought the baby ugly.

Anita's eyes widened. And yet it was just an honest reaction. Didn't all newborns look like either E.T. or Churchill?

She wasn't yet Anna, not in anyone's mind. We hadn't bothered with a shortlist of girls' names. Only boys': Billy, Thomas, James. Names that would remain unoccupied. I might occasionally hear another mother shout, 'Billy!' in the playground and would twist my head, thinking, There he is: there's my Billy, deserting Anna's pram to watch the child - the boy I was promised - making castles in the sandpit. Later I would wish I'd taken more of an interest in naming her. That I hadn't snapped at Ray as he made one suggestion after another, "Will you make your mind up!" And so he had chosen one. Just one. There was no middle name. It was only later that it seemed like an oversight.

I could see nothing of myself in this girl-child; nothing of Ray. If I had given my thoughts a voice - which was unthinkable - I would have demanded, 'Take her away from me.' But this child was no changeling. There had been no moment during which the midwife could have made a switch.

Attempts at breastfeeding only reinforced feelings of revulsion. At first, Anna refused to latch on and, when she finally did, it was agony. Fuelled by fear of failure, obsessed by the need to get it right, I forced her - rigid and angry - to feed on the hour every hour, resenting how much time the feeds swallowed up, how little sleep I managed to get in between. Clemmie had drummed into me the importance of being lady-like, but first there was childbirth and now this *slave-like existence. Closing my eyes, I would wish myself somewhere else, thinking myself back at work, taking dictation in shorthand, seated at the type-writer, and wake to find my bloated farm-animal self. Teats, not nipples, raw, bleeding and chapped. Leaking and spraying.*

There were days when I didn't get out of bed with my head pounding, when I said, "Right, you're just a tiny baby. You're not going to get the better of me." But I liked myself less for entertaining thoughts that bolstered the idea that Anna and I were at war; that every day should end with a winner and a loser.

Sitting forwards, hunched over the book, Anita was outraged. Ray and Anna. Her mother had protected her own name, but had barely changed theirs! Her life was there - in print. Anyone could order a copy and read it.

Rather than provide an answer to the fundamental question, 'Why am I here?' motherhood had me demanding, 'What the hell am I doing? I was happy before. I had everything I wanted.' On one occasion, afraid to admit to Ray that I was in danger of screaming the house down if I didn't get out for five minutes, pretending I'd forgotten to buy milk, I left him in charge of the baby. (He wouldn't have minded if I did this more often, but I obsessed about Anna being my responsibility and mine alone.)

Anita felt a tap on her thigh. The woman to her immediate left had nudged her hip with one of her feet. Anita looked at the open-toed sandal, horrified, and from there to the woman's smiling face.

"Did I disturb you? I just wanted to ask," she lowered her voice to a whisper, "is that a good book? I mean, it's obviously got you in its grip."

Anita had been so absorbed, she had succeeded in blocking out the train carriage. The woman was sitting back in her seat. Expensive hair, expensive scarf tied around her neck, crisp white blouse. Newly protective of her privacy, Anita was in no mood for conversation. She put one elbow on the text she'd been reading.

The woman held up the book she was cradling as if revealing a secret. Anita saw the cover: artwork made to look as if a page had been torn to show a picture of a goldfinch. "This is beautiful. *Beautiful.*" She shrugged her shoulders as if to emphasise the word. "So polished. Don't you wish you could write?"

Anita had no idea how to react, still less what to say, but it became apparent that her contribution wasn't required.

"I'm reading it in bite-sized' chunks, you know? Sometimes I find myself going over the same sentence three or four times, just to get the *feel* of it. I think that when someone's spent ten years of their life working on a book, you owe them that." She sounded like a person who collected opinions from reviews printed in magazines. Perhaps she tried them out on strangers to see how they sounded coming from her own lips. "Addie doesn't read, do you, Addie?" She nudged her friend with her other foot.

The slouched woman snorted, her arms folded. "No, I don't!"

The Goldfinch woman widened her eyes, as if they were sharing a joke. Almost as if reading was a bond between them. Anita thought that she might do anything to stop the American from talking. She rushed to fill the short pause for breath. "Look, I'm really sorry."

"Marcia." The woman offered her name like an invitation.

"Marcia," Anita tasted it. "I don't mean to sound rude - but I have to finish this book. It's for work." She sat back in her seat, in case it was sitting forwards that had somehow given the impression that she was approachable.

"Oh, that's OK," the American woman said, in a way that suggested the opposite.

Her heart hammering, Anita tried to locate her place on the page.

Freed temporarily from the need to push a pram, able to swing my arms once more, hear the click of my heels on the pavement, I felt liberated. There was no need to focus all my attention on a child in a pink bonnet. My eyes delighted in things I had stopped noticing. A date carved in the cornerstone of a building. The dolphins circling each lamppost.

Approaching the station, an idea took hold in my head. I had a little money. I could buy a ticket, get on a train and never go back! My soul swelled with songs of freedom. But it was too simple. The plan had to be flawed. Several times, I walked as far as the Empire Theatre and back, waiting for an objection to raise its ugly head. To be honest, there seemed to be little to stop me. There was no doubt that Ray and Anna would be better off without me. Because, by then, there was no longer any 'us'. It had become 'me' and 'them'.

And then, just as I had decided to go in, the midwife who had delivered Anna marched smartly out of Lime Street station. As though she was my conscience, the woman acted as a hand-brake, and it was the memory of this near-collision that would slam into me when I least expected it and, when the beating of my heart settled, I would almost weep, How many more times? *If I had hoped not to be recognised without my legs in stirrups, my face distorted, I was disappointed:* "So it's you, Mrs Ripley! And how's your beautiful little girl?"

My mother had trained me well in those automatic responses people expect when enquiring how you are and how's the family? "She's fine. Wonderful, in fact. Yes, we're all fine."

"Is she not with you today?"

It wasn't an accusation. I don't know why I lied except that, when the truth was impossible, even a half-truth seemed undesirable. "My mother's watching her."

"So you're treating yourself to an away day, are you?"

"Sorry?"

"Where are you off to?" *The midwife nodded in the direction of the queue at the ticket office, those at the end checking their watches and timetables; showing signs of impatience.* "New Brighton? Chester?"

"Oh, I'm not going anywhere." *My neck flushed.* "I'm just checking the price of a ticket for my husband. Somewhere he has to go for work next week." *I glanced over at the queue, shame and defeat in my longing gaze.*

The kind woman leaned in confidentially, "My advice, for what it's worth, is that you should always treat yourself if you're lucky enough to find a sitter."

I experimented with a smile. "I don't have time for treats."

"Even a quick cup of coffee can make the world of difference. Being a mother is an uphill struggle. Take my word for it. You have to look after yourself so that you're in a fit state to take care of a child."

But, beside myself with remorse at the thought of what I might have done, I was oblivious to this kindly-meant empathy. It was true that I'd let myself go. I wasn't looking after myself. I had started comfort eating. But she had seen right through me, seen what was - or wasn't - inside me.

Having not been near a church since Anna's christening, I sought out my local priest and insisted he hear my confession.

"Now? Can't it wait?" he asked, as if his was a job with office hours.

"What if I'm run over by a bus before then? You'd have me on your conscience."

Most irregular, I was told. Eleven o'clock on Saturday mornings was the time for confession, he muttered. "Take a seat and wait," he told me, and then kept me waiting so long that my humility was snuffed out, impatience welling until it filled my chest to bursting. Strictly speaking, it was another sin to add to my list, but one matter took priority and, in my mind, the priest should be held accountable for my anger.

When I gave a rough calculation of how long it had been since my last confession, the priest responded with a disapproving sigh. "It's little wonder you were worried about that bus."

Tempted to say, 'I'm sorry, but I've been a little busy!' I held my tongue because kneeling with your head bowed was not the best position for answering back.

While the priest waited for me to finish my penance (I wondered then, as I had wondered when I was a child, if you could admit to murder and get away with three Hail Marys and a Glory Be), he positioned himself rather obviously at the back of the church beside the cross-shaped slot in the wall. I posted just enough loose change to slacken his expression.

These days, of course, you'd see a doctor.

I see-sawed violently between dread and self-pity. Surely I'd be found out? Why did no one notice? I needed to hide who I was from my husband, hide it from the health visitor. And yet, *at the same time, I felt an overwhelming urge to yell, 'Can't you see me, Ray? Can no one see me?'*

Left in charge of a child who was screaming for no apparent reason, I would pick Anna up, holding her under the arms, and feel an overwhelming urge to shake her. Shake her until she stopped, until she was still and silent, regardless of what that would mean.

The skin of Anita's waist crawled with goose bumps. What she read repulsed her. Surely this wasn't just post-natal depression?

Knowing myself to be out of control, I would put Anna back in her crib, holding my hands at arm's length as if to measure the distance between us, repeating, "I know you're not doing it on purpose. I know you're not doing it on purpose," though the opposite was true.

Anita felt herself slipping further and further out of focus. No wonder her mother had been so keen for the books to be packed away in the loft! She clawed her way to standing and pulled the small window open. Standing for a few minutes, holding the metal of the frame, she filled her lungs, praying that the American woman wouldn't see this as an invitation to discuss contemporary literature. Then she sat - there was no option but to read on, to finish this thing.

...somehow imagining that I could see myself: my clenched fists; my manic pacing; saliva growing cobwebby at the corners of my mouth.

But no matter how many times I repeated the words, the message refused to reach my brain. Trembling with realisation at what I might be capable of, I would seek refuge in another room, barricade myself behind the door, the inside part of myself suffocating, the outside part horrified by the knowledge that my child was safer screaming herself to the point of exhaustion. Though I'd had my share of dark moments, I had always assumed I was a nice person. This now appeared to be an illusion I'd been clinging to. I barely knew myself anymore.

A decade later, when Shaken Baby Syndrome was spattered all over the news, people seemed reluctant to believe that the mothers who stood accused were guilty. This was the worst kind of murder - that of a defenceless innocent - and a woman? No, they shuddered at the thought. But I knew. I understood. Because there were days when I had dreamt of seeing my child's scrawny neck snap,

Anita's hand crept over her mouth. As she held the book away from her, the umbilical cord severed.

...and in my dream - though I'm ashamed to admit it - the sight of the neck hanging limp heralded relief. My chest relaxed and I could breathe again. I imagined laying the silent child back in the crib, tucking blankets around her, and being able to love her at last.

Anita thought she had already been dismantled, piece by piece. Why, she asked herself, had she skimmed over the baby photos in the photograph albums? That was where the clues would have been - in her mother's eyes.

I read about these tragic filicide cases in the day-old newspapers Ray abandoned on the kitchen table underneath his used breakfast bowl. Headlines labelled the women as evil, although in their make-up free photographs I saw exhaustion, I saw wretchedness: I saw myself.

By the eighties, there was no doubt in most doctors' minds that shaking could result in infant death. But the medical experts weren't infallible. They made false assumptions. The person in charge of the infant when symptoms presented wasn't necessarily the one who was to blame. For the first twenty-four hours after the damage was done, the child might simply be listless or grouchy. It might vomit. I felt betrayed by the women when they walked free from court, and husbands, boyfriends and uncles were handcuffed and taken into custody, faces hidden from the cameras. I had offered those women my understanding. I had touched the paper outlines of their faces, smoothed their paper brows. But they didn't understand me at all. They weren't like me. I was alone again, everything raw.

Anita tried to picture her mother, as she would have been (far younger than Anita was now): the first few grey hairs perhaps, the appearance of the first few lines. The woman who had given her life was elusive. In many ways, she was less knowable than her father. In life, as in photographs, Patti was often just out of shot.

Discovered by my own mother mid-crisis, both me and the child looking like banshees, it was Clemmie who'd said dispassionately, "Don't be too hard on yourself. It's not all or nothing. There are degrees."

And, clutching at hope, sensing that my mother might understand what I was going through, I dared say out loud: "But it is. It's nothing."

Anita slotted a fingernail between her top and bottom teeth.

Although that wasn't completely true. It wasn't always nothing. Sometimes it was the flipside of love. Though it's terrible to write this, after so much time has passed, sometimes what I felt for Anna was hate.

There it was on the page. Everything Anita had carefully pieced together was wrenched apart.

Hate with such purity and intensity that it appalled me. I was shaking so violently that you'd be forgiven for thinking I had locked myself out of the house in January without a cardigan.

"Give yourself time. It might be a year before you bond." As calm as anything, Clemmie tipped her head as if she was a plumber reconsidering her original assessment of a leaky tap. "Eighteen months, maybe."

"But I expected a boy! I wanted a boy!" Astonished that I had spoken of the taboo for the first time, I was quick to realise that, in doing so, I had made it true.

My mother sat, detached, non-judgmental, without offering comment.

Wanting forgiveness, needing to feel my hair being stroked, I knelt at her feet and rested my head in her lap. I wasn't sure how to phrase the question and so, rather than agonise over words, I came straight out with it. "At what point did it happen for you?" And, with the words, the fight went out of me.

"Love doesn't come into it. You bring a child into the world and it's your responsibility to care for it. It's as simple as that."

Responsibility was a word I recognised. It called me to attention. Sharpish, I sat back on my heels.

Not a flicker of emotion. What I saw, after all of the years of not knowing, but perhaps sensing a subtle undercurrent, was that my own mother hadn't been able to love me.

Anita reread the paragraph. She wished that Ed was sitting beside her so she could tell him that she finally understood what he had been trying to tell her about stars. It was possible to look up at the night sky, a blanket draped around your shoulders, and to see something that had ceased to exist thousands of years ago. But it was also possible to see something that had never existed at all. Most people saw only what they wanted to see: the illusion; the lie.

Moments of enlightenment don't erase everything that has gone before. They don't turn you into a different person overnight. Instead, you have to learn to live alongside another version of yourself. Perhaps she has always been there, but you haven't been paying attention. It's only now that you remember the days when the person who stared back at you from the mirror wasn't the person you expected to see. When you were told that a person in a photograph was you and you had to look again, struggling to find any resemblance.

Incensed, Anita blinked at the words. Having betrayed both her and her father, Patti was now providing instructions for how to live with the truth. To live with it, but not to resolve it. What made things worse was that Anita knew that second person in the mirror, the person who was no longer a stranger.

"The idea that love is all a child needs is nonsense," Clemmie said. "It's only one of a long list of things."

I had never been neglected or maltreated. My grazes had been dabbed with TCP, splinters had been removed, cuts plastered. I had no cause for reproach. If anything, I saw that my mother had compensated for absent feelings by becoming a brilliant actress.

"And you married a good man. Between the two of you, you'll manage."

I didn't dare ask the next logical question, the one I most wanted to know the answer to: 'Do you think things might have been different if I had been a boy?' What I said was, "There were no boys in your family, were there?"

She didn't want to read any more, but her eyes raked the page and settled on the words *hadn't been able to love me.* In a carriage occupied by unsympathetic strangers, Anita acknowledged the truth about her own absence of maternal feelings. Once accepted, other possibilities opened up and, with them, unpalatable questions. Had she selected politics that supported the fact that she'd never wanted children in the first place?

Her answer was a sigh. The heavy rise and fall of Clemmie's chest. The shake of a head.

And though I felt as if the rug had been pulled from under my feet, there was a glimmer of something I hadn't felt for a long time: hope. Perhaps I wasn't as hateful as I had thought. Might whatever I was suffering from - or whatever I was - be genetic?

The Ripleys, it seemed, were incapable of loving their children. Or, at least, we were incapable of loving our daughters, because neither of us experimented further for fear that our first shameful experiences of motherhood would be repeated.

CHAPTER TWENTY

Anita needed to be somewhere other than in the train carriage. Anywhere. As soon the announcement came that they were approaching their final destination, she grabbed her things from the overhead rack. When she excused herself, the American woman made it known that it was quite an inconvenience to move her feet from the seats for someone who'd had better things to do than talk about books.

Beyond the carriage lay an airless limbo. An in-between place of automatic doors that seemed to open and close at will, and an overpowering stench of ammonia. A sound like electricity filled Anita's ears. Head down, avoiding making eye contact with swaying people who had stood for their journeys, her anxiety gathered force.

She burst from the train, onto the platform. There was an unstoppable momentum in the way she skirted around pillars and slow-moving passengers; a man stopping suddenly to send a text; a large green container of sand; up the ramp and into the overcrowded forecourt. No, she didn't want a free newspaper. She contemplated stopping to wash her hands. Scrubbing them raw. But what she'd read couldn't be unknown. The damage was done. Anita had heard people disown children, declare that so-and-so was dead to them, and thought it harsh. The idea that her family was dead to her was almost unbearable. And yet...

She couldn't allow herself to think too far ahead. Only that she needed to add to the distance between her and Liverpool, her and a mother who... who... The word 'hate' clouded her vision.

Passing a row of taxis, she pressed forwards onto Euston Road, the bustling thoroughfare linking Euston and St Pancras, somewhere pedestrians looked out of place unless they were trundling wheeled cases. Anita came from a city built around a bustling river port, where journeys began and ended. Out went ships loaded with coal dug from Lancashire, salt from Cheshire, metal from Birmingham, livestock from Wales and gunpowder from Ireland. In came the bananas, the palm oil, the silk, the ivory, the raw cotton, the jute. In came brandy, rum, tea and coffee. On any other day, Anita would have relished being back in the big city; the flow of foot-traffic and the relief of anonymity. Today the British Library and the gothic extravagance of the hotel were red-brick blurs.

She hurried onwards as if St Pancras might offer sanctuary, forgetfulness. A gleaming cathedral of coffee shops, cafés, boutiques and champagne bars, willing to relieve milling Eurostar passengers of any spare sterling they might be hoarding. People glanced up from lattes, slim laptops and text messages to frown. There was something suspicious about an adult moving so fast in a place where others lingered and queued. They stopped in their tracks, looking to see who might be giving chase.

In her single-mindedness, Anita was greeted by melancholic chords coming from a shabby black piano. An offering for the homesick and the weary. Travellers straggled, some perching on upright cases, an inconvenience to anyone intent on walking in a straight line from one end of the concourse to the other.

As she said, "Excuse me," dodging a near collision, Anita veered off in a less congested direction, cutting directly in front of the piano. She was aware of the pianist's pork-pie hat, his rocking motion, but these peripheral things didn't concern her. She sidestepped the chains securing the battered instrument - as if someone might actually wheel it out of the station and up the Euston Road! The tune ceased without warning, then a sea-change: the opening bars of an old Tom Waits number. A lightness of touch and a gravelly drawl. A stab of longing, the music was inside Anita's head, her chest. The lyrics to *Martha* had once meant something. And then they stopped.

Heavy footsteps and breathlessness. "Anita! Nita! Couldn't you hear me calling you?"

That voice! Feeling as if she'd been caught red-handed she turned and saw the man in the pork-pie hat. The floor tilted, the pull in her stomach immediate and intense. In another lifetime they had sat on a plane with their foreheads touching and she had felt the flow of electricity pass effortlessly between them. For a moment, that single memory eclipsed everything else.

"I was looking at your photograph on Facebook five minutes ago, then I looked up and... well, here you are."

Then he was grinning, and his unrestrained delight made it difficult for Anita to explain that she had suffered a moment's madness.

That she would never ordinarily have contacted him.

But she hadn't expected. Least of all today, when there was nothing left to shore her up.

It was *him*.

Prior to her train journey to Liverpool, Anita hadn't thought about him for years, and now... The hat helped with the impression that the face was unaltered. Her focus on his eyes, shadowed by the brim, Anita's stomach somersaulted violently. She felt weakened by the knowledge that she had no control over it.

His face fell, as if it had struck him that it was inappropriate to look quite so pleased to see her. "I was sorry to see all that stuff about the fire. You've obviously been having a pretty rough time."

Jolted back to the here and now, Anita didn't say anything because she had no idea what she might say. The burnt-out shell of the house seemed vague and shadowy. *My mother never loved me* was hardly a suitable opener.

"Well, that's me done. I'm all out of small talk. It's your turn." He shifted his weight to his other foot and indicated over his shoulder with his thumb. "Or, if it's easier, I can go back to the piano and pretend I didn't see you."

Anita was afraid that if she opened her mouth to speak, the words *Do you remember that time we kissed in the lift of the Empire State Building?* would tumble out. But she didn't want him to go. She wanted to hold him there by whatever means it took, even if she appeared ridiculous. "Why do you use a photograph of a pig for your Facebook profile?" she blurted.

"Oh, that." He scratched the side of his nose, and the gesture was so familiar that Anita wanted to demand: *That! Do that again.* "My daughter managed to log into my account and change the photo for me. I could have reacted, but I accepted it as my punishment for being a shitty father."

Having been in such a rush to get somewhere, it struck Anita with an absolute simplicity: she had arrived. "I thought you said there were better things to do with your time than having children."

"Ah, you know what women are like with their witchcraft. But I caught on. I said, 'two is my absolute limit.'"

"And are you? A shitty father, I mean." Christ! What kind of a question was that to ask?

It seemed to amuse him. "From the point of view of a

fourteen-year-old? I'd say that I probably am. She's a good girl. She thinks that in order to support her mother she has to be anti me. Wants to believe someone's to blame. It makes things tidier. Also," his smile was wistful and he pushed the pork-pie hat back slightly, "I kind of like the pig. But what about you? Did you cave in?"

She swallowed. "Cave in?"

"Do you have any children?"

"No."

He laughed. "Probably very sensible."

"Do you want to get drunk?" Anita heard herself ask. It wasn't what she'd intended to say, but it was what her twenty-one year old self might have come out with, everything slightly exaggerated. The idea that you might live for the moment, damn mortgages, kids and the rest of the world.

"It's a bit early." He let his mouth shrug for him. "But what the hell? I suppose I could manage a small beer."

The barman wore a crisp white uniform shirt and a green apron. He seemed to float in front of a backdrop of gleaming bottles. She ordered Irish whiskies for them both. "Bushmills, please. And no ice." After stealing a glance over her shoulder - it was him! - she handed the barman her debit card.

"Now, that *is* a very small beer," he said as he examined the contents of the tumbler and clinked it against hers, a question-laden gesture. Sipping, he closed his eyes in pleasure. "You remembered."

Anita was pricked by a vivid recollection; another occasion when his eyes had closed in the same way. Fearing her expression might be transparent, she hopped onto the black leather seat of the bar stool. It was positioned a little too close to his and their elbows touched. She slotted the heels of her shoes into place. There was something reckless about sitting on a high stool, owning the knowledge that your feet couldn't reach the floor.

"You know, I like this train station," he mused, and taking the material of her sleeve between two of his fingers, he pulled lightly and said, "Did you ever see that film where Tom Hanks plays this guy who lives at JFK airport?"

She stared at his hand, slightly startled. "I don't think I did, no."

He laughed, closed mouthed. "Do you still sleep through as many films as you used to?"

She could feel the pull of her sleeve, as the material tightened under her wrist. He seemed to have no intention of letting go. His little finger had crept to the base of her thumb.

"More, I expect."

"War had broken out in his home country. He couldn't enter the USA and he couldn't go back. He was stuck in the airport."

While he was speaking, Anita sucked her bottom lip, letting a mouthful of whiskey flow over it, something else she hadn't done for a long time. Under the sweep of her tongue, her lip felt swollen, as if it wasn't part of her. Suddenly twenty-five years seemed to be a very short period of time. She felt like laughing. "I think I may be Tom Hanks."

"You can't be." There was only his face, his words. The moment was both dangerous and in its perfect place. "This is *my* story. I'm Tom Hanks."

"Why? Why should you get to be him?" Anita was conscious of her every movement, but it wasn't a self-consciousness she wanted to shy away from. Under his gaze, she was bold, attractive.

"You haven't even seen the film!"

"I don't need to."

She told him things - everything from the fire to her mother's book. She might have tried to fool herself that she was experimenting to see how it sounded to talk about her mother's book out loud, but this was an illicit conversation in an illicit setting. The barman removed glasses from the dishwasher, polished them, held them up to the light, and pretended not to be listening. Sentences came out in a rush, largely uncensored - although a clinging loyalty made Anita pause before spilling the details of her problems with Ed. After all, they might exist only inside her head.

"Fuck," he said when she had finished. "I hope you know I mean that in a sympathetic way."

She still couldn't quite believe that he was beside her, listening to her, their knees almost touching; a collision between what she had believed to be her neatly compartmentalised past and present. "Am I overreacting?"

Over the years, on the odd occasion when she'd thought of their relationship, she told herself it had been a disaster. Nothing more than a hormone-induced chemical reaction. She had convinced herself that you couldn't live like that in the long-term, with everything in razor-sharp focus. Now she wondered, had she sabotaged it?

"Who was that girl?"

"What girl?"

"The one you were singing to."

"Anita, flirting's part of my job, you know that. Every single person in the audience must be convinced I'm singing to them."

Had she run away from herself? Was that what she'd done? It was a shock to discover that they still shared a connection, that something had survived which was both rare and real.

"You react in the way you react. It's all you can do. You went back home to the people who know you best, and this is what you came away with." She breathed his words in, just as she always had. There was a quality to the way that he listened to her and understood her precise meaning. "Although." He checked the contents of his back pocket, let go of her sleeve, raised an index finger, and addressed the barman. "Can we get two more of these? Doubles. Thank you."

"Although?" She prompted, unwilling to share his attention, leaving her arm where he could take her sleeve between his fingers again, though he didn't.

He frowned; a moment's seriousness: "So, this book. It's a memoir?"

"I don't really know what you'd call it. It's written in the first person, but..." Anita shook her head, finding she was not quite as ready to discuss it as she thought she'd been.

"Is it possible that your mother told her story to someone and *they* wrote it down for her?"

Anita was adamant. "My mother would never do that. She doesn't *talk* about things."

He considered this. "You write what you know while you're learning your craft, it doesn't matter if it's novels or songs. So let's just say that your mother's written a novel and based it on her experience. It doesn't mean that every word is true. On the other hand..."

"I was willing to go along with that." She noticed the way that two of his teeth had overlapped. "Don't cancel out what you just said."

"I'm trying to offer a little balance. Or do you want me to only say the things I think you want to hear?"

Two more tumblers arrived and the barman pushed one closer to Anita. She raised her eyes, briefly. There was only one face she wanted to lose herself in. "Even *I'm* not sure what I want to hear," she heard herself say.

"Sarah. That's my..." He looked down and nodded, from which Anita understood that the word *wife* was no longer appropriate and *ex-wife* was too painful. "She persuaded me to go to the South Bank to see Esther Freud talk about this semi-autobiographical novel of hers. Hideous Something, I can't remember the title. It hadn't crossed the author's mind that her sister would take it personally when she put their childhood out there."

"It's good to know the Freuds are as screwed up as the rest of us." She hadn't intended to be funny, or not as funny as his hands slapping the bar and head-thrown-back laughter implied.

"Ah, Anita, you've still got it. But you don't think this book of your mother's is semi-autobiographical, do you?"

She shook her head slowly. "It explains too many things. I read it and... I don't know. It's as if I spent my life behind the lens of a camera, ignoring everything I couldn't see through the viewfinder. And suddenly it's all..." Her hands mimed an explosion on either side of her head.

"Panoramic vision," he said. "Sometimes it's best that everything's out in the open."

Anita resisted. "I'm a big girl. I know some people struggle to bond with their children. It's nobody's fault. But why did she have to publish a book about it?"

"So that others don't think they're the only ones going through it."

But Anita didn't want to believe that her mother had done something noble. "Then she should have written a self-help book."

"Maybe - but, if I'm honest, I've written some pretty personal songs over the years. I never *dreamed* that the people they're about would recognise themselves. People rarely see themselves as others see them. It's everyone else who claims it's about *them*."

"*You're So Vain.*" Anita gave a rueful smile. She wondered, but couldn't ask, if he had written a song about her. About their break-up. She remembered feeling as if her heart had been ripped out, surprised to learn through mutual friends that he'd made a similar claim. "What happened to your band? You were so good."

"As you can see," he swirled the whiskey around his glass, "I'm a highly sought-after musician."

"That's your job?" she asked, glancing towards the piano. "I'd assumed..."

"What? That I was doing it for fun? I busk when I'm between contracts. I still get a reasonable amount of session work. There's the possibility of an album coming up - I can't tell you who it's with. And before you ask, yes, I really *am* that superstitious. But if I pull it off, there might be a world tour."

"I'm glad you still play. I'd be very sad to hear you'd packed away your guitar."

"So, did you get to lead the life you thought you'd lead?"

"Yes." She sipped her second measure. Her bottom lip felt pleasantly numb. "And no."

"It's not all it's cracked up to be, is it?"

She didn't need to ask what he meant. "If we'd bumped into each other three weeks ago, I'd have said yes. No hesitation."

"Your fella..." He snapped his fingers.

"Ed."

"Right. He's one of the good guys?"

"Rock solid." Anita realised she'd overdone it, the result not nearly as convincing as she'd have liked.

"Well, that's something. I'm happy for you."

Anita felt confused. It wasn't right to be here, talking about Ed. He wasn't part of this other life. Or was it this bar - this second drink - that was wrong?

"I'm *less* happy for me. I thought you might whisk me away somewhere." He gave one of her feet a playful kick. (This was when it *was* acceptable to nudge someone with your foot.) "I have very fond memories."

As intoxicated by his words as she was, the admission that this was more than a drink caused Anita to call a halt. Coffee would have been safer. "You know, I should probably head off."

"You said 'drunk'!" he protested. "You're not even falling off your barstool."

"You know me. I always was a lightweight." She picked up her belongings, took what she intended to be one final look at him and waited for her chest to rise and fall. "Thank you. I needed that." She wondered whether... just a peck on the cheek perhaps. But he showed no signs of moving.

He raised his glass in salute. "Next time, New York."

She laughed and turned.

"Have you ever been back?" he called out, just as she was about to walk through the door.

Perhaps he had sensed her hesitation. This meeting shouldn't have happened. She might never see him again. "No," she said.

"Good."

"Have you?" Perhaps there would be a next time. Her hair would be cropped and grey and he would be fat. Elderly people looking back on this meeting as a missed opportunity.

"Yes." Anita felt deflated to hear this. "I had to. It was work." Then he grinned. "But you shouldn't. It wasn't the same."

CHAPTER TWENTY-ONE

adybird, ladybird, fly away home. Your house is on fire,
your children are... Anita came to with a jolt. She had
no idea where she was. Squinting through the grime of
the carriage window, ugly fencing identified the station her
train was pulling away from as Hackbridge. Hers was the
next stop. She settled back briefly, the makings of a headache
announcing that she was dehydrated. As conflicting thoughts
competed, she convinced herself that her mother's book
should take priority. Stepping off the train, queuing at the
ticket barrier, the idea of not thinking appealed. And it was in
this mood of trying not to remember that Anita realised her
feet had chosen the route back to Chalkdale.

She had suffered temporary lapses before. Once, back in
middle school, she'd gone back to her old desk in 4C and had
sat next to Gordon Greening for over five minutes before she
realised what she'd done. "Can't bear to keep away from me?"
he'd grinned, something repeated as fact in the lunch queue,
sprouting a rumour that she was quick to squash. But this was
unforgivable. And yet, standing in front of the carcass of her
house, part of Anita wanted to take her suitcase and carrier
bags and sit in its centre, among the wreckage of things she'd
been sure of.

"I was wondering where you'd got to!" Ed appeared at the kitchen door as she was busy untangling herself from the handles of carrier bags. "You should have called. I would have picked you up from the station."

She dismissed the slight hesitation she sensed before he stepped forwards to kiss her. Instead, conscious of the taste of whiskey in her mouth, Anita angled her head to avoid breathing on him. "I'm a bit groggy. I fell asleep and almost missed my stop."

"You've been drinking."

"Yes." She refused to react to the disapproval in Ed's tone. "I bumped into a friend I hadn't seen for over twenty-five years. A musician. He was busking at St Pancras. You know the piano they have at the station?" She hadn't lied. All those things were true, and yet she hurried to change the subject. "Something smells good. Is that lamb?"

"I've made a tagine. It's keeping warm."

Hearing Ed's voice reminded Anita how wounded he'd sounded on the phone. She had kept things from him Building up to an apology, Anita paused as she passed the living room door. The far wall was now a deep orange. "You've decorated!"

"Do you like it?"

She stepped inside the room - what had been two smaller rooms knocked together. The colour was the one Anita had chosen for their living room at Chalkdale. She had never been sure that Ed liked it, but he had brought it here, to their temporary home. "I do. It makes me feel more like my old self."

His expression brightened. "I spent hours in B&Q. I'm not sure it's exactly the same as the one we used before, but it was the closest I could find."

"It's perfect." Anita's eyes were welling. It was true that she felt more like her old self, but her old self was now armed with new knowledge. She was unable to hide the quiver in her lip.

"Come here," Ed said, and she allowed herself to be held

against his chest, letting him believe that his gesture had moved her.

Anita composed herself. "When did you find time to decorate? You were at Reuben's party for most of yesterday."

Did Ed colour slightly? "The walls were in good nick so there was no need for prep. I did the first coat on Friday evening and the second coat this morning." As her gaze drifted to the skirting board, he added, "Don't look too closely. I've still got a bit of touching up to do. The masking tape bled."

And so Anita broadened her view, taking in the two-seater. "I don't believe it. Matching cushions!" This time it was Anita whose arms circled Ed's waist.

"Actually, they're on loan from Natalie."

Experiencing a nameless shrinking feeling, she stepped back and looked again. "That was sweet of her." It was something Ed's mother might have said when unwrapping a gift - *"That was sweet of you"* - meaning that whatever it was would soon find its way to a charity shop. "I'll just take my case upstairs so it's out of the way."

"Shall I put the kettle on? Or will you carry on drinking now that you've started?"

Unsure if criticism was intended, Anita chose to ignore it: "Tea would be lovely, thanks." There it was again: that echo of a middle-aged person (and though Reuben thought her ancient, middle-aged wasn't how Anita saw herself).

She washed her hands, catching sight of her red-eyed reflection. Was this really how she'd looked just over an hour ago as she sat on a barstool sipping whiskey? Anita unpacked her make-up, applied powder and mascara, and brushed her teeth. After arranging her new clothes in the wardrobe - something she took satisfaction in - Anita pulled the matted black and white toy (supposedly, but not recognisably, a bear) from her case. It was difficult to know how to hold such a small toy with adult-sized hands. She thought of Reuben's snappable wrists. *Imagine Iris was a child. Imagine holding her under the arms and shaking her until her neck went limp...*

A wave of nausea passed through Anita. For a moment of perfect clarity, she was gripped by the knowledge that she might be capable of such a thing. Her thumbs pressed into the chest of the bear, so obviously not a human child, and yet... Blood surging, Anita appreciated her mother's need to remove herself from the room, knowing that the child would be safer left screaming.

This was madness. As a teenager, she used to babysit regularly. She had held Reuben when he was just a few days old. Other friends' children too - crying children.

Anita didn't know what to do with Iris, except that she needed to hide the toy. Somewhere out of sight. And so Anita snatched at the handles of the plastic bag containing all the evidence that remained of her frayed childhood and stuffed it inside. Unceremoniously, she crammed the bag into the bedside cupboard, rearranging it several times so that the door would shut.

Then, trying to create an illusion of being in control, she straightened the Buddha's head and stood the brass doorknob beside it. But there was something she had forgotten: her mother's book.

Strange. There was no bulge in the side pocket of her case. She felt inside it: empty. It wasn't in the John Lewis's carrier bags. Her handbag, perhaps it would be there! Trying to cling to hope, Anita ran downstairs and checked.

Seized by the urge to cry, she sank to the bottom step and sat with her elbows resting on her knees, head gripped in her hands. The last image Anita had of the book was when it lay on the table in the train carriage. She must have been so desperate to get off that she'd left it behind.

Beyond her open handbag, collapsed between her feet, Ed's shoes stepped into view. "Have you done your usual trick and left something at your parents' house?" he asked.

"A paperback." Anita bit down on the end of her thumb. She had hoped it wouldn't be necessary to explain everything. In her imagination, she had simply handed the book to Ed, watching him reach for his reading glasses, waiting for the moment when he recognised the anonymous woman he was reading about. "I must have left it on the train."

"That's what happens when you drink at lunchtime."

Anita bristled. "Not the Carshalton train. The one from Liverpool."

"We'll have to get you another copy." He returned to tending the couscous, tipping the Pyrex bowl towards his stomach and forking it. "Dinner's almost ready. Are you going to give your folks a quick call to let them know you're home?"

"I called from the station." Anita felt uncomfortable that the lie slipped so easily from her, but she couldn't risk her mother picking up.

"They're obviously not speaking to each other. Your dad's just texted me."

"Hah!" Anita could barely believe she was being checked up on. "I expect Mum's upstairs in her office and he's down the bottom of the garden."

Ed spoke over the scraping of a fork on glass. "I'll text him, shall I?"

"No, you've got your hands full. My phone's here."

"Your tea will be a bit cold. I've opened a bottle of red for dinner."

"I'll just have a glass of water." She put her phone away and went to help herself, draining the glass in a few gulps and then re-filling it. "Shall I lay the table?" She pulled open the cutlery drawer.

"It's all done. Why don't you choose some music?"

Confronted by the tablecloth and the unlit candle, Anita understood why Ed had appeared to be so upset when she'd arrived home, late and hungover. She scrolled through the list of artists on the iPod and paused. *Martha* had been playing on a loop inside her head. Even if Ed would never know the reason why, that choice would be inappropriate. After several moments' indecision, Anita settled on Elbow, one of the bands they'd seen several times. She chose their first album, trying to recapture something of their early years together. The drumbeat seemed to come from a place inside her chest.

Her smile felt painted on as Ed lit the candle and returned to the kitchen to fetch the plates of food. While he poured the wine, she recounted how her father had based his purchase of Merlot on Ed's recommendation. The tagine was excellent, the lamb especially tender. Ed expressed his usual reservations: it wasn't as good as the last time; he worried that he'd overdone it with the lemon.

"I'm going to have to disagree with you."

Though they said other things, the subjects they skirted around pressed heavily on Anita's mind. She needed to clear the air between them. But opening her mouth to apologise, Anita found herself clashing with Ed. And instead of offering *You go first*, he frowned. "Please. I really need to get this off my chest." It was as if he was calling to mind the first line of a carefully rehearsed speech. And as he said, "I did a lot of thinking while you were away," Anita had a sense that she was sitting very still and that everything around her was in motion, the plates and cutlery sliding off the table.

Ed thought they had a problem and he knew how to fix it. Anita had never suffered from migraines but, with pressure building inside her temples, she imagined that this feeling signalled the last chance to flee to a darkened room. The words kept coming, sentence after sentence. Ed knew that she'd never pressed for marriage, but thought that now was a time they both needed something permanent and real. "I had this all planned. But then something happened yesterday, and I can't ask you the question I want to ask until I've been completely honest."

Anita felt her fixed expression crack. This wasn't how the script inside her head went. She gripped the stem of her wine glass and hoped to neutralise what must have been an appalled expression.

Ed's eyes were clenched shut and he was shaking his head. "This is even more difficult than I thought it would be."

"What?" she asked, wanting and yet not wanting to know.

"Natalie and I had a few drinks last night. I don't know if she told you, but Phil had rung at the last moment and invented an excuse for not going to Reuben's party." A sickening dread preceded Ed's every word. "She managed to hold it together all afternoon. It was only after Rubes went to bed that I realised how upset she was." He had been there after Reuben *went to bed?* "So I gave her a hug and -"

It was as if Anita was outside the room looking in. Someone else was seated in her place at the table. Wanting to end this agony as quickly as possible, she heard herself prompt, "And?"

"And then I kissed her."

She had settled in the belief that Ed was not the bad guy. Funny. Now that she thought about it, those were Natalie's words. Confronted with a wall that she now saw was the colour of flames, Anita's eyes dropped to the remains of the tagine on her plate. The lamb that had been marinating for two days; the preserved lemon that Ed had gone out of his way to buy. All the evidence was here. There was no doubt that he had planned every detail. And the plain fact was that Ed wouldn't have *been* at Reuben's party in the first place if it wasn't for her. But simultaneously, Anita recalled the intense pull of attraction to another man, far more recent than the kiss Ed had described. Something she'd had no control over.

"It was totally my fault. Totally." Ed was contrite, she could see that. His hands clawed at the skin around his mouth and chin. "Natalie asked me to leave straight away. I've apologised - this morning, when I went to collect the car." *So you've been back?* "She said she wouldn't tell you -" *Oh, did she?* "- but I had to." Anita was aware that her eyebrows jumped slightly. "I couldn't lie to you. Even if this is the least romantic proposal you're ever likely to receive."

Ed still thought that it was appropriate to propose - under *these* circumstances? After it had waited fifteen years. Though she closed her eyes, Anita was calmer than she would have ever thought possible. The fingers of one of her hands flexed. "Can we stop right there."

"I understand completely if you're angry."

"I'm not angry. Not in the way you think I am. And I can see that you had this," she indicated to the orange wall, the table, her plate, "planned perfectly before whatever happened... happened." She was back in the road outside Chalkdale watching their house burn.

He clutched her hand. *"Nothing* happened."

His choice of words - his emphasis - made Anita bristle. Clearly, something *had* happened or they wouldn't be having this conversation. But the truth was that Anita had already heard more than she wanted to. "And I believe you. But I can't do this today. Not now."

"I think we need to start thinking about the future."

Resentment tugged. Even now, Ed thought he knew best. "Well, I can't," Anita said firmly, and with authority, but the flicker of her hand betrayed her. "Because I've just had the rug pulled from under my feet and I'm stuck in the past, rewriting history."

"Nothing's changed -"

"Ed, listen to me." She gripped the edge of the table and leaned forwards. Only suppressed rage can make a person shake the way she was shaking. "The kiss with Natalie? It can't hurt me, not today." She watched his jaw drop. "And if now's the time for honesty, the only time you've *ever* hurt me in fifteen years of living together was when you told me how you've had to stick at a job you hate because of me." Wide-eyed, Ed was breathing very hard. "But today, I found out that my mother..." Anita's voice cracked. Her throat had closed up. Her fist was a stopper for her mouth.

Ed sounded genuinely shocked. "Your mother's what? Oh my God, she's not ill, is she?" He infused the word *ill* with such finality, it was as though Anita was hearing the news. *Your mother has emphysema.* Patti wasn't a healthy weight. She shuffled and wheezed and was often breathless. Though Ron was ten years her senior, Anita's father was the fitter of the pair by far.

She shook her head, dislodging the image, then took a sip of red wine to loosen her throat. "It turns out that my mother didn't want me. She's never been able to love me."

For a moment, Ed looked as if he'd been slapped. "That's ridiculous."

Those were the words he chose.

"She *told* you this?" Ed seemed close to laughter.

"No, I read about it." She watched as wax dripped down the side of the candle he had lit.

"She wrote you a letter?"

Anita registered her disappointment. His questions irked. "Actually, she's written a book. It's been published anonymously. But it's her, alright. And it's Dad, it's me."

"*That's* the book you lost on the train?" Ed scraped his chair back and started pacing the pine floorboards. One of his arms was wrapped around his torso, the opposite hand at his mouth. He seemed to be coming round to the idea that this wasn't something Anita, with her wild imagination, had dreamt up. "I'm so... On top of everything else..."

She looked up at him. He had thought her capable of

coping with the news that he had kissed her best friend. But that was *before*. "I asked Dad not to tell Mum about my visit. I didn't want her to wear herself out cleaning the house from top to bottom - and she would have done. So she wasn't prepared. The books were stacked in my old room."

"The one we stay in?"

Anita nodded. Now that she thought about it, Anita had a recollection of cardboard boxes, but trying to follow the thread of how the boxes had come to be unpacked defeated her.

"Does your dad know?"

"I don't think either of us was ever meant to find out." Then it struck her. Ed was suggesting that she needed to tell him. "Oh, no. *I* can't -"

"He'll find out one way or another."

"But not from me."

Ed went around the back of her chair and folded his arms around her. A vision of how he had comforted Natalie seeped through the gaps, whispering, *If he had held Natalie like this, the kiss could never have happened.*

After what might have been several minutes or several hours Ed said, "You didn't phone your dad, did you?"

She wondered if he imagined he had mended something. One hug, and the crisis had been averted. "I couldn't. Not with this on my mind."

"Then I'll send him a quick text. He'll be worried."

Too exhausted to argue, Anita sat hugging herself.

Minutes later Ed returned, carrying his new slim-line laptop and rocked back onto the low sofa, his feet lifting slightly. "Do you mind if I look it up?"

"I don't mind." Only the echo of *That's ridiculous* stopped Anita from saying more. In fact, she minded very much. She wanted Ed firmly on her side, knowing what she knew.

"What's it called?"

Anita released a bitter laugh. *"An Unknown Woman."*

He frowned. "Isn't that -?"

"The portrait I wrote that article about. But it's more than that." She went and perched beside Ed as he set his mouth and typed the title into the search engine. There was only one result. Anita was curious to know how she would feel, seeing the story of her life for sale. Ed looked at her as if to say *Are you sure?* and she responded with a nod.

Be the first one to write a review, the page invited.

"OK," Ed said, steeling himself as he clicked on the *Look inside* feature. Anita no longer wanted to look. She knew what he would find. Instead, she folded her arms and sat back, while Guy Garvey sang lullabies of people and places, as if you would never find yourself exiled from your own life, as if everything was cyclical and, if you became unhinged, you could retrace your footsteps and try again. As if there were always second chances, and family waiting to welcome you with open arms. Before today, Anita's understanding was that home was the place you returned to when you needed to be understood.

She heard Ed sigh deeply. He didn't take back the hastily-spoken dismissal as she'd thought he might. Part of her needed to hear him say, *I'm sorry I didn't take you seriously.* And the fact that they were now united by knowledge was less comforting than it would have been otherwise.

Eventually he spoke. "How much of it did you read?"

"A few chapters. Six... seven..."

"And you don't think she exaggerated for the sake of a good story?"

"She didn't put her name to it. What does that say to you?"

He appeared to accept this. "Shall I download it?"

Anita's eyelids felt heavy. She pressed her cool fingertips against them. "I don't know."

"One of us should read it from start to finish." He clicked

on the *Buy now* button. There it was again: Ed interpreting her indecision as an invitation to take matters into his own hands. She understood immediately that, whilst Ed claimed to be on her side, whatever she chopped down, he would use to build bridges.

They had been lying in the darkness for some time. Freed from the fear that her expression might be transparent, Anita had been batting thoughts back and forth, trying them on for size. Let off the leash, there was no logic, no order. And, contrary to everything she'd told Ed, it wasn't her mother's book that monopolised them.

Gustav Klimt's painting came to mind. The woman turns her lips away, the kiss is planted on her cheek, and her face remains pure. Had Ed misread Natalie's need for comfort and been rejected? But Ed was five inches taller than Natalie. You can't kiss someone who's shorter than you unless her face is raised towards yours. Exactly how innocent had Natalie been?

The speed at which Ed had jumped to her defence had surprised Anita. It surprised her still. Had he claimed he was to blame so as to leave their friendship intact? Perhaps Ed and Natalie had agreed between themselves that this was what he would do.

Burn it down.

Watch it all burn.

Burn it all.

Had she suggested the precise words he might use?

Then Anita berated herself. Speculation wasn't only pointless, it was dangerous. Natalie had given up her bedroom for them. Who else would have offered them a room?

And Ed. He had sounded wounded on the phone. She had kept things from him, it was true. But would that have been enough to make him throw himself at her best friend?

If she was angry at anything, it was Ed's honesty. What

purpose had it served? Had he wanted to wipe the slate clean? Or remove the danger of surprise if, at some future date, Natalie were to say: "I suppose Ed told you that he tried to kiss me once. We were both very drunk."

On the other hand, what would Anita have confessed if she'd been completely honest? *I bumped into an ex-boyfriend and the pull in my stomach was so immediate, so electric, that it floored me.* Though the meeting had been accidental, if guilt was in premeditation, it barely mattered that Anita had jumped down from her barstool and left. Because there was little doubt. Had she stayed a moment longer, Anita would have acted - and it wouldn't have stopped with a kiss. This time, she was honest enough to recognise that she'd run away from herself.

Then the parallel: Ed had said that Natalie asked him to leave. Without this push, might he have stayed? Then it wouldn't have been *nothing*. But how far would things have gone?

It was true. These things *do* happen - but not without a build-up of sorts. She and Ed had been living in Natalie's house. Sleeping in her bed, for Christ's sake. Ed had seen Natalie making breakfast. She had poured his morning coffee dressed in pyjamas, braless. Anita had found herself staring at dark shadows as she sat at the breakfast bar. Though she hadn't caught Ed looking, he wouldn't have had much choice. Did Natalie undo another button while she was reaching for the coffee pot, her back turned? Had something started then, when Anita was there, *in the room?* Or had Ed always been attracted to Natalie? When Phil left, they had ceased to be a four. These past two years, dinner settings had been lopsided arrangements. Anita had imagined Ed must have felt as if he was intruding, but perhaps she'd been blind?

But she was the one who'd insisted they took Natalie up on her offer of a room. Ed made it all too clear that he would have preferred a hotel.

What was a kiss, when you thought about it? Wasn't thinking about another man while lying in Ed's arms the greater betrayal? Anita had experienced something far more significant than a kiss. Intimacy. Fear of re-igniting something intense and electrifying.

The cushions bothered Anita, now that she thought about them. Would Natalie have asked Ed to leave, then called him back from the end of the path and said, "Wait! Take these cushions. They'll go with the orange wall"?

But you dug at your peril. Far safer to burrow into yourself.

So what if Natalie *had* kissed Ed? Anita had no doubt that theirs was a sudden collision. They either regretted it or didn't regret it, but had decided in a terribly adult fashion that it couldn't go any further.

It had never been so clear to Anita as it was in that moment, masked by darkness, why her parents didn't communicate. They were perfectly capable of narrowing down possibilities for themselves. Did it matter which one of several equally unpalatable possibilities was the truth?

One thing was certain. Ed wouldn't have told her about the kiss if it wasn't over. The telling brought things to a neat end.

Or was she wrong about this? What about the next time Ed suggested that they drop round to play with Reuben's new computer game? Anita knew herself. Even though she'd told Ed that the kiss didn't matter, she would watch him. It didn't matter that Ed wasn't Jason, or that Natalie wasn't Lizzie. She would wonder what they were up to the minute they left the room. History demanded this of her, and she would grow to hate herself for it.

Rotating his head, Ed interrupted Anita's thoughts. "What now?" he said.

Anita had thought he was asleep. She took her time answering. "I think we should paint this room green."

"That's not what I meant."

She propped her head up on one elbow. "I know."

"I don't *hate* my job, but it *is* just a job. I need something more. Something outside work."

She was relieved to be talking about a subject that no longer seemed to matter quite as much. "You want to build a house."

"I'd like to take a stab at it, yes."

She fumbled for the switch of her bedside light, threw back the duvet, rocked forwards and let momentum carry her to her feet.

"We don't have to talk about it now." Ed turned onto his side, watching as she padded over to the chest of drawers. "I just wanted to say."

"Here," she said, examining the brass doorknob that she'd picked up. *What does betrayal look like? A knowing look or a kiss?* She handed it to him. "It's a present from my dad. He said we don't have to build a house around it, but perhaps you should - if it's a project you're after."

"I thought -" He stopped and Anita saw he had caught up. She had set herself apart.

"I can't promise that I'll want to live in it, especially not at the moment. But if it's really going to take two years to build, I may feel very differently by then."

With this clarification, Ed seemed to weigh the proposition. Would he want to go to all that trouble and then have to consider selling his dream home?

She climbed back into bed. "I'm sorry if it's not what you want to hear, but it's the only answer I can give you at the moment."

He was silent for a few moments before saying, "Are you going back to work tomorrow?"

"No." She switched off the light, keen to return to her private thoughts. "I'm going to see Dr Kernow."

She sensed his silent approval.

"Are you going to talk to your mother?" he asked.

"No."

Though Ed didn't force the subject, Anita knew he wouldn't let it go.

Resigned to the prospect of a sleepless night, she made herself comfortable, but shortly afterwards Anita entered the burning building of the Walker Art Gallery, securing the thermal imaging equipment over her eyes. What should she save from the priceless collections? Works by George Stubbs or Sir Joshua Reynolds? Claude Monet or Paul Cézanne? John Millais or Dante Rossetti? David Hockney or Patrick Caulfield? Or should she try to reach Hilliard's portrait of Elizabeth I? It wasn't one of Anita's favourites but she felt sure she could persuade Roz to find it a home at the Palace.

She woke, convulsed by coughing. Beside her, Ed was still. Rather than risk waking him, Anita decided to move to the spare room, but she hesitated in the doorway, looking at his shadowy outline. This was what the fire had set in motion. All of it.

CHAPTER TWENTY-TWO

She waited for Roz in a grey-walled café within sight of the curve of Hampton Court Bridge. Anita had chosen a table where she could see and be seen from the door. Lunchtime trade hadn't yet begun, although a pleasant hum of preparation was in progress. Empty picture frames of different shapes and sizes were hung on the upper part of the walls and they, too, were painted the same matte grey. It was a statement of sorts, although it wasn't clear to Anita what the message was.

She and Ed had breakfasted together that morning. "I heard from the loss adjuster," he'd said as he held a slice of toast vertically to butter it. "The site's going to be cleared on Thursday."

Her own knife had stilled. *Cleared.* It sounded so impersonal. "This Thursday?" she asked, though there was no room for doubt. The first house to be built in Chalkdale would be the first to go. They had failed as caretakers.

"I thought we should both be there. I'm going to take the day off work."

Anita imagined the stench when the charred remains were stirred up, pictured the garden turned to wasteland. She lost her appetite. "I don't know..."

"Please, Anita. I'd like us to do it together. I never thought that you could grieve for a house, but -" Ed's expression was as pained as she had ever seen it, and she found herself nodding.

So it was to be a funeral. They would stand side by side and watch the diggers move in. They would wear hard hats. Elderly slipper-wearing neighbours would cling to the frames of their front doors and pay their respects. She imagined the sickening scrape of metal on concrete; the vibrations of drills; rubble carted away by lorry. Anita wasn't sure that she would be able to bear it, but it would be her final chance to say goodbye.

Perhaps it would be a way to move on, she thought as she now stirred her latte, absent-mindedly, reducing the barista's artistry to a swirl. It would certainly be a point of no return.

"I'm sorry, I'm sorry. It's been a bit of a mad dash," Roz said, leaning down to kiss Anita's cheek, and even this she did efficiently.

Swallowing painfully, Anita attempted to look bright. "For what? It's me who was early."

"Then I take it back." Roz edged into the seat opposite. She looked up at the waitress who had appeared armed with her notepad and a hopeful expression. Having paid the entrance fee, most visitors to the Palace stayed for the day, eating in the Tiltyard café, or picnicking in the grounds. "Just a latte for me as well. Make that a skinny, please." Then with elbows pointing towards the corners of the table, fingertips touching lightly, Roz switched her focus to Anita. It was clear that she was speaking as her boss. "So, how are you?"

"I've been signed off work for another two weeks."

Roz did her best to disguise surprise. "Two weeks? I hadn't realised."

Flat-palmed, Anita slid an envelope containing the sick note she'd been given across the table, a furtive movement.

Roz delicately opened it and made a small noise in her throat, as though it confirmed what she'd suspected. "You should have told me. I would have come to see you."

Anita felt as if *Handle with Care* was stamped across her forehead. The doctor had used the words 'debilitating' and 'fragile'. It was shameful to be thought so weak that she was incapable of work. Anita's embarrassment manifested itself in the dip of her head. "I needed to get out of the house."

"Anita, look at me," Roz commanded and she obeyed. "How long have I known you?"

"Seventeen years." The high pitch of the coffee grinder whirred in the background.

Roz slipped into easy friendship, her mouth curling into a smile. "Christ, is it really that long?"

"I'm afraid it is."

"Well, then." She straightened her spine. "I have an even stronger point to make. In all that time, I can only remember you being off ill for a week."

"Two weeks."

"Big deal. You're hardly what I'd call a shirker."

"Perhaps that's why I feel so guilty. I hate letting the side down."

"Your latte?" the waitress asked. A young girl, she wore the obvious look of relief of someone who has walked very carefully and managed not to spill anything.

"Thank you," Roz said, pulling the oversized white cup and saucer towards her. It was full to the brim. "Liverpool wasn't very helpful, then?"

Anita gave a sharp laugh. "How long have you got?"

"I said I'd tag my lunch break onto the end of our meeting." She added a lump of brown sugar to her coffee, which sank slowly through the froth.

"And are we still in our meeting?"

"I think I'll take an early lunch." Roz took the cup in both hands and held it at chin level.

"In that case... Liverpool was helpful, in that it clarified lots of things I've never really understood before." And Anita began to slot the pieces together in an order that made sense as far as the sick note was concerned, because it wasn't fair on Roz to expect her to leave her status as manager behind completely. Anita omitted her accidental meeting at the station, though doing so made her feel like a fraud. Her thoughts lingered on small details. The nails that he grew long, as guitar players often did. The small overlap in his teeth.

Anita also hesitated before describing her return home. But Dr Kernow had said it was important to talk about her feelings, and - as she'd already asked herself - who else could she talk to? She decided not to skip the details about Ed and Natalie. Though Roz had met them both, she didn't owe them her loyalty. They weren't exactly what you'd call friends.

"And you believe him?"

"I believe that it didn't go any further and it won't happen again. But," she collected her thoughts, "he *was* a little too quick to jump to Natalie's defence."

"So you've lost your bolt-hole and you're less than certain about your best friend."

"But it's OK, because Ed thinks that getting married will fix everything." Immediately, heat flooded Anita's neck. It was cheap, saying this, and she didn't think of marriage as being cheap. She simply didn't think it was for her. Though Anita wasn't ready to discard a fifteen-year relationship over one relatively small slip, it bothered her that Ed had come within an inch of proposing. Was it making the offer that had been important? She wondered if, after serving a lengthy apprenticeship, he considered that the job of husband should automatically be his. Anita tried to imagine how she would feel in his place if he turned her down. Could they return to what they'd shared before, or would everything be left in ruins? The thought was frightening. No one knew Anita as well as Ed did. Right now, Anita needed Ed to remind her who she was.

"Men!" Roz appeared lost for words, although her happily-married status made this exclamation unconvincing. Like her, Brendan was quirkily attractive and passionate about his job (something in publishing). They even spoke in the same staccato tone that people who didn't know them mistook for shortness. Roz would only ever say *That's ridiculous* when fighting a friend's corner, and never without checking her facts.

"Roz, I don't know how you're going to feel about this." Oh, to hell with it. "But I'm nervous about coming back to work. So far, the Palace is the only place where I've had panic attacks."

Her manager's eyebrows pulled together. "I can see how that would worry you."

"Would it look strange if I visited a couple of times while I'm signed off sick?" What Anita didn't say was that she wanted to make sure the medication was doing the trick.

Roz pursed her lips. "I don't see why not. Certainly not from my point of view. We've done plenty of things to help ease people back into work before - although, admittedly, it's usually after longer absences."

"That's why I thought I'd ask. I don't want to do any work, just to -"

"You want to see how it feels to stand in the Cartoon Gallery."

Even mention of the place caused a perceptible acceleration in her heartbeat. "Yes," Anita said, humbled to be understood without having to go into detail. But there was something else she wanted to do. She felt the need to walk the length of the Processional Gallery in the Tudor palace, to place her hand within the etched outline of another, as if it was a portal from the past to the present, linking her with everyone who had done the same thing.

"I'll run it by HR. In fact, why don't you come with me

now?" Roz bent down, picked her handbag up and put it in her lap.

She was taken aback. "Now?"

"Not right now. After you've finished your coffee. Just as far as the office. I'll get an official answer."

Anita's gaze wandered towards the bridge. The tallest of the spiralling chimneys were just in view.

Roz grabbed her hand and tugged at it. "You can do this, Nita. I'll be with you. OK?" Her smokey-blue eyes were intense, challenging her to say yes.

She smiled, reluctantly, nodded. "OK."

CHAPTER TWENTY-THREE

Sitting at the breakfast room table, screwing the lid back on a jar of last year's home-made plum jam, Patti felt unaccountably twitchy. "Have you heard from our Anita since she visited?" she asked Ron, who had one elbow on his copy of the *Echo*. In the other hand, he held the spoon he was using to forge his way through a bowl of Fruit 'n Fibre.

"I had a text from Ed."

"But nothing from Anita."

"No." The page dragged as he turned it.

"Don't you think that's a little strange?"

"It's not unusual for a couple of weeks to go by."

"It's been three weeks."

"They're busy people. I expect this house business is taking up a lot of their time."

"But given -" Patti could have ended the sentence in any number of ways, none of which would have justified her concern. To seem unduly worried might cause suspicion. And yet, Patti knew daughters with children of their own who spared five minutes every day to check in with their mothers - though, admittedly, many of them were after favours. Anita wasn't that type.

Ron was looking directly at her. "Have *you* tried calling?"

"They don't have an answerphone in the new house." She

pushed back her chair, stood and set the kettle to boil. Then she opened a cupboard and brought down the big brown pot that had been her mother's. She stood the thermos flasks next to each other: hers for the office; Ron's for the garden.

"Why don't you email?" His voice was amused. "You're hardly ever off the computer."

Though Patti's mouth tightened, she couldn't dream up a suitable retort.

Upstairs, in need of distraction, she typed 'Novels set in Liverpool' into the search engine. She would see where the book blog was in the rankings. Google suggested Patti might also like to try *Fiction books set in Liverpool.* She shook her head: 'Fiction books' for goodness sake! She would stick with 'novels', thank you very much.

The Liver Bird Book Blog was holding its own, just below Wikipedia and Maureen Lee. But what she saw was fourth in the rankings stilled her fingers. *Will you help us find out who authored anonymous novel set in Liverpool?* The web address given in calming green was for an American book blog. And underneath was the smaller text; *A chance discovery on a Liverpool to London train has prompted book blogger Marcia Reynolds to call on the UK blogging community to help track down the author of an anonymous novel.*

The blood drained from Patti's face. Even before clicking through to the site, Patti knew that her worst fear had been realised. Anita had read what she'd written.

She had dared write all of the things she hadn't been able to speak of. The remorse, the sorrow, her fears, the people and the places. The words had poured down like rain. The gutters and the gullies, the downpipes and the drains had overflowed, slicking the cobbles and paving slabs, darkening the tarmac. Storm clouds had transformed the Mersey into an inky churning toxic mass. At times, Patti had thought she might drown.

A chill radiated from Patti's core, dissipating as it reached her fingertips. On the screen in front of her was a photograph of an attractive middle-aged woman dressed in enviably casual elegance, the sort that smacked of money: crisp white cotton with a silk scarf knotted around her neck, either Hermès or designed to look like Hermès. Her thick hair was cut in a slick ash-blonde bob. It was Patti's book that the woman was holding up to the lens of the camera. Any hope that there might be room for doubt evaporated.

Book blogger Marcia Reynolds was holidaying in the UK when she picked up this book that had been left behind by a woman traveling on the same London-bound train as her. **Watch the video here**.

She sat very still, a childhood trick she'd taught herself, hoping that everything would go away. Patti was just one woman with a computer. How could this have happened?

The admission of how naïve she'd been was gut-wrenching. Patti had felt the enormity of other people's indifference for so long that she'd imagined herself invisible. It seemed incredible that anyone would take the slightest notice of what she had written. But shouldn't she have known better? Hadn't she sat at her desk and typed what she'd thought was a throwaway message only to discover that it touched a nerve with someone in Australia? The internet magnified everything one-thousand fold.

And now a single copy of her book had made it to the United States, a country Patti, with her phobia of flying, was unlikely to visit. To New York specifically, a place Liverpudlians returned from, declaring how at home they'd felt. Having come this far, watching the video was compulsory. Patti sat with one hand over her mouth, as if it might shield her from the consequences of her foolishness.

"We were both on our way from Liverpool to Euston and I could see that she was absolutely engrossed in this novel. The

248

emotion was written all over her face. So, obviously, I was curious to know what kind of book had had this effect on her. I asked, but you could tell she couldn't bear to tear herself away from it. Anyway, as we were pulling into London Euston, something made her get up in a terrible hurry, and she left it behind on the little table these trains have. I thought I might be able to catch up with her, and so I grabbed it, but she was already way ahead by then - we had luggage to collect, you see. And so I ended up bringing it all the way home with me. What with one thing and another, it sat on my nightstand for the best part of a week. I was finishing The Goldfinch. *Do you know it? It's masterful. Anyway, what* this *book turned out to be is a 'warts and all' - I think that's what they say in England - exploration of motherhood, told by this narrator who had really struggled with it. I mean majorly. And I just thought, Wow! This book would really help people where post-natal depression isn't just a passing phase. You don't find this kind of stuff in a self-help book. Women would be too afraid to come right out and say it. This writing is so brave and raw. And so I lent it to a friend of mine whose daughter is finding it hard to bond with her eighteen-month-old. And, I have to tell you, she just wept with relief to know that there was one other person out there who understands what she's going through. And I began to wonder, what if the main character in the story is a real person? If the author had put her name to the book, I'd be able to ask her. What's more, I'd be able to thank her. But she hasn't. And so that's why I'm calling on the UK blogging community, particularly in Liverpool: do you know the identity of the woman? Someone must know the author. So come on. Let's make sure she gets the recognition she deserves!"*

Patti sat back in her chair and allowed the breath she had been holding hostage to escape. She knew what this meant - what it meant for all of them. Posting a video constituted a call to arms in the blogging world. Patti's own experience told her that this thing would go much, much further. People were so desperate for content, they would share almost anything as long as it was about books or writing, often without even reading it. The idea that it might be unstoppable lodged itself in her throat.

Christ, if *she'd* seen it, Sylvia would have seen it too! She'd want Liver Bird Book Blog to take up the cause - and what excuse could Patti come up with? Before she knew what was happening, she'd be part of it.

She logged onto Amazon.com and blinked as she saw that four copies of her book had been sold and it had been given a five-star review: *This book helped put into words the things I'd been feeling but couldn't explain. It helped validate the fact that I will get through this, as so many others have, and that I can be a good mother. There are some emotions not even your best friend can sympathize with. They say that for everyone there is a book that understands them. This is mine. If the author had put her name on the cover, I would be writing to thank her. In the hope that she reads this, I want to say thank you, from the bottom of my heart.*

Patti could take no pleasure in the praise. If Anita had a child of her own, perhaps... But Patti could never wish that her daughter had gone through what she'd experienced. Those first few terrible years. The feeling that, because you were incapable of something you believed was the most natural thing in the world - every woman's destiny - you were less than human. You were *un*natural. She was glad motherhood had passed Anita by.

Determined not to indulge in self-pity, she swiped a drip from the end of her nose. *Think, woman, think!* The quickest way to prevent the thing from spreading would be to claim ownership. But that too might become news. And she would have to explain why she didn't put her name on the book in the first place - although what business it was of Marcia

Reynolds's she didn't know. In her own mind, the answer was obvious. To protect those still living. And yet she'd failed to protect the two people who meant everything to her. The need to leave her mark had driven her to do this thing. Now, it would be her downfall.

She felt a sudden surge of anger. Why hadn't Ron warned her that Anita was coming home? And it struck her: Christ, she'd have to tell Ron. Tell him that she'd let him down. No, what she'd done was far worse. She had betrayed him. This thought possessed consequences immediate enough to set her lip quivering. She walked to the spare room at the back of the house, threw the net curtains over her head like a bridal veil, and looked down into the garden. There he was, sturdy and steady, potting clippings from plants and setting them on the benches inside the greenhouse. Completely unknowing.

She pressed one hand against the glass as if to reach out to him, but he had his headphones on. He talked about plants 'wintering' as if they were on holiday. He talked about his beloved Red Men as if they were old friends. He casually enquired what was for tea. Ron asked for nothing more. Until Anita's visit he hadn't expressed the slightest interest in her book blog. And then, after saying that he'd get out of her who the author of the book was, he hadn't pressed. He was always so perceptive about the things she didn't want to talk about. Patti felt ashamed to have lied to such a good and honest man. It pained her, what she would have to do; what it might do to their marriage. But there was nothing for it.

Only one other thing took priority. Patti had read plenty of blogs that said the act of publishing should be more difficult. There should be a big red button that said, 'Are you sure?' and then another that said, 'Are you really sure?' Perhaps 'Are you prepared for the consequences?' would be more appropriate. She logged onto the publishing platform, clicked on the title of the book and then on the word, 'unpublish'. The message

'Are you sure?' appeared.

Her nostrils prickled. Confronted by the hours spent at the keyboard, re-ordering a sentence, unpicking changes like knitting, Patti felt the pain of destroying something she had created. She had so little to show for her life. *Such a shame. After you showed so much promise.* She lifted her chin in defiance. In all probability, it was too late to think about damage limitation. But at least she could tell her husband and daughter that she'd tried. It was their opinion she cared about, no one else's - certainly not this Marcia's.

She clicked on 'yes'. It was done. No one else could order her book. Only the copies in the house remained.

As she walked under the hatch to the loft, it struck Patti. She would bring the books down right now, then she would ask Ron to help her burn them. One by one, Patti imagined throwing them into the rusted incinerator that stood crookedly to one side of the vegetable patch and her husband raking their cold ashes into the soil.

Ron's stomach had been rumbling quietly for some time, but still the call for lunch hadn't come. He pulled off his wireless headphones and looked towards the kitchen to see if Patti's silhouette was framed in the window. She must have lost track of time. He decided to surprise his wife with soup and a sandwich. It was probably his turn, if he was honest. Perhaps if he gave the plastic table and chairs a wipe down, he'd be able to tempt her out onto the patio for a spot of fresh air.

Back in the kitchen, having left two very soiled kitchen cloths soaking in the half-sink, Ron was investigating the contents of the fridge when he heard something that sounded like a distant mewing. Perhaps one of the neighbours' cats had crept in through the back door. It wouldn't be the first time he'd had to turf the black and white Tom out of the living room. Once, he'd found it perched on the back of the sofa, bold as you like, looking out of the bay window, eyes locked on a blackbird. It had acted most put out when Ron had clapped his hands, saying it had no business being there.

Out in the hall, the noise sounded less like a cat and more like those haunted noises he'd heard in hospital corridors those final few times he'd visited his mother. Blood began to charge around his body. "Patti?" he called out, rounding the end of the staircase with one hand on the banister.

"Ron," came the weak reply, followed by sobs of relief.

He launched himself at the stairs, two at a time. From the halfway point Ron could see that the loft hatch was hanging open and the rickety aluminium ladder had been pulled down. His stomach turned over.

His wife was wedged across the narrow landing between the bathroom and Anita's bedroom. She was lying on her back and her legs were at an unnatural angle. How high was she when she fell? "Oh, Patti," he dropped to his knees at her feet end. The thing was to emulate calm. There was no way to get around her and so, after adjusting her skirt so that it covered her knees, he put his hands wherever he saw a patch of beige carpet. It was like a nightmarish game of Twister. "What do you think you were doing, going up the ladder by yourself? Hmm?"

"I called," she said feebly, looking in the direction of his face, but her eyes were unfocused and her words were slurred.

As subtly as possible, he checked for signs of injury around her head, gently stroking her hair away from her ears, relieved by the absence of blood or fluid. "Well, I'm here now. I'm going to take care of you. First things first though, I think I'd better call an ambulance - just to be on the safe side." He manoeuvred himself awkwardly, walking his hands backwards, praying that he wouldn't fall on Patti and do yet more damage. Once on his feet, he said, "Don't go doing anything daft while I'm gone."

"I was calling for ages." Her voice was childlike.

"I know you were, I know you were. It's my fault. I had my headphones on." He pressed one of his hands against the wall for balance. "Stay right there."

Glancing up to the loft, he saw that the light was switched on. In God's name, what had Patti been thinking? She struggled with the stairs!

Halfway down, Ron suffered one of those rare moments of complete forgetfulness. Not quite sure what he was doing, or how he had come to be there, he slowed to a halt and tried to blink the fog away. Another moan put him straight, and his feet started moving again. The lady who answered his 999 call was good enough to prompt Ron, asking him to repeat everything to make sure he had understood.

Hanging up, he said to himself, "Right, Ronald. Stay with her. Make sure she's warm enough." It was comforting to be equipped with a strict set of instructions he could tick off, one by one.

He unhooked a short woollen jacket from the row of pegs in the hall - nothing that would put any pressure on Patti's poor legs - and took it upstairs with him. "Are you feeling cold, love?"

Ron couldn't really tell if what she said was a yes or a no, and so he held onto the shoulder pads and flapped the jacket out as if he was making the bed. Then he covered Patti's upper half as best he could from her feet end, and retreated to the top step. From a sitting position, he could keep one eye on his wife and one on the front door. Several copies of that book he'd helped stack in Anita's wardrobe were scattered about under the loft hatch. One had landed open with its cover up, as if someone had put it down to save their place. The woman on the phone had reminded him of the importance of keeping talking, and so he created a breeze with the pages while locating chapter one, and cleared his throat. "'*If family myths*

254

were to be believed, it all began when my mother, Clementina (never called anything other than Clemmie, unless her father was dishing out a roasting), tripped on the way up the aisle of St Xavier's. As a child, I heard elderly female relatives hiss behind cupped hands that the fall had been a bad omen.' Very apt for today, wouldn't you say, love?" He looked at his wife, but she had moved her head to one side and begun to sob. "Don't you worry. I know it hurts but the ambulance is on its way. And how often do you get the chance to hear me read? *'Although, it was probably nothing more than the combination of high heels, a hem that could have done with another inch taking off it, and the double brandy Clemmie had downed to quell her nerves.'"*

Ron continued reading even after, stumbling over a few words, his throat began to close. Though he seemed to have developed what felt like severe indigestion, he held one arm across his chest as if it were in a sling and carried right on. He imagined that he had been called to read aloud in front of his old school master. If anything, his words became louder and clearer. Even as a writhing shadow appeared behind the frosted glass in the front door, Ron continued to read. All of the way down the stairs.

The paramedic from the Fast Response Unit was very businesslike, waiting only for him to confirm Patti's full name and say, "Upstairs," before making sure the ambulance was on its way. Having relinquished control, and with nothing left on his to-do list, Ron stood guard by the front door. Once he'd let the reinforcements in, he felt for the wall behind him, absent-mindedly running his hands over the texture of the hessian-effect wallpaper. His last attempt at decorating. Thoughts were crystallising that had previously been vague. He wasn't sure how they changed things. You couldn't turn back the clock. He and Patti had got on as best they could, without all of those parenting guides you could buy on-line, without fear that the woman behind the counter at the bookshop would gossip about you. 'She was in here the other week buying that self-help book. The one on *post-natal depression*', a condition so unmentionable, it could only be whispered with exaggerated movements of the mouth.

But right now, the ambulance crew were bringing his wife downstairs. Strapped to a stretcher, she looked in a great deal of discomfort, to be held at such an incline. Feeling redundant, he watched as she was carried out of the front door, some kind of portable breathing apparatus covering the lower half of her pale face. Ron felt he should say something comforting, but he was embarrassed in front of the medics. The only thing that he could do to be of help was to hold the door open, stand well back and say, "Watch out for the step."

The man at the back of the stretcher twisted his head towards Ron. "Will you come in the ambulance or follow behind? Only you'll have to be quick if you're coming with us."

"Is she -?" he nodded, barely knowing how to ask.

"Your wife's in no immediate danger, but she's in a great deal of pain."

"Then I'll follow behind. I should probably lock up." He also needed to put something on his feet. He had left his gardening shoes outside the back door.

"In that case, take your time. We'll be going to the Royal."

"Right," he said, watching from the porch and raising his hand in a salute, fretting, just as he did when Anita backed the car off the drive at the start of the long drive to London. Patti wasn't a good passenger. "Sorry, was it the Royal you said?"

"That's right, mate. The Royal."

He stifled an urge to tell them not to drive at over forty miles an hour. The only other time he had taken Patti to hospital had been for Anita's birth, and then she had packed her own bag, which had sat by the front door in readiness at least two weeks before it was required. Pack a bag: that was what he would do.

A couple of nighties, a dressing gown. Ron was not a man who was comfortable opening his wife's underwear drawer, even though he saw its contents regularly pegged out on the line to dry, but it had to be done. Similarly, he felt as if he was invading her privacy by packing her washbag. Unsure what was appropriate for hospital stays, he stuck to the essentials. There was no spare tube of toothpaste in the bathroom cabinet: he would have to stock up at Boots.

Passing the open door of his wife's office, bag in hand, Ron heard the familiar ping that heralded the arrival of an email. The screen was blank. He paused, scratched one side of his neck. Ron didn't like to snoop, but he saw that there might be the opportunity to eliminate the need for lengthy explanations. Patti was going to find it very difficult to explain what she'd been up to. Because what was writing if it wasn't avoidance of actually saying the words? Dismissing his reservations, he hit the space bar.

The company name on the website Ron saw was familiar, but this wasn't the screen where he usually placed his orders. This was a 'dashboard', designed for self-publishing. When he read that the status of Patti's book was 'unpublished', he felt a small sadness. Lord, if he wrote down all of the things he was ashamed of, if he wrote all of the secrets he only shared with Aunt Magda, how many volumes would he fill? He logged off the site. It was replaced by another, an article titled *Who authored anonymous novel set in Liverpool?* And, feeling a renewed sense of uneasiness, he scanned the words written by a woman called Marcia Reynolds.

Patti hadn't made a secret of the doubts she suffered before their wedding. She was barely nineteen. It was Ron, then twenty-nine, who'd driven the whole thing forwards. But he'd held her freezing hands as they sat on a bench in front of

257

the palm house in Sefton Park and promised that everything would be alright, because he was going to take care of her. And that one simple promise had been more important to Patti than any number of long-winded marriage vows. How far had he lived up to it? Things had happened so fast, that was the problem. A rented flat would no longer do, and so, after being told that he would get the standard married man's raise, Ron talked himself up a notch or two, got a little extra, and booked an appointment with his bank manager to discuss a mortgage. He'd imagined having to sit some sort of written test, or that a set of old boys' rules would come into play but, surprisingly, they didn't see through his act. They hadn't noticed that, although Ron had worn a suit these past fifteen years, he was still the terrified schoolboy - albeit one who'd netted the girl of his dreams. "Sign here," was what they'd said. "And here, in this box." He would have gladly signed his life away, knowing that he could provide for Patti.

So out of his league, she made Ron feel alternately that anything was possible and that she might at any moment come to her senses. Wondering in horror who this scally holding her hand was as they stood on the ferry to New Brighton, watching The Three Graces getting smaller and smaller. When they had seen *Titanic* together, Ron had nudged Patti and said, "See that? That's us on the ferry," and she'd slapped his arm and said, "Don't be soft."

They should have courted. Enjoyed each other's company. But it had been such a shock when Patti had agreed to go with him to the Milk Bar that he'd kept chancing his arm, amazed that she kept saying yes.

For Ron, married life gave everything purpose. He was building a future. Sticking to the promise. Then Anita came along and there were two girls to take care of. And *of course* he'd been aware that Patti had struggled. He was no fool. Though it pained Ron to imagine how desperate Patti must have been, it didn't surprise him to learn that she'd come *that* close to getting on a train at Lime Street Station.

It wasn't that he hadn't helped. No matter what sort of a day he'd had - whether he'd been hard pressed to meet a deadline, if his manager had picked holes in his copy - Ron rolled his sleeves up the moment he walked through the door. "Come along, little lass. It's time for your bath. Let your mummy put her feet up." He was determined that Patti's evenings should be her own. He made sure she ate something nutritious, then, if she was too worn out to watch television or read her crime novels, he would massage her feet, make her a mug of hot chocolate, run her a bath. Sometimes he was both father and husband. *Up to bed with you. Plenty of time for that in the morning.* Constantly rallying the troops, he had tried to prove to the formidable Mrs Roscoe that he was worthy of her daughter.

"Ronald," she would greet him curtly as she took off her hat in the hall. Just that - although she might as well have announced, "Ronald, I shall be taking over now," as if she thought him incapable of anything but tea-making. No one else had ever called him Ronald, not unless he was in for a hiding. His mother-in-law liked things nice and formal, and so she was always Mrs Roscoe to him. He couldn't have imagined calling her 'Mum', not even after she softened towards him. It was their little joke in the end. 'Ronald' took on a teasing and - dare he say it - an affectionate tone.

And it was no surprise to him that Patti had held this world of unspeakable thoughts inside her. She used to confess to a priest - Father O'Farrell, his name was - though she rarely had a good word to say about him. As for Ron, he'd confided in Aunty Magda, and she had proven as good a listener as God ever had. The point was that you needed a conduit for secrets. Otherwise they might taint the marital home.

He disliked this American woman on the video. Her

soft drawl and overenthusiastic manner didn't fool him. To Marcia Reynolds, it was all a game. She was oblivious to the harm she was causing. He understood now that this Marcia Reynolds was the reason Anita hadn't replied to his texts. His daughter wouldn't realise that, in the writing of the book, her mother had been hardest on herself. How could she? He felt fiercely defensive of what Patti had written. Patti, who had shown so much promise before he came along, as Mrs Roscoe had frequently reminded him. "She could have had a career."

It struck him, right in the guts.

Winded, Ron hung onto the back of the chair for support.

Christ Almighty, he couldn't believe he'd never thought of it before. He was Jason Adams.

As far as the Roscoes were concerned, he was gobby, proud, cheeky. The 'boy' who had derailed their daughter's plans.

The order of events was immaterial to them. Ron had somehow imagined that, by marrying Patti, he would demonstrate that his intentions were honourable. But the Roscoes hadn't wanted him to marry their daughter. They'd hoped he was a passing phase.

How had he ever had the nerve? The Milk Bar to the register office in two weeks.

But it *was* a marriage. It was a good marriage, and he didn't think that Patti would have had it any other way. Even Mrs Roscoe had been forced to acknowledge it in the end, when she'd reluctantly accepted Ron's help. "Against all odds, you've turned out to be a surprisingly good husband," she'd said to him, just the once.

He'd been more than a little gobsmacked, but because she hadn't begrudged him this, Ron had played it down, saying the first words that popped into his head. "You only ever see me on my best behaviour. Most of the time, I have my feet up on the coffee table, a bottle of whiskey in one hand and a can of Cains in the other."

And he was overtaken by a yearning to be near Patti, to repeat his promise to take care of her and to protect her from all the Marcia Reynolds of this world. But the ambulance man had said that there was no call for rushing about. Things needed to be done in the correct order, and so he went and cut flowers from the garden - roses, which he dethorned by the kitchen sink, ox-eye daisies and a few cosmos - and he secured the stems with green garden twine and a couple of layers of cling film, just to be on the safe side.

About to change into something a bit smarter than his gardening clothes, Ron caught sight of his reflection in the mirror on the inside of the wardrobe door. Pulling himself up straight, it was as if he was looking at the person he had always pretended to be: a respectable son-in-law. Well, perhaps giving the appearance of respectability wasn't the most important thing. He scraped a few hangers along the rail on his side of the wardrobe and realised. All he had to wear was shirts and ties. And so he rummaged around in a drawer until he found a neatly folded round-necked jumper. Something Anita had bought several years ago, but he had yet to wear. It seemed to be a good and honest item of clothing, the sort of jumper Ed might choose (perhaps Anita bought his clothes too), so he pulled it over his head and stuck his arms through the sleeves. Unpretentious was the word that sprang to mind as he looked at himself.

Equipped with the bag, the bunch of flowers and a copy of his wife's book, he left the house. It was a strange thing to say at a moment when others might be overwhelmed by the crisis he had on his hands, but Ron was infused with the feeling of a man who was about to propose, not one who was about to see his wife in traction.

CHAPTER TWENTY-FOUR

Ron sat for what may well have been a very long time, but it barely mattered, because he was in the same building as Patti and, by being there, he felt happy that he was keeping his promise.

Eventually, Ron's arm was gently shaken. Immediately, he tightened his grip around his wife's book, which lay open in his hands. He opened his eyes to find a nurse standing over him. Everything had gone well, she said. It was strange, but Ron hadn't doubted the outcome. The paramedics had left him with such an impression of efficiency. They'd said that Patti was in no danger.

"You can come through, but don't expect too much."

It was not in Ron's nature to expect too much, and yet he knew only too well the power of asking. His prayers had once been answered (he thought of his poor mother, bent over double, the marks left by her teeth on her skin), and then Patti had said yes, and his pals had slapped him on the back and said, "How the hell d'you pull that one off, you gob-shite?" and he'd shrugged and said, "I'm a lucky git, I suppose." So when Anita arrived, Ron knew that he had more than a man was entitled to wish for. Add to that a steady job at the newspaper when there were few to go round. Happy-go-lucky Ron had received more than his fair share.

And so he exchanged his seat in the waiting room for a seat by Patti's narrow hospital bed, which was curtained off from the rest of the ward. He imagined it was much the same as being in a tent on a campsite, not that they'd ever gone in for that sort of thing. But he was aware of movement, of bulky shadows and the traipse of feet. You couldn't help hearing things - moans of pain, corresponding words of comfort - that were none of your business. Ron looked only at his wife's face so that, the moment she stirred, Patti would open her eyes and see him.

When at last she did, he said, "There you are," to reassure her. He would have squeezed her hand, but there was a needle sticking out of it and he was worried that he might hurt her. "How are you feeling?"

With a startled look, her eyes dropped to the book in his hands.

"I've been catching up on my reading. It's not often I get the chance."

"Ron -" she began, with a tone so heartbreaking that he immediately hushed her.

"Would you do it all again?" he asked.

"I should never have..." Patti turned her face away, making new creases in the worn white pillowcase.

"Not the book, you soft so-and-so. I'm talking about me and Anita. If you had your time over, is there anything you'd change?"

She turned back to him, as if he should know better, a hint of his old Patti asserting herself. "Nothing. You know I wouldn't, Ronnie." There had been no hesitation and it wasn't often that she called him Ronnie. "But Anita..." Patti was too distressed to make any further headway into that sentence.

"It'll be alright. I'll take care of things. She'll come round."

"Will you go and see her? Will you go now? I should have done it myself, but -"

He could see how much asking this favour pained his wife. A woman who wasn't prone to tears, she was embarrassed to succumb in front of him now. Ron averted his eyes as Patti regained her composure, but they were tented together and there were few places to look. Then her eyebrows twitched.

"Is everything alright?" he asked, though clearly things were far from alright.

"You look different."

"You can talk!" He smiled, nodding towards the lower end of his wife's sheeted body.

"The jumper..." She didn't mention the lack of a tie and what this might mean.

"Anita bought it for me. I've not got round to wearing it before."

"I like it on you. You look like a schoolboy."

This was the only conversation that was possible. Ron knew that. Part of him wanted to confess that he had always known Patti struggled, but he wondered if, after all these years, it would seem like a betrayal. If he had said something earlier, could he have encouraged her to seek medical help? Or would it - whatever it was - have become the thing their lives constantly revolved around?

And yet, at the same time, he felt that Patti had always known he had understood. But to be sure, Ron decided this was the moment to tell his wife the thing he'd always kept from her. Then she could decide if she wanted to talk.

"It's made me think, reading your book. It's made me think what I would write. Not that I'd make such a good job of it, but it's made me think." He scratched his head. This was going to be hard.

As hard as he had imagined.

But he told her. About the cellar. About his, the most heartfelt of prayers. *Please, God, please.* And about Aunty Magda. The teeth-marks on his mother's white knuckles. The tangle of metal. All of those things that made absolute sense when you kept them trapped inside your head, and didn't seem to make quite so much sense when you set them free. In a way - a comforting way - being enclosed in a small space, speaking what was for Ron a lengthy monologue, did feel a little like being inside a confessional.

And Patti looked on, a twist of a smile on her lips and unrestrained tears, performing that most sacred of duties. She listened to his meditation without interrupting, without judgement, without dismissing or belittling this thing that had been eating away at his insides for as long as he could remember. Without remarking, *If only you'd said something earlier.*

She listened as Aunty Magda would have listened, as priests *should* listen, except that, when he reached the point where he might have said, *That is all I can remember, Father,* Patti spoke. "The sweet peas. They're for your aunt."

One of his hands reached for his throat. In the telling, the stranglehold seemed to have loosened. Not completely, but just enough so that he didn't feel as if he was suffocating. Ron inhaled the word, "Yes." He knew that Patti would be thinking of how he had planted them out year after year - *Madga,* the *Chatsworth* and sometimes the *Fragrantissima* - brought them into the house and put them in his mother's vase on the mantelpiece. He knew that, by this, Patti would understand that he was not over his aunt's death, and never would be. A sigh juddered through his chest. "What a shower we are, the pair of us."

Though it hadn't been Ron's intention, he realised those words welcomed Patti back into the equation, reminding her of all the things she couldn't make right while trapped inside a body that was incapable of cooperating. "Well, *I* am. I don't know about you."

"We'll muddle through. We always do."

"And you'll pay a trip to London? To see our Anita?"

"I will."

"Now?"

"What? And leave you lying here?"

"I've got half a dozen nurses to keep me in check." Her eyes pleaded: *I'll need you once I'm home.* And there was some sense in it.

"I suppose I could be there and back in a day."

She acknowledged this silently, but gratitude fringed her attempt to smile.

He stood and put the bag he had brought with him on the chair. "I've brought you some bits and pieces to be getting along with. Nightclothes, your toothbrush." Best to leave it there.

"I'll be fine."

"I'd better tell the nurses that I haven't deserted you. They'll think it's very irregular."

"They can think what they like."

"That's my girl." He held onto her arm very gently as he bent down to brush his lips against her forehead. "Is there anyone you'd like me to call? Geraldine, perhaps. The lady you do the blog with."

"Yes, Sylvia! Sylvia Beckworth. If you log onto my computer, you'll find her email address."

"I'm sure even a Luddite like me can manage that. Although I'd better write her name down before I forget it." Lacking any paper, he scribbled on the back of his hand. "A strange woman's name written on my hand. People *will* talk."

He was making a parting in the curtains when she called out. "And Ron. There is one other thing."

"What's that, love?"

"I want you to burn the books. All of them."

He forced a smile, hoping it would be interpreted as agreement, but, painful though they were, he had already claimed those written words. They were part of his history. Part of *their* history. "Behave yourself while I'm gone," was all he said in response. "No more ladders!"

"No, Ron. No more ladders."

CHAPTER TWENTY-FIVE

It had been a good day at work. Anita hadn't been under the impression that people had pussy-footed round her. She had enjoyed a picnic lunch with Ruth on a bench in the Palace grounds. Sitting among the topiary, feet crunching past on the gravel path, the view of the long water stretched in front of them. She had coped fairly well with Ruth's inquisition about the fire and where they were up to with the plans to rebuild. Anita had replied honestly, "I've decided to leave it up to Ed. The project's his baby now."

Ruth dipped her fork into a Tupperware box full of some kind of salad. Tuna by the smell of it, niçoise without the anchovies. Loaded with hard-boiled egg, it hesitated halfway towards her mouth. "And you trust him?"

It had forced air through her nostrils, a question asked with good intent (although that wasn't to say Anita's answer wouldn't be repeated in the Tudor kitchen). There was a time not so long ago when discussing her relationship with Ed would have felt like breaking a trust. Now Anita had a better grasp of what betrayal looked like. And, with her GP's offer of counselling hovering like a threat, Anita had been told that it was important that she talked about her problems. "The site's been cleared," she said. There had been an honour in the unwavering vigil. The standing up straight. The refusal to cry.

Even the hated concrete path which, defiant to the end, had resisted the workman's drill. "I trust him to build a house. But I've warned him that I don't know if I'll want to live in it."

Ruth, who regarded Anita's relationship as unconventional, drank this detail in with horror and awe. "So what will you do? If you decide you don't want to live in the house, I mean?"

"That's a long way off. Neither of us has any idea how we'll feel in two years' time." In the border, red hot pokers were set off against a red-brick wall. She regarded Ruth, still in her twenties, thinking *I doubt even you do.*

"But just say."

Anita squinted against the sun. "I honestly don't know." Curiously, admitting this was liberating. "That would really depend on whether Ed decides that he does."

"You actually think Ed might choose the house over you?"

Ruth made the choice sound so simple - and perhaps it was. One of the Egyptian geese the Palace staff had watched grow from this year's batch of goslings waddled into view, snatching at the short grass. Spring had failed to deliver many of its promises, but not this. "He's investing two years of his life. I imagine that will be difficult to walk away from."

"But -" Ruth looked flabbergasted. "How can you carry on as you are in the meantime if you think that's even a possibility?"

It was possible to smile. "I don't see what else I can do."

In fact, getting up and going to work was all Anita had been focusing on. She had ticked off days in her diary, the passing of each one a small success. Everything else was secondary. Non-essential things hadn't happened at all. There were telephone calls she hadn't returned, both from her parents and from Natalie.

"Hi Anita, it's only me. I wondered if you wanted to go for that coffee we talked about."

269

"Hi Anita, I don't know if you got my message. Give me a ring when you've got a moment."

"Anita, give me a call. Just to let me know that you're OK."

"Look, I know Ed's told you. Please just ring to tell me that we're still friends."

And, perhaps worst of all, from Reuben:

"Hey Aunty Nita. When are you coming round to play my computer game? I'm going to thrash you. Ha, ha. Mum says any day but Wednesday."

Lack of time wasn't an excuse. She had found time to check Facebook during her daily commute. Those searches had focused on one particular name and a picture of a pot-bellied pig. He had accepted her friend request, but hadn't messaged. It was possible, she supposed, that their miraculous, accidental collision meant nothing to him. Or, it was equally possible that he was waiting for her to act. She was the one with the thoroughly good egg of a boyfriend. He was the one with the ex - not to mention the troubled teenage kids. There was no doubt that this diversion was contributing to a frame of mind in which Anita could smile at someone twenty years her junior and say, "I don't see what else I can do."

Anita's thirty-year-old self had once said, "You don't muck about when you're our age." She had draped her arms around Ed's neck, moved her hips and - hoping she sounded sultry - sung along to *Glory Box*. Commitment was sexy. Every decision had seemed monumental then. Choices made would impact on your whole future. In many ways, despite having added sixteen years to her quota, Anita felt younger. Since the fire, she had slipped out of adulthood. Life might take any number of unexpected turns. Its path was no longer fixed.

It was not that Anita didn't want to phone Natalie. It was simply that she had no idea what she might say. They could navigate around 'the kiss', but Anita's impression was that Ed had broken Natalie's confidence. If so, he would have contacted her and warned her he'd done so. Unfair though it seemed, Anita didn't know if she could trust Ed and Natalie to be together on their own, and she couldn't picture the three of them in the same room, with her feeling like a hanger-on. She felt as if she was being forced to make a choice. Ed, the man she'd made a life with. Natalie, whom she'd known even longer, who had seen her though any number of crises.

It didn't seem fair. Neither did it feel like the right time to make a decision that would be final. Anita didn't care that it might seem cowardly to others. She borrowed from Elizabeth I, adopting procrastination as a deliberate strategy. Sooner or later something would force one of the issues. The idea that there might be a variety of options was appealing. She wouldn't be pushed about. She didn't have to live in a particular house if she didn't want to. She didn't have to give up the job she loved. And if calls didn't get returned, then that was fine as well.

The anti-depressants - those small round red pills - were taking the edge off. Anita recognised that her brain function was trapped in perpetual early morning, slow to shake off the fug of sleep. Perhaps, she thought, as her gaze jumped from the manicured Palace grounds towards the unregulated yellowed grass of Home Park - was that a glimpse of antlers she'd seen? - this passive approach wasn't a natural reaction. But her unmedicated response had made colleagues avoid her. Refusal to take the anti-depressants would, in all likelihood, have cost Anita her job. Already, they had become a crutch. She had gone from someone who was reluctant to take an aspirin to someone who gladly swallowed whatever was on offer, without reading the list of side effects. Anita had no idea if she was actually getting better or if, without the drugs ("We'll wean you off them," Dr Kernow had reassured her), she would be straight back to square one. Palpitations, sweats, a desire to escape so overwhelming that nothing could stand in her way.

She had felt stronger in Liverpool, Anita reminded herself, buffeted by the Mersey breeze sweeping straight off the Irish Sea. But that was only because she'd been walking around with her eyes shut. Here, with the late summer sun warming her bare legs and the steady rain of the fountain, she was a long way from her childhood home, a long way from her mother. Here, with Ruth babysitting (Anita had overheard Roz asking the staff to make sure someone always knew where she was), she was insulated - even from the possibility that a tourist might take a seat beside her and strike up an unwelcome conversation. In many ways, sitting in the Palace grounds, she felt protected from the outside world.

Anita recoiled as she turned the corner at the end of her road and saw her father perched on his upright suitcase outside her front door. Then an urgent thought replaced that instinct. "Dad!" This could only mean one thing: he must have read those terrible things her mother had written. He had left Mum. This was how the fairy tale ended. She tripped into a run.

But he turned his head and his face didn't have the look of a man in agony. "It's a long time since I found myself sitting on a doorstep, waiting for the grown-ups to come home," he said, pushing himself to standing. He didn't sound in the least bit tormented. Neither did he state the obvious: that Anita hadn't returned his calls.

She broke the embarrassing impasse by stepping forwards and kissing his cheek. "So you found us." Anita fumbled for her key while he moved sideways with his suitcase.

"I didn't realise this was where you'd moved. I always liked the look of this terrace."

"It's handy for the station." She jammed the key into the lock. "There you go. Oh," she faltered.

"What?"

"I've just realised what's different about you." Anita raised one hand to her throat, as if loosening a tie.

"It's the jumper you bought me."

"About ten Christmases ago! I assumed you didn't like it."

"I've been saving it." He hauled his case over the lip of the step, and squared it with the wall while Anita closed the door behind them. "You don't look surprised to see me."

Anita opened her mouth to speak.

"It's alright, Tilly Mint. You don't have to say anything. I've pieced it together for myself. But there are a few things I need to bring you up to speed on. Things best done in person." His smile was taut and she wondered what lurked behind it. "Well," he looked into the living room, then held onto the doorframe as if checking its stability. "This is nice. Very... cosy."

Abandoning her handbag at the foot of the stairs, Anita sidled past in the direction of the kitchen. "Grab a seat. I'll put the kettle on."

"Got anything stronger?"

She retraced her steps and leant into the doorway. Her father was seated on the small two-seater, his arm positioned as if he was in a furniture store, considering whether to make a purchase. His backdrop the burnt orange wall, he had rearranged Natalie's cushions.

"Am *I* going to need something stronger as well?" When his glance said what he didn't, her chest rose and fell in response. "I'd better see what we've got."

The contents of the fridge door rattled. Anita was supposed to be watching how much she drank. Between the milk and the orange juice nestled an expensive Chablis Ed had brought home with him. He'd said that he would keep her company by cutting back, but that if they were going to drink less, they might as well explore the good stuff. She called out, "There's a bottle of white wine open."

"Then wine it is."

Though Anita had nothing to be nervous about, she felt apprehensive. The living room setting didn't help. She and Ed had yet to make any good memories there. After pouring a large glass for her father, Anita was about to stop at the halfway mark for herself but, seeing how little was left in the bottle, she held it upside down. "Waste not, want not," she muttered, waiting for the last drip to fall.

"Ah!" Seeing her approach, Ron took the glass she held out to him. "Good to see you."

She frowned uncertainly. "And you."

They clinked and both sipped, neither taking pleasure in the content of their glasses, though Ron gave a murmur of approval.

"Aren't you going to sit down?" he asked.

"This sofa's not very good for conversation." She perched on an arm. "It's too small."

"Too small for -? That's a first on me."

"I'll demonstrate, shall I?" She moved herself next to him, and they found themselves anchored, shoulders touching, with a view of the oversized flat screen television (another new purchase).

"Perhaps we'd be better off at the table."

Anita stacked the scattered paperwork and squared the architect's plans into a neat pile.

"House plans?" her father asked.

"They arrived just as Ed was leaving for work. Going through them was to have been his job for tonight." Relocating did little to dissipate the awkwardness. Clearly, her father was finding it difficult to make eye contact. Eventually there was no option but to ask, "What is it you've come all this way to say, Dad?"

He winced. "I'm just putting it all in the right order."

"Then I'll start, shall I? I thought you didn't know about

Mum's book, and I couldn't be the one to tell you. But you *do* know, don't you?"

He nodded, his look resigned. "Yes, love. I know." She hadn't noticed that he was holding a copy in his lap. Now he placed it in front of her.

The orange wall seemed to press in on Anita. She rested her forearm on the table, holding onto the base of her glass. "Have you known all along?"

"Only since yesterday."

She felt relieved to hear this. "And you've read it?"

"Right to the very end." He raised his glass to his lips and drank.

So he was one step ahead of her. "And you're not *angry?*"

"I'm angry with that awful American woman. Marcia blooming whatsherface. I could bloody well murder her."

Anita's forehead tightened into a frown. She wasn't going to let her father go off on one of his tangents. "How can you be so calm about it? I -"

"This is where I'm going to stop you." Ron raised a hand and splayed his fingers. "Before you say something that might later be used in evidence." It might have been an attempt to lighten the mood but, from his expression, Anita got the impression that she was in some way on trial. "Your mother's in hospital. She's had an accident -"

The room tilted. "What kind of accident?"

"I think she'll be out of action for some time. She's had a nasty break. Her hip."

"She's broken her hip?" She must have fallen down the stairs! Anita had witnessed for herself how out of breath Mum got. It was easy to imagine how it had happened. A clumsily-placed foot, the loss of balance, flailing arms. But that image was replaced by something far more disturbing. Anita's heart was racing. Had her mother -? No, she tried to dismiss it...

But her father continued. "I found her wedged across the landing. Lord only knows how long she'd been calling for help. She'd fallen from the loft ladder."

Though a relief of sorts flooded Anita's veins, her mother's injuries could have been far worse. "What was Mum doing up there?"

"Trying to bring her books down from the loft. I've no idea how they got up there in the first place!"

"That was me. She asked me to put them up there." Remembering the creak of the ladder, how flimsy it felt under her weight, Anita lifted her wine glass to her lips. Her hand was shaking.

Her father responded with a throaty sound.

"How will they treat her?"

"They'll give her a new hip joint. The surgeon hopes to do it within thirty-six hours, provided he's happy with everything else."

"Then shouldn't you be there with her?" It was madness that he was here, with all this going on.

"Your mother wanted me to come and see you. I asked the nurses and they agreed there was nothing I could do. I'll be out of your hair first thing in the morning and, if by any chance they find a slot for her tomorrow, I can still be back by the time she's in Recovery."

There was no point arguing that he shouldn't be tiring himself out, running up and down the country. The only reason her father was here was because Anita hadn't returned his calls. She glanced at the skirting board: a strip of masking tape was still in place. Orange paint had bled through it.

Remembering that she'd interrupted, it occurred to Anita that her father might have been about to say something important. "You mentioned an American woman."

Ron grimaced. "Were you missing anything when you arrived home after visiting us?"

As an image of the woman's nudging feet came to Anita, she felt the colour drain from her face.

"One of your mother's books made it across the Atlantic." He gritted his teeth. "And this Marcia so-and-so has been posting messages all over the internet. She says she found the book on the Liverpool to London train." One of Anita's hands found a path to her mouth. "It's all a big game to her. *Let's see if we can't solve the mystery of who the author of this anonymously published book is.*"

One moment's carelessness, and this!

"Just before her accident, your mother was watching a video this woman posted. And from what she did next, I know she was horrified. She unpublished her book. Now she's asked me to burn all of the copies in the house."

"Why publish it in the first place? That's what I don't understand. It wasn't just her story she was telling. It was yours, and mine. And the things she wrote -"

Her father's glass rang as he tapped the band of his wedding ring against its stem. His expression said *Enough!* "I can understand why you're so upset. But there are things you need to understand." He lifted his chin and laughed. A single self-deprecating syllable. "This would be so much easier if I had just picked you up from one of your parties and we were driving through the empty streets after midnight. Through the tunnel, along the Strand. Do you remember?"

Anita's nostrils flared. An unwelcome build-up of tears caused her eyes to itch. She blinked, remembering the freedom of driving through dark and sometimes damp city streets, drunk on false promises of what adulthood had to offer, alive in dozens of ways she'd never experienced before. "You went through a red light once," she said.

"Once that you noticed." And suspended in the look father and daughter exchanged was other knowledge.

The secrets she had imparted, confident they'd go no

further. Never had her mother begun a sentence, *Your father tells me.* It took Anita by surprise, here sitting opposite her father, that she hadn't thought this extraordinary - especially given the things she'd come out with.

"Imagine for a moment you'd written your story. Not after reading your mother's book, but before. You might have written that you had a different relationship with your mother than you did with me, but that's to be expected. She got the raw deal, doling out the tellings off while all I did was show up at bedtime for a cuddle." Anita had intended to protest when he posed the question, "Do you honestly think, at any point, you would have written that you felt unloved?"

The answer was a resounding 'No'. It didn't need saying. What Anita remembered most was her mother's calm. Even when dishing out a telling off, Patti would appeal to Anita's better nature. "You're not just letting us down, you're letting yourself down. And you're so much better than that." Always that little ray of hope.

Her father took her hand and squeezed it. "What your mother wrote... It says far more about how she feels about herself than how she feels about you. She's harder on herself than anyone else I know." He didn't miss the fact that Anita's lips had fallen further apart. "Yes, without exception. Her parents didn't want us to marry, you see. I was ten years older than her, and she had *A-levels,* for God's sake. *I* was the one who pressed for it. I told her everything would be alright.

'In the space of a year, your mother went from being a young woman with a promising career ahead of her, to a stay-at-home mum. Can you imagine that?" He shook his head. "I look at nineteen-year-olds now and I think, they're *children.*"

"But you were in love."

"Yes." He said it with a sadness. "The kind that makes you take ridiculous risks. I don't know if you ever had that with Ed." He glanced at her, looking for affirmation.

But it wasn't Ed Anita was thinking about. There had been no risks with him. No, it was Jason. All swagger and talk. Cocky charisma of the kind teenage girls have always fallen for. And she was thinking about a far more recent encounter, and then backtracking to the middle distance: foreheads touching on a plane; an exchange of electricity taking place at thirty-eight thousand feet. Eight hours, and their lips didn't once touch.

"There was an incredible amount of pressure on you to compensate your mother for everything I stole from her." Her father smiled a crooked smile, but his voice turned thick and fierce. "I don't believe for one second that your mum didn't love you. I think she'd listened to all those people who told her what she could expect to happen when she held you for the first time. We still had that incredible chemistry, you see - and I don't mind telling you that I *still* get a little lurch in my stomach whenever I see your mother."

This made for uncomfortable listening, but Anita had always taken pride in being born from what, as a girl, she'd assumed were romantic circumstances. Love at first sight. Star-cross'd lovers. Later, she'd been glad not to have been the product of a dark fumble after her father had arrived home on a Saturday night, having drunk half his week's wages. Was there ever such an ugly phrase as conjugal rights?

"I think she expected Catherine Wheels," her father said. "She built it up so much in her head that when they didn't happen... well, it was more than an anticlimax. It was a disaster and it took a long time for her to recover. She came out of the other side liking herself a lot less."

Anita recognised the truth in this - and not just because the words seemed to slot neatly into places that had been there, waiting inside her. It was the fact of her First Holy Communion, the only occasion on which she'd worn a white dress and a veil. Anita had not felt transformed. Though, outwardly, she might have looked as devout as any of her classmates, Anita had assumed that the reason she felt nothing was because Jesus hadn't wanted *her* for a sunbeam. Then she'd transferred the blame to the priest. She stared hard at the knots and swirls on the surface of the oak table. How many other people were helping to propagate the myths they'd been fed? Not wanting to be the one to admit? Perhaps even wanting others to share in their fathomless disappointment?

"To me, what's so telling are the bits your mother left out. She didn't write about how difficult your birth was. Perhaps she thought that you didn't discuss these things, but the midwife told me, or perhaps she didn't tell me. Sometimes it's the things that aren't said... It's a look."

They both drank, Ed's extravagant purchase bland and tasteless.

"And your mother didn't write -" He reached again for Anita's forearm and this time he left his hand resting there "- and I'm *not* trying to make you feel bad - but you weren't the easiest child. You cried a lot." He widened his eyes and nodded. "I'd come home and, from the redness of your face or the look of defeat on your mother's, it was obvious - even to an eejit like me - that you'd screamed yourself beyond the point of exhaustion. And blow me if you didn't fall asleep the moment I threw you over my shoulder. I'd give you a little pinch so your mother didn't think I had the magic touch.

'Even when you were older, sometimes you'd cry until you made yourself sick. What your mother really needed was something outside the home. A job."

Anger surfaced uncharitably before Anita could stifle it. "Then why didn't she -?" She left the sentence stranded.

"This was Liverpool. You know yourself how hard work was to come by. Just look at the lengths *you* had to go to."

Anita pondered the fact that her father thought moving to London had been a sacrifice. Even after their night-time excursions, he hadn't grasped how much she'd wanted to break free. One visit to the V&A, and there had never been anywhere else she'd considered living. It was housing prices that had driven Anita outwards, to a place with a Surrey post-code that stubbornly clung to pretensions of being in London.

"Mum seems to think the problem was that I was a girl."

"Don't you think that might have been the explanation your mother fed herself - that it could have been different if you'd been a boy?"

Anita's mind wandered to those contented gurgling babies whose smiles she returned - and those she found herself glaring back at. And, though it might not have been the truth, it seemed that the children Anita smiled at were dressed in blue. Not because blue happened to be Anita's favourite colour, or because she disliked seeing babies with pierced ears and ridiculous Alice bands. No, it was because something about girls repelled her. "No," Anita said with finality. "No, I don't. And Grandma obviously felt the same."

"But, Tilly Mint," her father persisted, "the Roscoes only ever had girls. As far back as the family tree goes. Your mum and your Nan - they had nothing to compare the experience with."

Though she stopped short of telling her father that she disagreed, Anita knew with certainty that she'd inherited her mother's genes.

"The point I'm trying to make is that you had a wonder-ful mother. A far better mum than the ones you see gushing over their children and never saying no. And if she overcame everything she wrote about, well, then I have even greater admiration for her. The fact that she's done this thing - written a book - and I didn't even *know* she was doing it - it's knocked me sideways. *I* was supposed to be the writer in the family. Not that family notices and sports columns ever counted for much. But this American woman seems to think it's a good book."

"The issue isn't whether it's good or not!" Anita would have said much more, but her father's warning glance cut her short.

"No, you're absolutely right. The issue is that your mother is lying in hospital, thinking that you hate her."

To Anita, still raw from the impact of reading the word 'hate' in relation to herself, it was as if Ron had slapped her. She blinked, stunned.

"I'm sorry to put it so bluntly, but that's the truth." Ron was trembling with the effort of speaking, not just his hands, but his head, his lips. "And I really don't think she deserves to suffer that way. She's punished herself these last forty-odd years. Surely that's enough?" His face contorted. Her own father, who had never failed to fight her corner, was taking Patti's side. Anita had never seen her father cry before - hoped never to see him cry again. "Besides, what about all your talk of preserving the stories of ordinary people? History can't always be as convenient as we'd like it to be. You had choices that weren't open to your mother."

They spent the next few moments not looking at each other. Whatever Anita might have said in response was interrupted by the sound of a key being turned in the lock and Ed's shout of, "Bloody trains! What's this doing here?" and his slightly more urgent shout of "Anita!"

"In here!" she replied, realising Ed would have jumped to conclusions on seeing a suitcase in the hall. "We have a visitor." Glancing at Ron, Anita saw that he, too, had registered the sound of panic, and understood her interpretation. They had seconds to compose themselves before Ed appeared in the doorway. The top button of his pale blue shirt undone and his tie dangling from one hand, his fluster softened. "Ron." Ed attempted to turn his greeting into a joke. "To what do we owe the pleasure?" He looked from one subdued face to another, his gaze dropping to the mirror images of hands curled around wine glasses. They were betrayed by very thing they had staged for his benefit. His face lengthened. "Is somebody going to tell me what's going on?"

CHAPTER TWENTY-SIX

All three were seated at the small square table, Ed's laptop open in front of them, among the debris of a fish and chip supper. A smudge of tomato ketchup on a white plate. The tang of salt and vinegar.

Marcia hadn't been idle in the last twenty-four hours. New posts had sprung up. Numerous Tweets. '*Latest Development: Unknown Liverpool Author has Unpublished her Book.*' '*Someone must know who #mysteryauthor is.*' '*Unknown Woman provides stark insight into the reality of Post-natal Depression.*' Charities providing support for sufferers were latching on. Marcia was no longer asking: she was demanding.

Ron admitted that social media baffled him. "When I worked at the paper, you wanted the exclusive. The minute you went to press, the story was yesterday's news."

Anita exchanged glances with Ed.

"It's got legs," he said, giving her growing unease a voice.

"Even *I* know what that means," Ron said. "It's out of our hands."

When Anita looked grimly from her father to Ed, she was dismayed to see excitement reflected in his eyes. "Oh, no," she said.

He was quick to protest: "I didn't say anything."

"You didn't have to!"

"So tell me." He folded his arms.

"You're thinking that J K Rowling's PR company couldn't have come up with a better campaign."

Ed shrugged. "You have to admit, as marketing plans go, this would be killer."

"The question is, how do we stop it?"

The room was shrouded in silence, all eyes locked on the computer screen.

Refusing to accept there was nothing they could do, Anita attempted to answer her own question. "We could appeal to Marcia's better nature."

"Once we make contact, whatever we say becomes news," Ed pointed out. "She'll go public with it."

Looking pale and drawn, Ron curled a hand over his mouth, as if he didn't want his thoughts to be disturbed.

"Dad?" Anita prompted gently.

"Playing devil's advocate," Ed held the copy of the book that Ron had brought with him up. "Besides the two of you, how many other people know it's true?"

No one spoke.

"I know this isn't what you want to hear, but the only way to stop Marcia is by reclaiming it."

Anita twisted bodily towards Ed. "That won't stop Marcia. She'll want to be known as the woman who made the big discovery."

"Obviously, it's up to the two of you." Ed began to shut down his laptop. "Why don't you sleep on it? It's getting late." The screen blanked out, their focus lost.

"Patricia Roscoe," Ron said.

Anita had been too preoccupied to notice the moment her father removed his hand from his mouth. She looked at him now. It was a name Anita rarely heard used. Her mother's maiden name, and now it summoned her home.

"I want you to be able to tell your mother that you're

proud of her. What's more I'd like you to mean it." Her father reached across the table, picked up the book and pressed it into Anita's hands. Her blood curdled. The title seemed to mock her childhood ambitions, everything she'd worked for. "Think about it. Finish reading the book and when you come up this weekend to visit your mother, you can tell me what you've decided."

"So, it's up to me?" Anita was incredulous. "Why is this *my* decision?"

"You've heard what I have to say, but I won't go ahead unless you're in agreement."

"All you said was Mum's maiden name!"

"I was agreeing with Ed."

"You think we should claim the book?"

"That's what I'd like to see on the front cover. The name of the girl I fell in love with. The name she exchanged for mine." He slapped his thighs and pushed himself to standing. "I'm ready to call it a day." He looked older than his age as he took in his surroundings. It was as if Ron had only just realised he wasn't in his own home. "I'm assuming you have a spare bed for me. And I'll need an alarm call. Five thirty sharp."

CHAPTER TWENTY-SEVEN

As soon as she'd seen her father off to bed, Anita opened the book and began to read. It was uncomfortable going, and she had to pause frequently, closing the cover, using her index finger as a bookmark, repeating a sentence to herself, thinking it through. The next day she read, jostled shoulder to shoulder on the train. She read in the Palace grounds during her lunch break and, after a hurried dinner, she locked herself in the bathroom, stopping only to top the hot water up when she began to get cold. And while she read about her mother's struggle to bond, Anita remembered the smell of her mother's perfume, the warm crook of her arm, the sound of her singing in the kitchen when she thought no one was listening. And while she read about her mother's desire to be normal, Anita remembered her waiting by the school gates and waving, Germolene being rubbed on her grazes, being allowed to lick cake mix from a spoon. Instead of recognising this woman who described feeling overwhelmed by anger, she remembered butter spread on Rich Tea biscuits when she was feeling ill; she remembered her mother squirrelling away money for treats, saying, "Don't tell your father." It was hard to reconcile these opposing images, but what was clear was that motherly love wasn't only a noun. It was also a verb.

Anita rushed through St Pancras Station with ridiculous optimism, trundling her suitcase past the queues of Eurostar ticket holders and the gleaming glass to the place where the piano was tucked neatly beneath a staircase. What had she expected? That he would be perched on the stool at the keyboard waiting for the occasion when she might happen to arrive? After all, it was just before eight o'clock on a Saturday morning, an hour unheard of as far as musicians were concerned. On that last occasion, bumping into him was implausible. Why shouldn't she have expected the impossible?

So there it was. They would not sit in a café and drink coffee while she told him about the next stage of her journey. The scene had been so vivid in her imagination - his hands curled around the white china - it came as a blow.

Perhaps he was part of her past; New York something of its time. A photograph album that had been stored in a wicker box in the eaves, never looked at, now reduced to ash.

And yet... she ran her fingers over the lid of the keyboard and felt the indentations of the chipped black paint; the carved-out names of people passing through. Then, on impulse, she reached into her handbag and ripped a blank page out of her diary. Using the lid of the piano as a tabletop, she wrote, *It turns out that I am not Tom Hanks,* then she slid the message behind the stand intended for sheet music. Had Anita been looking for certainties, she could have sent a Facebook message, but she liked the sense of chance, the idea that fate might decide whether or not the message reached him. Now was not the time for decisions. Decisions were final.

You're fooling yourself if you think this is an ending, she told herself as she turned and wheeled her suitcase out onto the bustling Euston Road. *This is a beginning. Mum has her book, Ed his big building project to focus on. You need to decide how you're going to leave your mark.*

CHAPTER TWENTY-EIGHT

Everything about being in hospital reduced Patti's stomach to oil: the particular cocktail of clinical smells, always with an unpleasant undercurrent; the residue of anaesthetic; the processed colour-drained peas that accompanied evening meals. And perhaps most: the shame of being here, under these circumstances.

"Don't you worry, love," the woman in the nearest bed had consoled Patti when she'd been as sick as a dog shortly after her arrival. "We've all left our dignity outside the door."

At least she was now less conspicuous, camouflaged in full view on a ward of people recovering from hip and knee replacements. She was no longer the infamous fat woman who had fallen from the loft ladder; someone who was sniggered about.

Ron had prepped Patti. He had assured her that everything was going to be alright, squeezing her arm tenderly, afraid he might damage her. He lent her his certainty, and she believed in it all the time that he sat in the visitor's chair. Yet, left alone for an hour or two, the idea that she'd done something irreversible, unforgivable, crept back to engulf Patti. She was that very thing she thought that she'd put behind her - an unnatural mother. Propped up on numerous pillows, pinned to her hospital cot - a sensation caused by the morphine

- dread peaked and troughed with each coming and going on the ward.

Expecting Anita's arrival didn't prepare Patti for the moment her daughter walked into the ward. So different from the occasion the midwife had placed her daughter in her arms, the repulsion she'd felt. Younger looking than Patti had been at the same age, considerably slimmer, and with that air of self-possession people who go out into the world acquire. Like armour, Patti supposed. Lord knows, she could do with a complete set. She found that she couldn't call out, couldn't wave, could barely remember how to blink.

Intercepted by one of the crepe-soled nurses Patti knew as Carole ("Chances are," Carole had confided, "with your weight problem, you'd have needed a new hip before long anyway.") Anita asked for directions. Her gaze followed the nurse's pointing arm. Anita hesitated, as if she might turn to Carol and say, *No. There's been a mistake. That's not my mother*.

As their eyes met, Patti held her breath, waiting to see if her daughter's face would break into a smile. The corners of her own mouth dragged downwards, messages dispatched by her brain diverted elsewhere. Her daughter seemed to alternate between being a very long way off and close-up. Patti's head felt as if it were clamped in a brace. As Anita approached and placed her hands on the rail at the foot of the bed, it was difficult to read what she was thinking. If Patti was to hazard a guess, she would say that her daughter was steeling herself for some unpleasant duty she couldn't avoid.

"Hello, love," Patti said in her new cracked voice.

"How are you feeling, Mum?" Anita cast her gaze around the ward, as if she was looking to see if there was an empty visitor's chair beside a different bed.

"My own stupid fault. It's painful, that's to be expected. But they don't let you lie in bed for long. They've already started me on physio. They get you back on your feet as soon as possible, even if it means cranking up the meds." She was gabbling. This cheerful front had to go. "And how are you?" she ventured, feeling her way in the dark. *How do you think she is? You've destroyed everything she had left, you stupid old woman.* But what other way was there to begin a conversation?

"Yes." Anita sat in the visitor's chair. She appeared to be checking for damage, trying to make up her mind. "I'm surprisingly OK."

"Listen." Patti closed her eyes briefly and sighed. An apology simply wasn't enough. "I'm so relieved to see you." Words tumbled from her mouth. "Both you and your father, to be honest. So very relieved." In this, too, Ron had not let her down.

"I'm sorry I couldn't come earlier in the week, but I've only just gone back to work, and they've been very good about all the time I've taken off. It didn't seem fair to just drop everything."

"Don't be daft. I wouldn't have expected you to."

Anita's gaze sank to her lap. She gave a few sharp nods. "I should have returned your calls."

"Oh." Patti would have given a flick of her wrist if such a thing were possible.

Anita now reached into her bag. "I didn't bother with grapes." The corners of her mouth twitched. "But I did bring you this."

As Patti saw the book, the hand with the shunt in it jerked involuntarily, the needle pulling painfully. She winced, sucking air through her teeth.

Anita was on her feet. "Are you alright? Shall I fetch a nurse?"

Patti shook her head, waiting for the breathlessness to subside. When she looked again, Anita was back in the visitor's chair. "I didn't expect... I asked your father to burn all of those. He promised -" But Patti realised she hadn't extracted a promise from Ron.

"We've made a minor change to the cover." Anita's smile quivered, and Patti understood something extraordinary: her daughter was *nervous*. "I hope you like it." She held it in both hands at Patti's eye level. Sellotaped to the front, underneath the stolen title (the sight of which now made her cringe) was a narrow strip of paper with careful handwritten lettering on it. *Patricia Roscoe.* It reminded Patti of the home-made cards Anita had drawn for birthdays, Christmases and Mother's Days over the years.

A noise erupted from deep in her throat, wrapping itself around what she tried to say. "No one's called me Patricia since my mother passed away."

"We can change the font. Obviously."

"Oh, Anita." Patti clutched her daughter's hand. "It's a lovely gesture. Really. I can't tell you how much that means to me. I'm so very sorry."

"There's nothing to apologise for. We're the same, Mum. I can see that now."

Unsure of her daughter's meaning, she felt her brows pull together.

Anita didn't expand. She simply nodded.

"I want you to know that I unpublished the book -"

"Which is reversible."

About to add that no one else would be able to read it, Patti registered what her daughter had just said.

"We checked." Anita's eyes were pooling, but her chin was held high. "You're Britain's most wanted woman. Enjoy your anonymity while you can. You're going to have to get used to being the centre of attention." She was reaching into her handbag again, pulling out a plastic folder full of sheets of paper and a pen.

Patti was glad that she was lying down. "What's all this?" she asked, staggered.

Anita leafed through the top few. "Reviews, blog posts, interview requests, an invitation for you to become an ambassador for a charity..."

She felt nauseous. "Oh, no, I -"

"Yes," her daughter said firmly. "People out there need you. You'd better hurry up and get yourself better. Specifically," Anita reached to the back of the folder. "You need to be fully recovered by 4th July." Anita placed a single sheet in her hand.

"I can't read without my glasses." Patti frowned at the blur of receding letters.

"Let me, then." Anita swivelled round. *"The Queen Mary 2 will recreate history when she sails from Liverpool on July 4, 2015, to commemorate* RMS Britannia's *sailing 175 years ago, which started the first regular transatlantic service. The last time a Cunard liner sailed from Liverpool to New York was January, 1968, when* RMS Franconia *made the last scheduled voyage, starting from the same berth.* I knew I wouldn't get you on a plane, so I've booked two tickets. You and me."

Patti had no idea how to react. It wasn't the morphine that had struck her dumb. This time she wasn't going to get away with a mumbled three Hail Marys and a Glory Be.

CHAPTER TWENTY-NINE

In the Wolsey Rooms, Anita stood once more in front of the painting that had long-since fascinated her. She looked at the heart-shaped face - a face that wouldn't suffer fools; the delicate flush of the cheeks. She admired the confident pose, the right hand resting on the head of the stag, the pearls dripping from her wrist.

"So, who's our unknown woman today?" asked Roz, coming to a standstill beside her.

The truth Anita now saw was that, regardless of whose face appeared in the portrait, it was what it had come to represent that was important. Every woman who has been cut out of the picture; whose name has not been recorded for history. Every woman born in the wrong place, at the wrong time. There was no hesitation in her voice: "Patricia Roscoe."

Roz gave a start. "I don't think I've heard of her. *Why* haven't I heard of her?" Intrigued, she narrowed her eyes. "Have you dug up some juicy secret and kept it all to yourself?"

"No," Anita said, her gaze dropping to the woman's swollen stomach. "She's my mother." And the swell of pride she felt in saying those few words took Anita by surprise.

Roz's heels swivelled. "That's cheating." And then she added, "To be honest, I've never understood the rules of your game."

"My mother's never seen this painting, but she borrowed

its title for her book. She's the unknown woman." The corners of Anita's mouth lifted. Although she had lost many things, this emerging curiosity about the woman who had given birth to her was one thing she'd had gained. Not for the first time, Anita imagined Vita Sackville-West's eighty-page autobiography, locked in a Gladstone bag, waiting for the day some time after her death when someone would discover it in her turret writing-room at Sissinghurst. Her son, Nigel Nicholson, questioned his motives for a decade before he took the decision to publish the story of Vita's three-year affair with a woman, which took place early in his parents' fifty-year marriage. A toddler at the time, he'd been blissfully unaware. Anita was thankful that she'd discovered her mother's book while there was time to ask questions, time to build a new and more honest relationship.

"Is there any point in asking who wrote the poetry?" Roz asked.

Fourteen days from first date to wedding. That must have been some line Dad sold her mother; some dream he painted for her. Like other Liverpool poets - Roger McGough, Adrian Henri, Brian Patten - Dad's poetry began with a small 'p'. But Anita had fallen for less. Jason's cocky *'Alright.'* The glamour of a week in New York. Ed's '*So you haven't sold* your *soul.*' "Like you said," she shrugged, "they're all at it."

Roz looked exasperated. "So that's *it?* Seventeen years, and that's the best you can come up with?"

"That's my final answer." She looked at Roz's blinking face. "Coffee?" she said. "I'm buying."

Roz adjusted the strap of her bag and looked thoroughly put out. "I should bloody well hope so."

ACKNOWLEDGMENTS

To Ken, for entrusting your story to me, in the hope that I have done it justice.

As always, a mounting debt of thanks is due to my team of beta readers, especially Matthew Martin, Anne Clinton, Delia Porter, Amanda Osborne, Sarah Marshall, Mary Fuller, Lynn Pearce, Karen Begg, Sue Darnell, Joe Thorpe, Kath Crowley, Liz Lewis, Liz Carr, Julie Spearritt, Kevin Cowdall, Les Moriarty, Will Poole, Kate Hutchins, and Sarah Diss. Special thanks to Helen Enefer, Liza Perrat and Louise Davis for editorial advice and assistance, and to my proofreader, 'Happy' Harry Matthews. IT guru, Jack Naisbett, has responded to my cries for help on many occasions. Payment will be made with coffee and cake.

ABOUT THE AUTHOR

Jane Davis is the author of six novels. Her debut, Half-truths and White Lies, won the Daily Mail First Novel Award and was described by Joanne Harris as 'A story of secrets, lies, grief and, ultimately, redemption, charmingly handled by this very promising new writer.' She was hailed by The Bookseller as 'One to Watch.' Compulsion Reads wrote, 'Davis is a phenomenal writer, whose ability to create well rounded characters that are easy to relate to feels effortless.' Jane's favourite description of fiction is that it is 'made-up truth'.

Jane lives in Carshalton, Surrey, with her Formula 1 obsessed, star-gazing, beer-brewing partner, surrounded by growing piles of paperbacks, CDs and general chaos.

For further information, or to sign up for pre-launch specials and notifications about future projects, visit the author's website at www.jane-davis.co.uk.

A personal request from Jane: "Your opinion really matters to authors and to readers who are wondering which book to pick next. If you love a book, please tell your friends and post a review. Facebook, Amazon, Smashwords and Goodreads are all great places to start."

OTHER TITLES BY THE AUTHOR

Half-truths & White Lies

I Stopped Time

These Fragile Things

A Funeral for an Owl

An Unchoreographed Life

Printed in Poland
by Amazon Fulfillment
Poland Sp. z o.o., Wrocław